MW00634805

Merry Cherry Christmas

Also by Keira Andrews

Contemporary

Honeymoon for One
Beyond the Sea
Ends of the Earth
Arctic Fire
The Chimera Affair

Holiday
The Christmas Deal
The Christmas Leap
Only One Bed
Merry Cherry Christmas
Santa Daddy
In Case of Emergency
Eight Nights in December
If Only in My Dreams
Where the Lovelight Gleams
Gay Romance Holiday Collection

Sports
Kiss and Cry
Reading the Signs
Cold War
The Next Competitor
Love Match
Synchronicity (free read!)

Gay Amish Romance Series
A Forbidden Rumspringa
A Clean Break
A Way Home
A Very English Christmas

Valor Duology
Valor on the Move
Test of Valor
Complete Valor Duology

Merry Cherry Christmas

BY KEIRA ANDREWS

Merry Cherry Christmas
Written and published by Keira Andrews
Cover by Dar Albert
Formatting by BB eBooks

Copyright © 2020 by Keira Andrews
Print Edition

All rights reserved. This book or any portion thereof may not be reproduced or used in any manner whatsoever without the express written permission of the author or publisher except for the use of brief quotations in a book review.

Print ISBN: 978-1-988260-54-9

This is a work of fiction. Names, characters, businesses, places, events and incidents are either the products of the author's imagination or used in a fictitious manner. No persons, living or dead, were harmed by the writing of this book. Any resemblance to any actual persons, living or dead, or actual events is purely coincidental.

Acknowledgements

Many thanks to Anara, DJ, Mary, Leta, and Rai for their friendship and assistance. <3

Chapter One

FLAT ON HIS back—and not the way he wanted—Jeremy couldn't breathe.

I'm going to die a virgin.

The campus pathway's icy concrete was brutally unforgiving. Freezing-rain pellets peppered Jeremy's face like Mother Nature opening fire with a machine gun. Falling had completely knocked the wind out of him, and he blinked up at the blur of a lamp post wound with holiday lights. Without his glasses, the starbursts of blue and white were massive in the darkness.

He could hear laughter and wondered if he'd said the virgin thing aloud. Male voices hooted and howled, and if Jeremy hadn't managed to knock off his glasses when he'd flailed on the ice, he'd probably see the guys pointing at him too.

"Shit, bro, that was epic!"

"Wipeout!"

"Too bad we didn't record it."

"Stop being dicks." A baritone cut through the laughter, coming close to Jeremy, a shadowy figure blocking the blurry light as the person leaned over him. "You okay, man? You went down hard."

Jeremy's lungs still didn't want to work, and when he tried to answer, it came out as a gasping squeak. More laughter echoed in the frosty night. He needed his glasses but couldn't seem to make his arm move to feel around for them on the treacherous pavement. His body had seized up, pain radiating from his back. He probably wasn't going to *die*, but it hurt like hell. His face stung as more freezing rain pelted down.

"Did you hit your head?" the husky, concerned voice asked before snapping, "Guys, shut up already! It wasn't that funny!"

"Dude, come on. Holiday Hootenanny waits for no one. If we miss the Santa and his little helpers strip show, I'm gonna be pissed. He's fine. Right, buddy?" Another figure bent over Jeremy, and a fist punched his shoulder in a way that was probably supposed to be encouraging but just added to the throbbing pain. "Like a hard tackle. Knocks the piss outta ya, but you're okay." Then the hand was hauling Jeremy to his feet.

The deeper voice protested. "Stop! Seriously, he might have hit his head." This guy's hands were gentle, taking hold of Jeremy's shoulders with comforting strength. Without Jeremy's glasses, his rescuer's face was still a blur even at arm's length.

Jeremy forced a breath, although the cold air didn't help his seized lungs. He rasped, "I think my head's fine. Thanks."

"You sure?" His rescuer still held Jeremy's shoulders, his breath clouding in the cold air. "What's your name?"

"Me?" Jeremy asked, because he was never *not* awkward AF. He flushed, but at least his pale cheeks were probably already pink from the cold. Like most redheads, his blushes could be seen from space.

The guy chuckled with another puff of warm breath. "Yeah, you. I'm Max. What's your name?"

"Oh. Uh, Jeremy?"

"You don't sound very sure."

Someone else said, "Come on, this weather sucks. The kid's fine. He's standing and talking."

"Considering how many concussions you've probably had, you should know that doesn't mean shit," Max said, his tone sounding like an eye-roll.

"I'm definitely Jeremy. Jeremy Rourke."

"Okay, Jeremy Rourke. I guess I have no way of verifying unless I check your wallet. So, what day is it?"

"Friday?"

There was a frown in Max's voice. "You don't sound too sure about that either."

"I've been studying for exams all week. It's a blur. My last one's on Wednesday. So yeah… It's Friday."

"Okay. What's the date?"

"Uh…" Jeremy worked backward from the Wednesday exam date. "December thirteenth." He groaned. "Friday the thirteenth—it figures. Really, I didn't hit my head. I'm good. Thanks." He shivered, his thin rain jacket not doing much to block the wind, jeans soaked from where he'd sprawled on the ground. The freezing rain whipped around them.

"Pimenta, let's GO!" someone huffed. "Kid doesn't need a babysitter."

Ignoring his friends, Max prodded the back of Jeremy's head. "Not tender at all?"

"Nope!" Oh lord, this Max guy was touching him. Jeremy kept his hair short and neat but barely resisted the urge to smooth it down on top in case it'd gotten messy in the fall. "I managed to keep my head up when I went down."

Max leaned back, dropping his hands. "Okay, if you're sure."

There were five blurred figures around them on the pathway. "Can you just find my glasses?" Jeremy asked. "I can't really see anything."

"Totally," Max said. "They must be—" The *snap-crunch* was sharp in the night, and everyone seemed to freeze. "*Motherfucker*," Max breathed.

After a beat of silence, Max's friends howled with laughter again, one of them wheezing and exclaiming, "Holy shit, dude. They are toast!"

Max barked at them to shut up as he crouched. He stood again. "Yeah, uh, I stepped on your glasses. The frame's broken in half and the lenses are cracked. Well, one is cracked and the other is, like…"

"It's trashed," someone said.

Hot and cold all over, Jeremy ordered himself not to panic. How was he going to get across campus to his dorm room without his glasses? He blurted, "But I can't see!" and cringed at the terror in his voice.

It hurt to breathe. *Oh God, please let this be a bad dream.* But he wasn't waking up. He was out alone in the dark and might as well have been blindfolded. The U of T campus was huge, sprawling over dozens of blocks in downtown Toronto. The thought of trying to cross busy streets without being able to see made him sick to his stomach. Even in daylight, he would have felt horribly exposed and unsafe, but at night?

He reached blindly for Max's arm, almost pleading, *Don't leave me!* He managed to bite his tongue to keep from sounding even more pathetic.

Max seemed to hear the unspoken words. He took hold of Jeremy's shoulders again. "It's okay, Jeremy. I'll help you get home."

"Are we going to this party or what?" someone demanded. "This ice pellet bullshit is hurting my face."

"I'll meet you guys there," Max said. "I broke his glasses. I'm not going to leave him out here alone."

There was some grumbling, but also agreement. One voice said, "Hope your night gets way better, kid."

"Hey, you should come to the party!" the guy who'd punched his shoulder said. "Get your contacts or whatever and come get hammered. I bet you could use a drink."

Another added, "This is why you were captain of the team, Maxwell—taking the clueless little frosh under your wing. Always so responsible."

Max huffed. "Whatever, Honey."

Honey? Jeremy squinted, wishing he could see more of this other guy. Had he heard right? Had Max called him that? Maybe Jeremy had a concussion after all.

Another voice called as it got more distant, "We'll chug a few beers for you, bro! Hurry up!"

Jeremy braced on the slippery sidewalk, his sneakers no match for the ice, the mix of snow and rain—practically hail now—not letting up.

He said, "I'm sure I'll be fine. You should go to your party," although he desperately wanted this Max to stay with him.

"I'll get you home first. Do you live in res?"

"Yeah, on St. George." The adrenaline spike of losing his glasses seemed to be dulling the pain in his back, at least. "I'm really blind without my glasses. Sorry."

"It's cool. Honestly? I don't really want to go to that party. My ex is going to be there. You okay to walk? This weather sucks ass. Guess they haven't had a chance to salt the paths yet. Need to bust out my real winter boots."

"Me too. Well, I need to buy some."

"Yeah, those Chucks aren't going to cut it." With a gentle hand on Jeremy's shoulder, Max guided him off the path. "Better to walk on the grass. More traction."

It crunched under Jeremy's sneakers, crusted with a thin layer of ice. Jeremy blinked at the old buildings rising around the grassy area. They were looming brown shapes, and the path's streetlamps were big pinwheel sprays of light. The holiday decorations and lights just added to the confusion.

"Um, can you tell me when we get to a curb or anything?" Jeremy asked. "The world's like the crappiest Monet painting ever without my glasses."

Max laughed. "Gotcha. Blurry lily ponds and shit."

"Yeah. I'm really near-sighted. My prescription's minus-nine if that means anything to you."

"Not really. What are most people?"

"Zero is good. Twenty-twenty, I guess. I read somewhere minus-three prescription is the average for people who wear glasses."

"Whoa. You don't wear contacts?"

"My eyes are too dry. Lucky me."

"That sucks. You have a spare pair of glasses in your room, right?"

"My old ones. They'll do for tonight." He'd have to get the copy of his prescription and——

Jeremy tensed with the now familiar clench of hurt and dread. His mom had always handled that kind of stuff, but their most recent text exchange had been awkward at best, and his parents were the last people he wanted to deal with. That the feeling seemed to be mutual didn't help. At all.

"You okay? You look like you're gonna hurl. Shit, if you've got a concussion after all, we should get to the ER." Max leaned closer, but he'd have to get six inches from Jeremy's face for Jeremy to really see him, and he was still blurry.

"I'm good. Just thinking about my prescription. I'm not sure where it is. My mom's probably got it."

"Just tell her to take a pic with her phone."

"Good idea." Jeremy nodded, pushing away the thoughts of home and walking carefully on the crunchy grass that now looked faintly white. The wind gusted, the freezing rain morphing into snow.

"Why don't you have boots? I'm assuming you're a first-year. You're not from here?"

"Victoria."

"Oh, cool. I love BC. Vancouver Island is gorgeous."

"Yeah, I guess so? We don't get snow very often. Usually just rains. I had winter gear, but I outgrew it."

"You definitely need boots in Toronto." Max grasped Jeremy's bare hand, the leather of his gloves cool and soft. "And you need gloves. Dude, you must be freezing!"

Jeremy's heart went *BOOM,* and he hoped it was too dark to see his red face. Max had only held his hand for a second—and he hadn't really *held his hand*—but it was a thrill. A sad, pathetic little thrill.

"Yeah, forgot to bring my gloves from home, and I've been meaning to go shopping. It was still mild and now all of a sudden winter's here, I guess."

"Take mine while we walk back." Max pressed the leather into Jeremy's hand.

"No, that's not fair."

"I'm used to the cold. Besides, I think you might be in shock a little, so put them on." His tone was commanding but kind.

"Okay, but I'm fine." Jeremy had to admit that it was a relief to slide his numb hands into the warm, fuzzy lining of the gloves. They were too big for him, so he clenched his fingers to stop them from falling off. "Thank you." It was an even bigger relief to have someone taking charge. Taking care of him.

"No prob. Okay, we're going to have to cross the street in a minute."

The bursts of streetlights filled the dark sky as they came to the end of the grassy area. Cars zoomed by, headlights and red taillights huge, going fast despite the conditions. Jeremy stared down at the slick, blurry sidewalk, stepping gingerly. His sneakers didn't grip the layer of ice at all, and he flailed and clutched at Max.

Max laughed good-naturedly. "I've got you." He wrapped a big arm around Jeremy's shoulders.

Jeremy's breath stuttered, and not just because his ribs ached where he'd smacked the pavement. He was tucked against Max's side, and Max was a good foot taller than him. And *buff*. And it was warm like a hug. Jeremy hadn't been hugged in months, not since...

"Put your arm around my waist," Max said.

"Okay." Jeremy did, loving how that felt, to hold onto another guy like that. Like they were boyfriends or something. Another pathetic thrill ran down his bruised spine.

"We've got about ten feet, and then there's a curb. I'll tell you when."

Max walked slowly, his steps careful. Jeremy couldn't really see his feet but assumed Max was wearing something sturdier than sneakers since he seemed able to grip better than Jeremy could. They shuffled to the curb, where they stopped for the light.

"Thanks for this," Jeremy said, blinking at the massive balls of light all around. He realized how much he took seeing the world in focus for granted. "It's kind of scary when you can't see."

"Dude, I'd be shitting myself." Max squeezed Jeremy's shoulder where he held him securely. "Okay, we're stepping down onto the road. It's not salted yet either."

They shuffled across, and Max guided him back up onto the curb on the other side. They continued along the sidewalk with arms around each other.

Do people think we're boyfriends?

Despite everything, it was exciting. Which was cringey and probably why Jeremy had never actually had a boyfriend in real life. Because he was the biggest loser on campus.

"Do you know what your major's going to be?" Max asked.

"Biochemistry."

"Wow. You must be smart."

"I guess?" He was, but he obviously wasn't going to say that. "I'm really interested in gene expression and development."

Max whistled. "That sounds very science-y."

"That's what they said in the brochure." Jeremy was stupidly proud when Max chuckled at his weak joke. He asked, "What's your major?"

"Sociology. I've always planned on law school. Assuming I didn't blow the LSAT last month."

Max's voice had tightened, and Jeremy gave his waist an awkward pat. "I'm sure you did great."

"Thanks. Still another few days for the results. Waiting's the worst."

"Totally. I—" Jeremy's foot slipped, and he clung to Max, wheeling his left arm wildly. Max skidded, and they fought for balance.

"That was close," Max said, a warm puff of his laughing breath brushing Jeremy's cheek. "One more street to cross, right?"

Jeremy's heart raced as he glanced around. "Um, I think so?" The precipitation was fully snow now, and the world was just shadowy buildings, blinding starburst lights, and white. He shuddered at the thought of navigating it alone. "Thanks for helping me."

"It's cool. There's another curb coming up."

They made it to the residence building, sudden wind slamming the outer door shut behind them, the glass rattling. They stamped their feet on the mat, and Jeremy tugged at Max's gloves, which came off easily since they were so big.

He handed them back. "Thanks again. I'm sure I'll be fine now." He pulled out his wallet and held it close to his face, looking for his access card.

"Dude, you really can't see, huh?"

He grimaced. "Nope. But I'm okay. I've taken up enough of your Friday night."

"I've brought you this far. Don't want you to take a header now that we're in the home stretch. Besides, I'd rather wait until they salt before I go back out. If it's cool to hang for a bit?"

Jeremy's heart skipped. Hang? With *him*? "Of course." He fished out the card, immediately dropped it, then finally buzzed them in. "I'm on the fourth floor."

Max handled the elevator buttons. Under the glare of the fluorescent lights, Jeremy could see that he had medium brown skin and was indeed tall, which made sense the way he'd tucked Jeremy under his arm. The details of his features were still a blur under a blue and white hat— probably a U of T toque—and Jeremy was eager to see his rescuer in all his glory. When they reached his floor, he unlocked his door quickly, almost dropping the key card again.

Now he just needed to find his old glasses.

"Um, sorry for the mess." His sheet and duvet were a rumpled pile on his bed, which he knew not because he could see them clearly, but because they always were. He'd never been one for making his bed, which his mom had always nagged him about.

The hurt was a swift throat punch, and he choked it down.

Max laughed. "Yeah, this isn't a mess, trust me. Can I help find your glasses?"

"I just need to think about where I'd have put them." He sighed. "I'm sure it was in a very logical, safe place."

Max chuckled. "I'm sure. It's not a big room. Do you even have a roommate? This side barely looks lived in."

"Yeah, Doug. He's from Hamilton and goes home every weekend to see his girlfriend. He's only here Monday to Thursdays, and he's gone already since his program doesn't do December exams."

"Lucky bastard."

Did Max mean having a girlfriend or not having exams? Jeremy just murmured in agreement. "Oh! I think I know where they are."

He pulled a plastic storage container out from under his twin bed and fumbled with unsnapping the lid. Practically sticking his head in the box, he went through the random contents—health coverage paperwork, a spare power cable for his laptop, double-A batteries for his mouse, condoms—

Swallowing an embarrassed yelp, Jeremy thrust the Trojan box—unopened—back into the bottom of the container, hoping he was blocking Max's view. The thin throw rug on the floor didn't do much to cushion his knees, and he rooted around with increasing frustration.

"They have to be in here!"

"It's okay. We'll find them." Max sounded completely confident, and somehow it helped, even though he had no way of knowing if it was true.

Jeremy's fingers closed around the hard leather case, and he pulled it out with a triumphant cry. Max applauded, and Jeremy had to laugh. He quickly opened the case, hinges creaking, and put on the wire-framed glasses.

His prescription had gotten worse, so the periodic table poster he'd tacked up over his bed was a little fuzzy. But old lenses were still a heck of a lot better than nothing. He looked behind him at Max.

Holy. Crap.

Max's short, dark brown hair was wavy and a little longer on top, messy from wearing the woolen hat that sat beside him on Doug's bed. He had rich brown eyes, full reddish lips, and a strong and stubbly jaw with a little cleft in the chin that Jeremy wanted to lick.

He'd taken off leather ankle boots and left them beside Jeremy's sneakers, his coat hanging on the doorknob. There was a hole in the big toe of his red sock, and jeans clung to his muscular thighs, one knee up as he lounged on Doug's bed, leaning back against the wall. The forest green of his thin sweater outlined trim arms and a narrow waist.

Max waved. "You can see me now?"

Could he *ever*. "Yep!" Jeremy shot to standing, stifling the burst of attraction before he humiliated himself with a boner. What was he going to do now? Max looked like he was staying for a bit—right, waiting out the weather.

Jeremy belatedly shrugged off his raincoat. His jeans were uncomfortably damp, but he wasn't about to take them off in front of a guy he'd just met. Especially since the guy in question was all *sprawled* and threatening to make him hard. His socks squelched, so he peeled them off, dropping them with a wet slap by his shoes.

"Do you want a drink?" Jeremy opened the bar fridge in the corner. Doug had brought it and said Jeremy could use it as much as he wanted as long as there was always enough room for a six-pack.

"Sure."

Jeremy squatted and pushed up his old glasses on his nose. It felt strangely familiar and foreign to wear them again, like trying on old clothes that didn't quite fit. "There's water and Moosehead and…milk."

Max laughed. "Hey, calcium's important, right? But I'll take a beer."

When Jeremy stood, he tried to hide a wince. He gave a bottle to Max and kept one for himself, making a mental note to replace Doug's stash. He walked gingerly to his own bed and perched on the side. His pasty feet were bare, and he scrunched the thin rug with his toes.

"You sure you don't need a doctor?" Max frowned as he twisted the cap off his bottle. His extended leg was so long—and the space between the beds so narrow—that Jeremy could have leaned forward and touched that exposed toe without hardly moving at all.

"My lower back's sore, but I'll ice it. My butt took most of the fall."

"Be careful with your tailbone, though. If your ass is sore tomorrow, get it checked out."

"Yep. Right." *Just talking about sore asses, as you do. No big deal.*

"Um, I'm sure it's fine." Jeremy gulped from his bottle and stared at Max's toe peeking out through the red sock. Otherwise, he'd stare at Max and probably look like a total creeper.

There was an electronic ping, and Max took his phone from his pocket and groaned. "I'm definitely not going to that party. My ex is asking where I am. Like I owe him anything after he dumped me."

Jeremy almost choked. *He*? Max's ex was a *he*?

Max scoffed, muttering more to himself than Jeremy. "We only went out for, like, a month in September. It wasn't serious at all. I'm too young for serious. And I was already thinking about ending it when he did, so." He shrugged. He paused and read another message. "Now he's acting like we had *plans*. What the actual fuck? No. Hell no."

"Right. So you're…"

Max tapped his phone. "Gay. Uh-huh."

"Oh." Jeremy's head spun at the casual way Max said that. Fearless, like it was nothing.

Now Max frowned at him, still holding his phone. "What?"

"Nothing! I'm not—it's totally okay with me. I just didn't expect someone like you to be…" *Like me.*

Max arched a thick brow. "Someone like me?"

Oh God, Jeremy was screwing this up epically. *This is why I don't talk to people!* He waved his hand. "You look like you're the stereotypical captain of the football team. Or maybe soccer? Baseball? Hockey? Lacrosse? But I'm guessing football because you're so big." His face went hot.

Thankfully, Max laughed. "Yep, football team. The season's over, and it's not like we're in the States. Not a ton of people at U of T care about football. We were two and six, so can't blame them."

"Right. It's not a big deal like being captain of the hockey team." He quickly added, "Not that it isn't impressive! I'm not captain of anything." *Please shut up now.*

Max chuckled. "It's cool."

Sweat prickled the back of Jeremy's neck, and instead of shutting up, he said, "And that's good that you're, um, gay." He got up and went to his desk in his corner of the room, suddenly unable to sit still although he was aching. He put down his beer and gulped from the tepid glass of water on his desk from earlier. "I mean, not *good*. Not that it's bad!"

"Dude, relax. I'm not going to jump you."

"I know!" Ugh, he didn't want Max to think he was a homophobe. "Was one of those guys your boyfriend now?"

"Huh?" Max lifted his hips and slid his phone into his pocket. "Why would you say that?"

Jeremy tore his gaze from Max's crotch. "You called one sweetheart or something."

"What? We need to revisit the concussion discussion, because—oh! You mean Honey. He's my roommate—we've got a basement apartment in the Annex. His real name's Cedric, but way back during frosh week, he won a wing-eating contest. Downed fifty wings in a few minutes."

Jeremy winced. "I feel sick just thinking about that."

"He felt sick doing it." Max grinned. "Hurled before he even got his dollar-store trophy. The sauce was honey garlic, and that morphed into the nickname. It's normal to us, so I forget what it sounds like to other people."

"Is he a football player too?"

"Yep, he was our quarterback. We're all pretty tight."

"And they don't mind that you're…" Jeremy's heart kicked up. It was surreal to talk about it. It was surreal that he was talking to anyone! That this guy was in his room. That this gorgeous guy was *like him*. Aside from being a billion times more confident and good-looking. He was surely smart too if he was applying to law school. Like everyone else at school, Max seemed to have his shit together.

"That I'm queer? No, man. It's not an issue. I'm sure there are still some ignorant assholes around, but you usually don't have to worry about them here on campus or downtown. I've never had a problem." He paused and gave Jeremy a knowing look. "If you're nervous or curious or anything…"

Now Jeremy's heart was pounding so hard he could hear it. "I'm not. I mean, I know I'm gay. I'm definitely gay. I've known for as long as I can remember. That's not the hard part." He forced himself to keep looking at Max. He'd actually said it out loud for the first time in months. The words floated in the air. In the world.

Max nodded. "Cool."

Jeremy drained the water glass and fidgeted. There—he'd told someone at school. It wasn't so bad. Even though he might throw up, he'd done it.

"You dating anyone? Having fun?"

He shook his head rapidly and opened his desk drawer to rearrange the paper clips.

"Why not? You're really cute."

Jeremy scoffed. "You're just being nice." He pushed paper clips around, his ears going hot. He could imagine how stark the freckles across his cheeks looked as he blushed. How ugly.

"So this is the part that's a struggle?"

"Part of it, I guess."

"Dude, you're totally cute. Everyone loves redheads. Did you join the queer club on campus? You'd meet a ton of people. Are you nineteen?" At Jeremy's nod, he said, "Hit the Church Street bars and hang out in the Village. Or there are plenty other queer spaces in the city. You don't have to be nervous."

Barking out a laugh, Jeremy closed the drawer with a thud. "You don't know who you're dealing with. Being nervous is my usual state of being. I've only said it out loud twice now."

Max's brows drew together. "Wait, which part?"

"That I'm...you know. Gay." He needed to get used to it already. He needed to stop cringing when he said it, waiting to be rejected. He needed to get his shit together like everyone else on campus. Everyone else in Toronto, it seemed like. The sidewalks and subways were crammed full of people rushing around, and they all seemed to know exactly where they were going.

Too restless to sit, he went to the window between the beds in the shoebox of a room and pulled back the curtain. "Still snowing."

"I won't stay too long, don't worry."

"No, I don't mean that you should go!" Now he was being rude when Max had gone out of his way to help. When he'd been a *hero*. "Really." Jeremy paced over to the desk to grab his beer before sitting on the side of his bed again, facing Max.

"Cool." Max sipped his beer. "So you're not out to many people yet?"

"Just my parents. I'm not allowed to tell my little brother yet, or anyone one else in the family. I think they're hoping it's a phase. Or they're just completely ashamed of me. Or both."

"Shit. That's brutal. I'm sorry."

Jeremy shrugged it off. "Anyway." The last thing he wanted to do was burst into tears. "My roommate Doug knows. Although I never told him myself—we had to fill out these info forms with allergies and likes and dislikes. I wrote it on there." He cleared his throat, putting on an announcer voice. 'Hey, I'm Jeremy. I'm from the West Coast, I have a pineapple allergy, I always heat up cold pizza, and I'm really into dudes. Great to meet you.' Maybe not those exact words."

Max narrowed his gaze. "Wait, you heat up cold pizza? In the microwave or oven?"

Jeremy was relieved Max was letting the stuff about Jeremy's parents drop. "Oven preferred, but microwave will do."

"Whoa. I'm shook. Cold pizza left out all night in the box is basically a food group at my place. I don't know if we can be friends."

"Oh." Friends? Was that on the table? Jeremy knew Max was joking, but the idea of becoming friends with this gorgeous, confident senior had apparently fried his brain. "Uh…"

Max shot him a wink, and *Jesus*, that cleft in his chin should be illegal. "I suppose I'll allow the reheated pizza. So your roommate's cool with you?"

"Yeah. He doesn't seem to care. He's chill. Comes in every week and goes to class and does his assignments. Then takes off home for three days. Perfect roommate, I guess."

"Not so much when you're trying to make friends."

Jeremy shrugged. "That's on me, though."

"Hmm. And what's the deal with your parents?"

He tried to shrug that off too. "It's… It didn't go great. Coming out, I mean." Understatement of the year. The hurt swelled, so huge and terribly hollow at the same time. "I don't want to talk about it."

"Sorry. That's rough."

Nodding, Jeremy took another sip from the cold beer bottle. His fingers were wet with condensation, and he peeled at the green label.

"No high school friends out here?"

"Nope. Kara's at McGill, and we said we'd totally get together since Montreal's only a six-hour drive—not that I have a car, but there's the train." He sighed, trying for a careless smile. "We got busy, I guess. She has a new boyfriend. All my high school friends seem to be having an amazing time at university. Having a blast. Which is great! I'm really happy for them."

"Sucks to lose touch though. Happened to me too. Is Kara your best friend?"

"Not really. I never had a best friend, even when I was little. The people I hung out with are scattered all over now and…moving on. I see them on Insta or wherever, but I have nothing to post myself."

"You've got a whole city outside your door. I bet people would like to see your pics."

"Maybe." Jeremy groaned. "Talk about a pity party. I'll shut up now."

Max didn't seem bothered. "Nah, it's cool. So what's the prob? You're too nervous to make friends?"

"Dumb, I know. I'm living in downtown Toronto with a million people, and I can't meet anyone."

Max shifted on Doug's bed, crossing his legs. His exposed toe still poked from its red sock. "I get it, man. The city can be really lonely. So many people around, but they're strangers."

"Yeah. But it's not like I've never been to the city before. Victoria's not huge, but I've taken the ferry over to Vancouver enough times. Toronto shouldn't be so intimidating."

"This place is a lot. University's a lot. Leaving home's a lot. Especially if it's tense with your parents."

Jeremy exhaled a long breath. He wasn't sure how the captain of the football team could even begin to understand not fitting in, but somehow Max seemed to. "I got here just before frosh week, and I tried to have fun. Meet people and make friends. But after a couple of events, it was just…" He shook his head. "I kept thinking about home and my parents. My brother who I can't even talk to besides emails to his monitored school account. He's in grade seven, and our folks won't let him have a cell yet. He actually sent me a postcard as part of a school project, but he's busy being a kid."

"Was the project on ancient communication?" Max nodded to the bulletin board nailed up over Jeremy's desk. "Is that it?"

"Something like that, and yeah." Jeremy went over and plucked the glossy postcard of the Rockies from the top corner. The only other thing he had tacked up was his class schedule, which was dumb because he'd memorized it by day two. He handed the postcard to Max.

"Wait, he calls you 'Cherry'?" Max grinned. "And you thought 'Honey' was weird!"

"No, not weird!" *I just thought he was your boyfriend, but apparently you don't have one, which shouldn't be as exciting as it is.*

"I'm teasing."

"Right. And yeah, Sean couldn't say 'Jeremy' when he was little. Called me 'Cherry,' and with my hair, it stuck."

Max smiled, reading the postcard, which was only a few lines saying that Sean missed him and would kick his butt at Super Mario when Jeremy came home. Jeremy had read the messy scrawl of words a hundred times. He wished he knew when exactly he would be going home. They hadn't kicked him out, but…

"Must be fun to have a little brother."

"Yeah." Jeremy took the postcard and carefully tacked it back up before sitting across from Max again.

Max carefully said, "Must've been tough to leave him and come here and not know anyone and have drama with your folks on top of it."

"Yeah," Jeremy repeated. "Frosh Week was like torture trying to be social and smile when I just wanted to cry."

Max's brow creased, his mouth turning down in sympathy, and *shit,* Jeremy's eyes burned. No. He would not cry now. He refused, forcing a laugh. "Man, this pity party is turning into a rager. You sure you wouldn't rather brave icy sidewalks and your clingy ex?"

Max laughed softly. "I'm good. And I don't blame you. That all sucks. Hard."

The sympathy and kindness from this stranger made Jeremy's throat tighten, but he breathed through it. No tears shed. "Thanks."

"What about classes? There must be kids in your major you can get to know."

"First year it's all prereqs in these massive lecture halls. In September, I should have talked to people, but I was so…" He tore off a strip of wet beer label, not knowing the right word. Pathetic? Cowardly?

Raw. Breakable.

That felt too…real to say aloud. Instead, Jeremy said, "It seems so easy for everyone else. I just want to hide. Like… I don't, but I do. You know?"

"Yeah. And don't be too sure other people are doing so great. They might just be better at faking it."

Jeremy smiled. "Maybe."

"I'm telling you, all the confident people you see rushing around campus are probably just as fucked up as you are."

"Not possible. I've made zero friends, I'm unloading all my trauma on a stranger who is being way too nice, I'm going to be alone for Christmas, and I'm definitely going to die a virgin."

Oh fuck. *That* he'd said out loud. For sure this time. He flushed so hot his head spun and he tasted bile.

"Aww, buddy." Max laughed, a deep, sexy rumble, but it wasn't unkind. "You really are having a shit time of it."

"I'm sorry. You're not my therapist. I don't even know you! I don't know what I'm saying anymore. Ignore me."

"And you're not even drunk." Max grinned—lord, the dimples. "At least, I don't think so."

"Definitely not. Can I blame this confessional on a concussion?"

"Absolutely." But Max's smile vanished, and he unfolded his big body, fluidly moving to kneel at Jeremy's feet. He held up his index finger. "Follow this with your eyes."

"I was kidding. I really didn't hit my head." Jeremy was very aware of Max's other hand resting a few inches from his hip on the rumpled duvet. "I swear."

"Humor me. Concussions are no joke. Honey kept playing once when he should have gone to the hospital." He shuddered. "It was bad."

So Jeremy submitted to Max's experiments, finally standing and closing his eyes to test his balance. When he opened his eyes again, his gaze rested on Max's Adam's apple. A bristly five o'clock shadow was visible over his smooth brown skin, and Jeremy followed the shadow up over that chin cleft to Max's full, smiling lips. Then he met brown eyes through lashes so thick that this close, Max looked like he was wearing eyeliner on his bottom lids.

Jeremy had never wanted to climb another person like a tree so much in his life.

"Did I pass?" he croaked.

Smiling, Max flopped back onto Doug's bed and drained his beer. "You passed. Okay, what are you doing tomorrow?"

"Studying." Jeremy perched on the side of his bed again, running through the periodic table in his head to avoid a humiliating erection.

"Study in the morning, and then we'll knock out our to-do list." Max ticked off items on his long fingers. "One: get your glasses replaced. Two: new boots. There's a good place on Queen West that usually has a sale going. Three: get you a winter coat and gloves and all that. We can hit Winners."

For a moment, Jeremy could only stare. "You—you don't have to do that. I can figure it out on my own."

Max ignored him, tapping another finger. "Four: get you laid. We'll go to the Village."

Excitement and fear jackknifed through Jeremy. "What? Me? To-morrow? That's... *Tomorrow?*"

"Why wait?" Max asked it like it was a genuine question, as though he just did things all the time without analyzing them for days first. Weeks. Months. *Years.*

Max stood, and he had to be six-two. Jeremy was only five-seven, and Max towered over him—which was oddly pleasing. He'd liked being tucked under Max's arm. Max grabbed his coat off the doorknob and fished something out of the pocket.

"I guess these aren't much use now, but it seemed wrong to leave them murdered there on the sidewalk." He deposited the twisted metal remains of Jeremy's glasses on the desk. "Sorry I smoked them."

"It was an accident. You've already done way more than most people would."

Max shrugged. "'Tis the season for giving, remember? Think of it as an early present. Besides, I need a distraction from waiting for my LSAT scores. It'll be fun. I'll be your fairy godfather."

Jeremy probably should have protested more, but his chest was strangely warm and tight. Max's friend had said something about him taking frosh under his wing, so apparently this was a thing he did? It didn't mean Jeremy was special—just that Max was generous.

"I'll get my glass slippers ready," Jeremy joked, but his smile faded. "Thank you. Really."

"Sure." Max pulled out his phone. "Give me your number." Jeremy did, and then Max was gone with a wave.

Jeremy honestly might have thought the whole thing had been a figment of his lonely mind, but the blue-and-white toque sat forgotten on Doug's bed. Letting his dick get hard freely—which took about three seconds—Jeremy picked up the hat by its fluffy pom-pom. The wool had a soft fleece lining, and he buried his face inside, inhaling deeply.

It smelled like any hat would—stuffy fabric and dried sweat and a hint of coconut, maybe? Probably from Max's shampoo. If Jeremy pressed his face to Max's actual head, dipping his nose into that tousle of almost-curls, would the coconut fill his senses?

Jeremy carefully folded the hat into his coat pocket so he wouldn't forget it tomorrow. *Tomorrow*, when he'd see Max again. When he actually had plans to hang with someone. And not just anyone. Max had spent time with him and listened to him and seemed like he really gave a shit.

Even if Max was just being nice to the pathetic frosh virgin, Jeremy couldn't deny that it felt really, really good to have someone look after him. To have someone care enough to give up their Saturday to hang with *him*. It was the best Christmas present he could hope for, even if it was only for a day.

Chapter Two

WHEN MAX'S ALARM blared, he automatically threw back the covers, rocked to his feet naked, and yelped at the cold. He'd left his phone plugged in on his desk, and he crossed the few steps to jab the screen before Honey banged on the wall and knocked down his cheaply framed Maple Leafs poster again.

Max knew the tyranny of the snooze button well, and he had to keep his alarm out of reach if he had any chance to getting his ass to the gym for leg day. As usual, his first thought after *too cold* and *make the noise stop* was about law school looming closer, accompanied by the familiar acidy drop of his stomach.

But today, that was followed by a burst of memory that made him smile. He broke the cardinal rule of mornings and let himself flop back into bed and pull up his duvet. Just for a minute. His brain was whirring too fast for him to go back to sleep anyway, replaying the strange night he'd had.

Maybe not strange—more like…unexpected. He'd been planning to get buzzed and have fun with the guys, but he wasn't sorry about missing the party. Hanging out in res with a sad little frosh having a weirdly intense conversation about his anxiety had been…

What? Not *fun*, exactly. Max's dad would say poor Jeremy had more issues than *TV Guide*. Then Max and his sis would ask, *"What's TV Guide?"* to be assholes, and Dad would throw up his hands theatrically and bellow, *"Kids today!"*

Max laughed, missing his dad all of a sudden. He'd see him soon enough for the holidays at least. And by then he'd have the LSAT results.

Stomach twisting, he threw back the duvet and forced himself up, tugging on his track pants. He shuffled into the hall and closed the bathroom door behind him, ordering himself to stop thinking about it. Hey, maybe he'd bomb the LSATs and the decision would be made for him.

He didn't know what the hell to hope for these days.

Yawning widely as he pissed, he remembered his plans for the day and found himself smiling again, changing gears back to the Jeremy train of thought. It wasn't that he *enjoyed* that Jeremy was so lost. But he'd liked hanging with him. He'd liked getting him home safely.

Maybe Honey was right, and he had a thing for helping out clueless newbies. It made him feel good. So did donating to charity or dropping a loonie in a hat when someone asked for change. Nothing wrong with that.

Cute baby gay definitely needed a nudge in the right direction. It would be fun to take him shopping and help him find his way around the Village.

Brushing his teeth with his hip against the counter, Max wondered if he'd ever been so clueless. Maybe he had, but he'd definitely never been as anxious as Jeremy seemed to be about meeting people and getting laid. Shit, that was the best part of university.

But Max would get him sorted out. In no time, Jeremy would be strutting confidently across campus, his virginity a distant memory. The kid clearly had no clue that he was sexy as hell. In other circumstances, Max would have been tempted to pop that cherry himself.

Cherry was a fitting nickname, he thought, remembering the postcard. He smiled around his electric toothbrush. Mmm, the ginger hair and adorable freckles. The way Jeremy bit his lower lip and blushed. That earnestness—like a puppy with zero chill. A sad puppy in need of a bone.

Laughing at his own dumb joke, he spit toothpaste into the sink. A white film of soap scum had built up, and it was probably his turn to clean the bathroom, but he'd deal with that later. He popped his toothbrush back on its charger, ignoring the gross ring on the bottom that also needed scrubbing.

His mind easily bounced away from any more thoughts of chores, and he went to pull on his workout clothes, thinking of Jeremy again with a smile. Jeremy needed a friend, which was why Max had left before he'd been tempted any further to see how deep he could make him blush.

He would fairy godfather the shit out of this. Build up Jeremy's confidence and get him to relax and have fun. He'd be catnip to so many guys. Hell, they'd definitely be lining up to be Jeremy's first.

Max frowned as he dug in his knapsack for his earbuds. There were plenty of creeps out there. He'd have to keep an eye on Jeremy and make sure his first time wasn't with some asshole who would use him and throw him away.

In the kitchen, he grabbed a too-ripe banana, grimacing as he ate it. Bleary-eyed and groaning, Honey dragged ass past him to the coffee machine, fumbling a pod into it. He rubbed his hand over his tightly braided hair. His Raptors shirt was ripped at the collar, revealing a fresh hickey on his dark skin.

"Morning!" Max practically shouted because he was a dick.

Honey grunted.

"Good party?"

He grunted again. "You should have showed. The strippers were epic." He whistled softly in appreciation. "There was one chick with the biggest tits I've ever seen. And you would have loved the Santa guy." Honey flexed his muscular arms in demonstration. "Where'd you get to anyway? You hook up?"

"Nah. I hung out with that frosh. Jeremy. The weather was shit and I didn't feel like going back out across campus."

Honey jabbed the coffee machine as if that would make it dispense faster. "I forgot about that." He frowned. "The kid's okay, right?"

"Yeah. No thanks to you assholes."

"Eh, who needs us when Saint Maxwell's on the case?"

Max flipped him the finger before filling his water bottle from the ancient Brita in the fridge. "He needed a hand. Actually still does. I'm gonna help him pick out new glasses."

"Huh. Okay."

"And I'm taking him to the Village later, so count me out for poker."

"Dude, it's the last session before the holidays. Ty will be pissed if you don't give him a chance to even the score before we pay out."

"He'll live. I told Jeremy we'd hang."

After taking a noisy, grateful sip of his coffee, hands cupping the mug reverently, Honey said, "Can't you take him to the Village tomorrow?"

"Maybe. I can ask." Jeremy likely didn't have any plans, so Max could leave it up to him.

"You gonna tap that?"

"What? No!" Despite his quick denial, a low pulse of desire at the idea tugged in Max's belly. "I'm just helping. He's nervous."

"Baby bird got a broken wing?"

"Something like that. He just came out and his parents aren't really talking to him."

"Oh, shit." Honey shook his head. "That sucks."

"Yeah. He doesn't have any friends. I feel bad for him."

"You can always bring him tonight. If you're not into him and he knows how to play, he's cool."

They'd had a strict no-dates policy since first year, when Tyler had brought a new girl every week and was more interested in her boobs than playing the game. "Okay. Maybe. You coming to the gym?"

"Do I look like I'm coming to the motherfucking gym?"

Max laughed and grabbed another banana on his way out, making sure to slam the door as noisily as possible.

A FEW HOURS later, his quads aching, Max spotted Jeremy pacing outside the optical store on Bloor West. As Max approached with a wave, Jeremy visibly unclenched.

"Hey!" Max called. "Sorry I'm late. Subway delay. You know, the usual with the TTC."

Jeremy smiled but looked on edge. "Right. I thought maybe you changed your mind."

"Nah, man. I wouldn't leave you hanging. No service in the tunnel or I would've texted."

"No problem." He shook his head. "Sorry. I'm all..." He flapped his hands.

Jeremy seriously had some anxiety issues. Part of Max wanted to give him a hug and tell him everything would be okay, but that would probably be weird, so instead he said, "It's cool. Come on." He led the way into the store, a bell chiming overhead. The bright ceiling lights were augmented with garlands and white fairy lights across the top of the rows of frames and mirrors on three walls of the store. "Santa Claus is Coming to Town" played.

"Any brands you like in particular?" Max asked. The store was crowded, and the salespeople were all busy.

"Not really. Whatever looks okay."

"You mean whatever looks *spec*tacular." He shot Jeremy a wink. "See what I did there?"

"Uh-huh!" Jeremy grinned, looking a little flustered, his cheeks going pink. "I wish I had contacts. It's so hard to see myself in the new frames. Maybe I should just get them to replace the lenses in these ones." He pushed the wire-rim glasses up his nose. "Had these for most of high school. I know they fit my face okay."

"Yeah, but 'okay' is not what we're going for. Let's have a look."

They perused the racks, and Jeremy found a few to try. Max figured Jeremy knew his style, although they all tended to be the thin metal frames. Jeremy carefully tucked his glasses in the pocket of his raincoat. The other pocket bulged.

Max asked, "You happy to see me, or what?"

Jeremy blinked up at him owlishly. "Sorry?"

He nudged Jeremy's stuffed pocket. "Bad joke."

"Oh! That's your hat. You forgot it." He pulled out the toque and handed it over.

"Shit, thanks. I didn't bother with a hat today since it's above freezing. But I'll need this in Pinevale at Christmas for sure. Not that I don't have other hats, but this one's my fave." He tossed it in his bag.

"No problem." Standing very close to a mirror, Jeremy tried on the frames.

Max nixed one pair that were too narrow, but the other two were fine. He asked, "You ever try plastic frames? Something a little bolder?"

"No. My mom says darker frames overwhelm my face."

"Ah. Assume you got the prescription from her?"

"Yeah." Jeremy put his old glasses back on. "We texted. It was fine." He grabbed one of the prospective frames. "I'll just get these."

"I don't think those fall into the *spec*tacular category. Come on, you should be excited about whatever you pick." He scanned the rack nearest them and chose a few. "Try these."

"Really, these are fine. You're going to be bored if I try on everything."

"You're not trying on everything. Humor me. Unless you genuinely like those ones."

Jeremy sighed. "Not really. Okay."

One by one, he tried on frames, leaning right into the mirror that sat on a desk. Max couldn't help but enjoy the view. Damn, he had a sweet little ass in those jeans. "How's your butt?" Max asked, struggling to tear his eyes away. "Sore?"

"A bit, but it's fine." Jeremy glanced around nervously, seeming to check if anyone was listening.

Max realized a sore ass could sound…suggestive. Before his brain could dive down the rabbit hole of Jeremy's ass any further, he was distracted by Jeremy trying on a bigger pair of black glasses. He sat up straighter. "Oh yeah. Love that look."

Jeremy leaned in closer to the mirror, his jacket riding up even more. "You think?"

"Hell yeah. I like that classic vibe, but not too thick and chunky on the plastic. They still look sleek. It's hot. The big, dark frames really make your eyes pop."

Said hazel eyes widened a fraction. "Mine?"

"No, that lady over there who's been bitching out the salesgirl for five minutes about a scratch on her new glasses as if she wasn't the one who dropped them."

Jeremy laughed. "Shh!" He turned back to the mirror until he was only a few inches away. "You don't think they, like, take over my face?"

Max stood behind him for a closer look. "No. I think they bring more attention. Your other ones are just there. No statement. No style. Just functional. These are like, 'Bam! I've got glasses, bitch!'"

"Right." Jeremy bit his lip, and *damn*, that was adorable.

"Trust me, these are keepers. But it's up to you."

"I guess it can't hurt to try something new."

"That's the whole idea, right? You're going to get laid in no time."

A middle-aged couple nearby laughed, and Jeremy ducked his head. He fished out his old glasses and put them on, but Max stopped him.

"Put the new ones on and gimme your phone for a sec," Max said. When Jeremy handed it over, Max swiped up for the camera and told him to smile. He took a few shots and examined them, quickly determining the winner and deleting the others. He gave back the phone after Jeremy slipped his old glasses back on. "There's your next Instagram post. What's your handle? I'll follow you."

"Oh. Um, it's 'Jeremy-underscore-science-nerd.' I know, I know."

"What? It's cute. Very on brand." Max opened the app on his phone and searched the user name. "Request sent." He watched as Jeremy checked his app.

Jeremy laughed, his eyebrows shooting up above the metal rims. "Future-lawyer-jock," he read. "Guess that's on brand too."

"Yup." Max smiled, but unease nagged. Was he a future lawyer? Would he have to change his social media handles if he didn't go to law school?

As if that's what I should be worried about.

"I'm sure you did great on the LSATs."

He blinked at Jeremy in surprise. "Guess I can't hide it, huh? Thanks." Max sidestepped a woman in a puffy winter parka dragging a wailing kid wearing light-up reindeer antlers. "Anyway, we should get your order in and get to Winners."

They sat at one of the desks and an optician took Jeremy's eye measurements with a ruler-looking thingy. Jeremy had pulled up his prescription on his phone, the photo in a text thread. The phone was sitting on the desk, and Max glanced at the messages.

Okay, he more than glanced. Curiosity spiked the ball in the end zone and he went into creeper mode, reading the visible messages. The first was from Jeremy, a polite hello and asking how everyone was, then the request for the prescription photo. Then his mother's response.

We're fine. Busy packing. You're still covered on our insurance, so send me the receipt. Try to be more careful with this pair. Let us know when you have your exam results.

Max quickly looked away and spun a carousel of reading glasses on the corner of the desk, squirming in guilt for having read the texts. Which were weird. Like, they were polite, and it was good his parents weren't making him pay for the new glasses. But then there was the dig about being more careful. And busy packing for what? But then she wanted to know about Jeremy's exams. There was this push and pull.

Jeremy had said he was going to be alone for the holidays, so whatever his family was busy packing for, apparently he wasn't going? Was he going to be stuck in res? Max supposed there would be a handful of other people there, so maybe it wouldn't be so bad? Maybe he'd actually make friends with some of them. Maybe.

The optician said the new glasses could be delivered express by the end of day on Monday and rang up Jeremy's order. He paid with a credit card, and Max wondered if that was a card his parents paid off. Obviously none of his business, but Jeremy hadn't mentioned having a job. They headed out, walking a few blocks to Spadina to catch the streetcar.

There were glittery wreaths on lampposts and greenery with red berries in planters that held flowers in the summer. Store windows looked like Christmas explosions, and shoppers bustled by with bags, reminding Max that he had to get his family's presents before he went home because there were way more options in Toronto.

They sat next to each other on a two-seater as the streetcar made its way south in fits and starts. It got crowded fast, catching every red, people squeezing on and off at every stop.

Max finally broke as they inched toward College Street. "You said you'll be alone over the holidays? You don't want to head home to BC?" *And what are your parents packing for? Why aren't you going?*

Jeremy's smile was tight-lipped. "They're going to Hawaii with Sean. Taking a cruise around the islands and stuff. They're spending a lot on me being here, and with my exam schedule, I can't go anyway. It's totally fine."

"Right." Max nodded and pretended he believed for a nanosecond that anything about the situation with Jeremy's folks was "totally fine." He shifted, his knee jammed into the seat in front, imagining Jeremy in his barebones little dorm room on a deserted campus for weeks.

Max didn't like that idea one little bit. In fact, he hated it.

How could he help? He automatically began formulating a plan, flipping through options in his mind like the different plays on a football field.

"The best way to meet up with guys who are around over the holidays is a dating app. Well, 'dating' can be a little euphemistic. Have you signed up for any?"

Wide-eyed, Jeremy shook his head. "I've looked at them in the app store, but..."

Strangely, Max was glad to hear he hadn't cruised for guys online. Which made zero sense, since if he wanted to help Jeremy get laid, this was going to help. He pulled out his phone and pointed to an icon. "This one's good if you want to check it out."

"Uh-huh. Okay!" Jeremy squeaked. "So, that's exciting about going to law school," he said, clearly eager to change the subject.

"I guess." Now it was Max's turn to be reticent.

Jeremy frowned. "You don't sound too sure."

Busted. He laughed it off. "Just stressed about the LSAT."

Truth was, he hadn't discussed his doubts with anyone, not even his sister or Honey. But Jeremy had told him all sorts of things. He'd trusted Max with his secrets even though they'd just met. Maybe Max could confide in him too.

It was kind of nice that Jeremy was new—that he didn't know all about Max already and have preconceived notions. He wouldn't judge him the way Max's family and friends might. Not that they were judgy. Max was probably being totally unfair to them.

But he was supposed to be Jeremy's fairy godfather—confident and in charge. Captain of the team. He wasn't about to dump all his internal drama on the kid he was helping out.

Jeremy said, "I get not wanting to talk about it. There's a lot I usually keep to myself. Until I basically have a nervous breakdown and unload all my crap on unsuspecting good Samaritans. You're welcome."

Max smiled. "Oh, you've done that before?"

"Actually, you were my first."

The words were innocent, but they stirred a tug of lust that made Max's balls tingle. He'd never had a virgin kink, but he had to admit there was something about Jeremy that drew him in. Maybe it was because Jeremy was physically smaller, and Max typically went for muscular guys more his own size. He wanted to take care of Jeremy in a way he wasn't used to. Not paired with sex, at least.

He'd always been a mentor on the field and in the locker room, but that was about brotherhood and the team. He'd never let himself think of teammates as sexy. But it was different with Jeremy. The idea of being his first made his dick throb.

"Have you always wanted to be a lawyer?"

"Yeah. Probably a boring story."

Jeremy shrugged. "We're going to be here a while."

Metal screeched as the streetcar slowed at Dundas. All the restaurants and shops had signs in Chinese and English, and people thronged the sidewalks at the heart of Chinatown on a Saturday afternoon. Some pushed their way off the streetcar as others squeezed on. A bulky purse smacked Max on the head, the woman apologizing profusely as he waved her off with a smile.

He realized he couldn't remember the last time he'd told someone about his mom. The guys knew she died when he was a kid, but it wasn't like they'd sat down and had a deep and meaningful conversation about it. Not that there was any reason to have one now with Jeremy on the Spadina streetcar. Weird that he kind of wanted to?

"The thing with becoming a lawyer has a lot to do with my mom. She died in a car accident when I was nine. She was a lawyer with Legal Aid."

"Oh. I'm really sorry." Jeremy quickly added, "That she passed away—not that she was a lawyer."

Max gave him a smile. "I knew what you meant."

Jeremy grimaced. "Sometimes I say the wrong thing, or I just think I do, and I make everything worse by being super awkward. Like now."

They were sitting closely—streetcars were built for unrealistically small people—and Max gave him a friendly nudge with his shoulder. "It's cool. You don't need to be so worried. We're just talking."

"Easy for you to say. But yeah, I'll try. So, your mom was like a public defender?"

"Right. She worked her ass off to help people. My grandparents were originally from Goa in India, and they came to Canada before she was born. They gave everything to help my mom get to law school, and she worked so hard. She was top of her class, and there was pressure to become a Crown Attorney. But she was determined to represent people who really needed her help."

"Even if they were guilty?"

"Yep. But the justice system is so fucked up. She really wanted to fix it, you know?" He breathed deeply, thinking of her passionate speeches about racial and gender inequality at the dinner table. "Easier said than done, but I wish she'd had the chance." Before he could get stupidly emotional, he said, "Anyway, my dad was a part-time marketing manager, and he did the school runs and cooking. Now, he and my stepmother run a maple syrup farm."

"Cool. Or should I say, sweet." Jeremy wrinkled his nose. "That was bad."

That was adorable. "I'll allow it," Max said in his best judge voice. "How about you? Your parents, I mean." Shit, sensitive subject. He added, "Where's your family from?"

"Originally Glasgow and Cork."

"You'd never guess from looking at you," Max teased.

Like he'd hoped, it made Jeremy laugh. "Shocking, I know." He pushed up his sleeve and jacket to reveal the lower half of his pale, freckled forearm. "Part leprechaun for sure."

Before Max knew what he was doing, he skimmed his fingertips over Jeremy's skin. "So many freckles."

"Um, yeah." Adam's apple bobbing, Jeremy tugged down his jacket.

Max made himself look anywhere else and jumped to his feet. "Shit! This is us." He announced, "Excuse me!" and squeezed a path for them to the middle doors. They escaped into the fresh air and headed down Queen Street. Max checked the address on his phone. "You know, we probably should have taken Bathurst down. Sorry."

"S'okay. You can tell me more about being a lawyer. And I'm really curious about how a maple syrup farm works."

"Didn't you take a class trip as a kid?"

"Nope. Not really a BC thing, I guess? They probably make maple syrup somewhere in BC, but I'm not sure."

"Yeah, that makes sense. There's a lot of production in Ontario, but Quebec is the epicenter. Maple syrup is very intense there. The business, I mean. The syrups vary."

Jeremy stepped into the doorway of a fabric store to make room for two mega strollers coming toward them. "Do you know how to make it?"

"Yep. My stepmother's the boss, but Meg and I helped out when we were in high school. Meg's my sister. Technically my stepsister— Valerie's daughter from her first marriage. Valerie's my stepmom. She's cool. She and my dad got married when I was twelve and Meg was ten. Dad and I moved from Scarborough to the farm near Pinevale."

"Sounds nice."

"I didn't think so in grade seven, but I came around."

"You and Meg get along?"

"Yeah, I lucked out there." He smiled, wondering what Meg would think of Jeremy. He decided she'd really like him. "She's the best. Your little bro sounds cool too."

"He is." Jeremy's smile was tense. "And that's really cool your mom inspired you to be a lawyer."

From one sore spot to another. Not that becoming a lawyer should be a sensitive topic the way Jeremy's brother was. Max should be excited about it! He shouldn't low key feel like puking. As they reached a corner, a streetcar rattled by. A taxi horn blared and a guy in front of the Tim Hortons yelled about cows eating grass.

"Totally. Anyway, time to get you geared up for winter." He motioned to Winners, and they crossed the street.

This day was about helping Jeremy—he didn't need to hear about Max's angst and the idea about going to teachers college instead of law school. Even thinking the words *teachers college* made him antsy with shame. As he led the way into the store and an explosion of holiday sparkle, the voice he'd been working so hard to silence hissed.

I can't disappoint my mom.

Time for Max to focus on his fairy godfather mission. He slung an arm over Jeremy's shoulders, enjoying the snug fit. "Winter is coming, and you may not have to deal with dragons, but windchill is worse."

"Dragons?" Jeremy's ginger brows met.

"Sorry, random *Game of Thrones* moment."

"Oh! Duh." Jeremy grimaced. "I'm so stupid sometimes."

"Whoa. Ease up on yourself there. It's cool." He had a feeling this kid beat himself up over *way* too much. He nudged Jeremy's shoulder playfully. "That last season was so bad I wouldn't blame you for wiping it all from your memory. And you know, I actually wouldn't mind dragons in winter. At least they breathe fire."

Jeremy grinned at Max's dumb joke, and Max steered him to the wall of hats. More Insta pics coming right up.

Chapter Three

"GOOD TIMING! HEY, little bro. How's it hangin'?" A stocky blond with shaggy hair held up his hand for a clasp-shake.

"Uh, good!" Jeremy said, taking the guy's hand and trying not to be completely awkward. The porch creaked under their boots. It was just past five o'clock and already dark, colored holiday lights glowing on the porch railings.

"Ty, this is Jeremy," Max said. "Jeremy, meet Tyler." He took Tyler's hand and did a clasp-shake with a lean-in and partial hug.

"How's your ass?" Tyler asked. "You went down hard."

"Fine!" Jeremy squeaked. He really wanted people to stop inquiring about the state of his ass.

As Tyler rambled to Max about his fantasy football league, Jeremy followed them inside and peered around curiously. When Max had asked if he minded postponing going to the Village until the next night, Jeremy had agreed eagerly. The idea of actually getting laid was both thrilling and terrifying. This way, he got to spend even more time with Max and could put off the stress of potentially picking up a guy.

He realized picking up someone wasn't supposed to be stressful, but his brain whirled and stomach churned, and he was only too happy to postpone. Especially since it meant going to Max's place like they were officially friends or something. Acquaintances at least.

Max's place was the basement of a house in the Annex, accessed via a locked staircase just inside the foyer. There was another locked door to the main floor. Jeremy took off his new boots at the bottom of the stairs and added them to the collection on a plastic mat.

His new purchase was what Max had called "in-between boots," for when it was icy or slushy enough not to want to wear running shoes, but not freezing or snowy enough for the big guns. They were brown Blundstone knockoffs made of synthetic leather but surprisingly comfortable. Jeremy actually had a similar pair back home that he stupidly hadn't thought to bring since he'd planned to buy something suitable for real winter.

Max had insisted he needed both, since you didn't want to go cruising the bars in clunky boots. The thought of cruising bars in any kind of footwear made Jeremy break out in a cold sweat, but he'd kept that to himself.

He added his new navy peacoat to one of the hooks on the wall already bulging with coats. His rain jacket was inside one of the shopping bags he tucked into the corner, along with a new puffy parka that the tag promised would keep him warm to minus-fifty Celsius. God help him if it ever got that cold, which Max assured him it didn't in Toronto. Apparently minus-thirty or even minus-forty with the windchill happened a few times a winter, though. Jeremy was already shivering at the thought.

The apartment wasn't as dark as Jeremy had expected for a basement. There were IKEA standing lamps in every corner of the living room, along with surprisingly big windows near the ceiling that probably let in a fair amount of light during the day. A huge TV was attached to the wall across from a saggy red velour couch, and a square dining table sat off to the side by the entrance to what looked like a narrow galley kitchen.

The walls were painted plain beige and had a few art posters tacked up, also IKEA by the looks of them. He wondered if it was Max or Honey who'd chosen the black-and-white photo of the Brooklyn Bridge. There were no decorations or Christmas tree, but Honey was probably going home for the holidays like Max was.

The flare of hurt as Jeremy thought about his parents and Sean flying to Honolulu for their Christmas cruise stabbed hot in his chest. He'd checked the news earlier to make sure there hadn't been any plane crashes. So far, so good. Jeremy took a deep breath and locked away all those messy worries. Max was taking a chance inviting him for poker, and he was going to make a good impression.

Even with his slightly blurry old glasses, at least now he could get a good look at Max's friends. Carrying bright plastic bowls piled high with chips, Honey greeted Jeremy with a bright smile. He was Black, tall, and built like, well, a football player. Mike was big too, chubby with buzzed dark hair and light brown skin.

They crowded around a square dining table that was surely a hand-me-down judging by the nicks and a big stain on the pale wood that had probably been red wine. The basement had wall-to-wall carpet with its fair share of faded stains as well, although the apartment didn't seem dirty. There were some used glasses sitting on the coffee table by the couch, but it was clean overall. Jeremy wondered what Max's room looked like but couldn't exactly go poke around.

He fiddled with the sleeve of a new sweater Max had encouraged him to buy. Max had liked it on him so much that Jeremy had said he was chilly and changed into it in the café bathroom at lunch. It was fuchsia pink, which Jeremy would never have picked for fear of looking too gay. Which he knew was bullshit internalized homophobia, but he still braced for Max's friends to make some kind of comment. They didn't, eating chips and talking more fantasy football while Max and Honey served drinks in red plastic cups.

Jeremy wondered what his parents would say if they saw the pink sweater. Also what they'd say when they got the credit card bill, even though he'd mentioned to his mom he had to buy some winter clothes. He'd bought more than he planned, but they wouldn't be mad, would they? He'd always been responsible with his card, which they'd given him for emergencies and stuff when he turned eighteen.

Even though everything was weird and tense now, they wouldn't cut him off. Would they? He had some savings from working at an electronics store all through high school, but that wouldn't last long if his parents stopped paying. He'd have his meal plan for the rest of the school year, but what then? What if—

"You good?" Max asked quietly, nudging Jeremy's knee under the table with his own.

Nodding automatically, Jeremy picked up his cup and gulped the mix of Jack and Coke that was kind of gross. "Just going over what you taught me about poker."

Honey's eyes lit up. "What do we have here? A virgin in our midst?" He shuffled two piles of cards together with a flourish, thumbs releasing each side.

Jeremy helplessly felt his face go hot and knew he was beet red even if Honey had just meant a virgin at poker. He fiddled with his glasses and took another gulp.

Max said, "He's a natural, so don't get too excited."

"Don't worry, buddy," Mike said. "We'll be gentle. While we take alllll your money."

"I thought we were just playing for change." Jeremy thought about the credit card again and the what-ifs. He and Max had stopped by a laundromat to use the ancient change machine that still serviced equally ancient coin-operated washers, so he had a baggie of quarters as well as whatever random change he'd had in his wallet.

"We are," Max assured him. "But these morons get real excited about nickels and dimes."

"That's the fun of it," Honey said as he dealt. "All right, let's see what you got, kid."

Jeremy was confident he didn't have much. Max had bought a pack of cards from the random stuff at the checkout line at Winners and taught him the basics over lunch.

Now they played poker and snacked. When a pizza showed up, Max insisted it was on him. They'd stopped for booze earlier, so at least Jeremy had contributed by buying a bottle. It was definitely going to his head, his face pleasantly flushed.

Here he was playing cards and drinking like an actual university student instead of hiding alone in his room studying. Sure, he still had two exams, but he could study tomorrow before meeting up with Max again.

You're going to get laid in no time.

No. Jeremy ordered his asshole brain to stop worrying about that. It wasn't as though he *had* to hook up with someone. Besides, that was tomorrow. Tonight, he was one of the guys. He drained his cup and squinted at his cards. He wasn't doing too badly, although his pile of quarters was diminishing.

"Are we gettin' you drunk for the first time?" Honey asked.

"No!" Jeremy insisted, with honestly more offense than was warranted. "I've been drunk plenty of times."

Max raised an eyebrow. "Define 'plenty.' Are we talking double digits?"

Jeremy opened and closed his mouth. "Well. Probably not. But I've been drunk more than once!"

"We've got a wild man on our hands here," Tyler said. "So what did you first get drunk on? For me, it was Baby Duck."

Everyone groaned, and Jeremy shuddered at the thought of the super-sweet bubbly. Max said, "Meg and I skimmed off the top of Dad and Valerie's random collection of bottles in the liquor cabinet and mixed it all with Coke. We puked so hard."

Jeremy grimaced, rearranging the cards in his hand. "For me it was Smirnoff Ice."

Everyone groaned again, laughing. Mike said, "I haven't had that in ages."

Honey snorted. "Right, because your palate is so fucking refined these days."

"This is *craft* beer, I'll have you know." Mike lifted his bottle. "I'm refined as fuck."

"Since when is Rickard's craft beer?" Max asked. "That's Molson, you tool."

Mike took a gulp from his bottle of Rickard's White. "This is wheat beer. I squeezed a motherfucking lemon into it."

"Do you even know what craft beer is?" Tyler asked.

"Clearly not," Jeremy mumbled, then flushed, shocked he'd said it aloud.

The rest of them howled as Mike puffed up his chest. "Easy there, Smirnoff Ice." Then he grinned and gave Jeremy's shoulder a playful punch. Jeremy returned his smile as Mike took another gulp of his beer. "I don't care what it's called. I like it."

They finished the pizza and Honey won just about all the coins on the table before saying, "Let's go skating. The rink at Nathan Phillips is open to midnight this weekend. We've still got a few hours since we started so early."

Everyone seemed into it, and Jeremy wondered if he should leave them to it. They probably didn't want him hanging around all night. Max had already spent the whole day with him and had been way nicer than he had to be. Besides, Jeremy hadn't been on skates since he was a kid.

Max nudged his arm. "You up for it?"

Jeremy said, "Uh, I'm not so great on ice. You might recall."

"Now's your chance to get revenge for us laughing at you," Honey said. "Because I guarantee some of us will be falling all over the damn place."

"Come on, it'll be fun." Mike grinned. "We're drunk enough, but not too much to get kicked out or anything. I'll order a ride."

So Jeremy found himself squeezed into the back seat of a Lyft after Tyler convinced the driver to let them all pile in. Not just squeezed—he was sitting on Max's lap. Max's arm was slung around Jeremy's waist, and Jeremy sat rigid, hardly breathing.

They bumped over streetcar tracks, and he mumbled, "Sorry."

But Max only chuckled. Then he leaned forward and said quietly, "Relax. You're good." His breath ghosted over Jeremy's ear, sending a ripple down his spine.

Beside them in the middle seat, Honey said, "Maxwell enjoys a cute boy sitting on his lap."

From the front seat, Mike added, "Lap. Face. He's easy."

The guys laughed, and Max shrugged. "Where's the lie?" He gave Jeremy's waist a squeeze.

Was that a friendly squeeze? To get Jeremy to relax already? Or did it mean that Max really *did* like having Jeremy on his lap? Was Max hitting on him? Or was this all just friendly joking around? It had to be that. Max was way out of Jeremy's league. Like, in another stratosphere.

No, Jeremy could not even think about going down that road. Max was only being nice. The end. Jeremy was not going to daydream about anything more. He was not going to start crushing on Max.

Fine, he already was, but he was nipping it in the bud. No more crushing. No more enjoying the warmth of Max's body under him. The weight of his arm. The tickle of his exhalations on the back of Jeremy's neck. He wondered—

Nope. No wondering. Abort the wondering. He needed to focus on ice skating and not humiliating himself.

Which didn't go amazingly well but could have been worse. The rink was packed, Nathan Phillips Square decorated to within an inch of its life for the holidays with a giant menorah and Christmas tree, Toronto City Hall looming over the scene. Even though he lived right downtown, Jeremy realized he'd seen more of the city today than he had since school started.

Holiday music blasted, and he wondered how the people living in condos near the square felt about it. He supposed it was cold enough that their windows were shut anyway. The temperature had dropped enough that he was glad of the new winter gear. Max had assured him he could leave most of his purchases at the apartment to avoid carrying them around. Jeremy was pleased to have at least one more excuse to see Max and get his stuff.

Breath fogging the chilly air, they shoved their feet into rented hockey skates—no toe picks, thankfully. They also somehow passed the security guards' sobriety screening and were soon clomping around the crowded rink. Jeremy took baby steps, his arms wide. This was such a terrible idea.

Yet when Max grinned at him, he grinned back. It was surely going to end with his ass hitting the ice again, but it was fun. He was having *fun*. Max was there, and if he fell, he wouldn't be alone. His old glasses could have used a tightening and slipped down his nose too much. Jeremy was careful to keep pushing them up.

The lights were a bit blurred with his old prescription, the strands strung around the three massive arches over the rink a mess of golden light. The rest of the square was crowded with people and lines of stalls for a pop-up holiday market. A few fat snowflakes drifted down.

Over laughter and chatter and happy shrieks, "All I Want for Christmas is You" filled the air, and Jeremy shuffled a few steps on the ice. *Help me, Mariah.*

Honey whipped past, shouting, "Bend your knees!"

Max snorted. "Easy for him to say. He grew up playing hockey."

"You didn't?" Jeremy asked, performing a stiff-legged progression of inches.

"Nah, it was all football for me. Okay, bending knees. We got this."

Jeremy watched Max get up some good speed, his choppy crosscuts miles better than Jeremy's as he rounded one end of the rink. Then a little girl on figure skates whizzed by at an alarming speed. For an endless moment, Max pinwheeled his arms, the blades slipping and his feet flying forward.

Bam!

On his ass, he burst out laughing, and Jeremy walk-skated in short, faster strides toward him. "You okay? Oh shit!" Jeremy hadn't realized how much speed he'd quickly gained, and now he was heading right for Max with no way to stop. Max reached up to grab his hips with strong, leather-clad hands.

Tyler and Mike were laughing their asses off, and Max called "Bite me!" with a good-natured smile. He was still holding Jeremy's hips. "You good?"

"You're the one on the ice." Jeremy would probably join him shortly but tried for cocky. At least confident? Probably failed miserably.

But Max laughed. "Yep. That little girl was merciless. You gonna help me up, Cherry?"

Jeremy's heart flipped. His dumb nickname sounded different when Max said it. Almost sexy or something. Which was obviously all in his head. "Sure." He gave Max his hand and pulled.

In a twist that shocked no one, Jeremy ended up sprawled on top of Max on the ice. They were laughing too hard to do anything about it, and Honey arrived in a spray of ice to laugh and point. Max's body felt so good under Jeremy—muscular, but also warm and soft. His gloved hand was on Jeremy's thigh, and Jeremy was practically straddling him as he tried to push himself up.

He might not have been trying quite as strenuously as he could have.

In the end, Tyler and Mike made their way around, doing the walk-shuffle-skate move, and they helped Honey get Max and Jeremy on their skates again. Jeremy clutched Max's arms, and Max smiled down at him, his brown eyes crinkling, stubbly cheeks dimpled. That chin cleft was tantalizingly close…

Honey cleared his throat. "You losers want a few tips on how not to clean the rink with your asses?"

They tried a few more laps before returning the skates and grabbing cups of minty hot chocolate. A "Little Drummer Boy" mash-up filled the air, and Jeremy sipped the sweet, warm cocoa.

Max slung an arm over his shoulders. "This was a fun day."

"Yeah." Jeremy's throat was suddenly thick. He wanted to thank Max for being so kind to him. For being—he hoped—a friend. But if he said anything more he might burst into tears, so Jeremy took another sip of his hot chocolate.

Flurries of snow increased as the temperature hovered around the freezing mark. A fluffy flake landed right on the end of Max's nose, and

Jeremy swiped it off with a laugh. He watched it melt on the end of his glove, wondering what the unique pattern would have looked like under a microscope. When he looked up, Max was watching him.

Their gazes locked, and Jeremy's breath stuttered. Snowflakes drifted between them, and Max's eyes dropped. He'd taken off his glove, and he brushed Jeremy's bottom lip with a fingertip.

"Snowflake," he murmured.

They watched it melt on Max's finger.

Max cleared his throat. "So hey, you wanna go out tomorrow night? We need to get you laid, right?"

Jeremy could only nod and for a minute, he let his growing, undeniable crush on Max expand to fill every lonely corner of him, shining as brightly as the golden bulbs illuminating the night.

Chapter Four

THE RED COUCH sagged even lower as Honey flopped down next to Max, tilting him toward the middle. Eyes locked on the screen as his player scaled a wall while a bomb exploded in the distance, Max said, "Hey." Gripping the controller, he swore under his breath as he jerked too late to avoid an ambush.

"You're dead," Honey noted.

"Really? I hadn't noticed." Max tossed the controller on the cushion between them. "I should hit the gym."

"It's already three. Fuck it. Although you probably want to get in some last-minute curls before your date."

Idly watching the game's restart menu repeat on the screen, Max said, "Not going on a date. Told you I'm taking Jeremy out to the Village, remember?"

"Oh, I remember." Honey tapped his phone.

"What's that supposed to mean?" When Honey didn't answer, Max nudged his knee with his bare foot.

Honey's gaze was still on his phone as he said, "What did you two do yesterday?"

"Went shopping. Had lunch. Then here for poker."

"Mm-hmm. Then skating. Then hot chocolate. Then walking around the Christmas market. You know, like a *date*."

Max scoffed. "With you and the guys! That's not a date."

"Spent all day together." Honey scrolled lazily with his finger, eyes on the phone screen. "Like one big-ass date you didn't want to end."

"What? That's ridiculous. I spend plenty of days with you. Are we on a date right now? Should I have brought chocolates?"

"You know I never say no to chocolate." Honey flashed him a grin before going back to his phone. "The big difference is you don't look at me like you're drooling for a mouthful of my dick. Not anymore, at least."

"You wish." He nudged Honey's knee again with his foot—harder. Honey kicked back, and they foot wrestled for a few seconds. "And what the hell are you talking about? I'm helping Jeremy. He needs a friend. That's it."

"Uh-huh," Honey agreed, tapping out a text with his thumbs. "You're doing your broken wing thing. *And* you want a piece of that."

"I do not!" Max froze, shocked at the ferocity of his own denial.

Slowly, Honey swiveled his head up and met Max's eyes, his brows sky high. "Then why are you so pissed right now?"

Max forced a laugh, making a *pfft* noise. "I'm not."

"If you say so, bro." Honey went back to his phone.

Grabbing the controller, Max started another game, the familiar shooting sound effects filling the silence. He played for a few minutes, his shoulders up around his ears, controller movements jerky. He got killed again and tossed down the controller. It bounced onto the carpet.

"I'm just trying to help him."

"Okay. But so what if you're into him?"

"I shouldn't be. He's a baby."

Honey abandoned his phone, brows meeting. "He must be eighteen at least?"

"Nineteen."

"You're twenty-two. What's the big deal?"

"He's a virgin, okay? So even if I am attracted to him—"

"Which you are. Even *Mike* noticed, dude. *Mike.*"

Max groaned. "Fine. Jeremy's cute." Saying it out loud made him squirm. He'd really, really, *really* tried not to think about it. "But he doesn't need me taking advantage of him."

"Yeah, but you wouldn't. That's not how you play. You're the most responsible person I know besides my mom. You were captain for a reason. That virgin ass couldn't be in safer hands."

Max ruthlessly shut down all thoughts of Jeremy's fine ass. "Look, it doesn't matter if I'm into him. I said I'd help him get laid. That's why we're going out tonight."

"Then *help him get laid*." Honey swigged from a bottle of orange sports drink. "I know you'll be all tender and shit. Want me to sleep at Alicia's tonight?"

"*No.* I'm not screwing Jeremy. It wouldn't be right. I'm going home to Pinevale in a few days." The mess of feelings of both looking forward to Christmas while dreading his LSAT results was now joined by guilt over leaving Jeremy to spend the holidays alone. He hated to think of Jeremy all by himself in a depressing dorm room.

He was struck by a memory of his mom saying, *"Christmas can be a very lonely time for some people."* He'd been baffled—Christmas was the *best*. Presents and food and time off school. His seven- or eight-year-old brain hadn't been capable of imagining people lonely at the holidays.

Now, he imagined Jeremy's family apparently off on some trip, leaving him in that bare dorm room. Max's chest tightened. This was stupid. He barely even knew Jeremy. This was, what, day three? He shouldn't feel attached to him already.

Sure, he was attracted to Jeremy. He could admit that. He was attracted to plenty of guys! It didn't mean anything. But it was more than that. How was it more than that already? Why had he been watching the clock all damn day, counting down until he got to see Jeremy again?

"Even if Jeremy wanted me—"

"Oh, he does. You're both real, real bad at hiding it."

Despite himself, Max's belly swooped like he'd just intercepted a pass. "You think he likes me?"

"Yeah, he passed me a note after third period. I put it in your locker. It said, 'Does Max think I'm cute? Y-slash-N.' So tomorrow in homeroom—"

"Okay, okay." He had to laugh. "Fuck you." Max slouched back on the cushions, blowing out a noisy breath. "This wasn't the plan."

"You and your plans." Honey shrugged. "Roll with it. Now we gonna play, or what?"

They both grabbed controllers and started a new game. Max kept getting killed as his mind wandered again and again to Jeremy. T-minus five hours.

Not that he was counting.

"JUST A SEC!" Jeremy's flustered voice came through the flimsy door.

Max could hear him scrambling around, and when Jeremy flung open the door, his wire glasses were askew and half his hair stood up in a mess. Max laughed. "Were you jerking off?"

Jeremy flushed even redder, shaking his head and tugging at the collar of his blue, too-big polo shirt. Which was inside-out. For a second, Max thought someone else was there and he'd caught Jeremy getting busy.

For a second, the jealousy burned so hot Max couldn't breathe.

Which was ridiculous! He should be glad if Jeremy had found the confidence to hook up. They'd just met—Jeremy didn't owe him anything. There was no reason to be jealous. Definitely no reason to feel weirdly hurt.

But when Max went inside carrying Jeremy's shopping bags from yesterday, the room was empty, and Max was undeniably relieved. His mind circled back immediately to the idea that he'd interrupted Jeremy jerking off, and *boy*, did Max's dick like that. Imaginary slideshow images of Jeremy working himself clicked through Max's head, and his twitching cock was going to jump up to a full salute if he didn't lock that shit down.

He cleared his throat. "Sorry if I'm early. I brought your stuff." He put the bags on the floor. "I can wait in the hall if you want?"

"No, of course not. I lost track of time. I..." Jeremy was still wrestling with the shirt collar.

"It's inside-out."

"Oh!" Jeremy rubbed a hand over his face. "Oh my God, I'm an idiot." His hands dropped to his sides. "I was trying to take a picture. For that app you recommended. I figured I should set up a profile, right? And I don't want to show my face, so..." He motioned to his body, now draped in the huge inside-out polo.

"Gotcha. Want me to help?"

"Sure. It's not like I could humiliate myself any more in front of you. Although I'm sure I can find a way if I put my mind to it."

"I mean, you're a bright kid. You should never limit yourself," Max teased, fighting through another surge of jealousy at the idea of thousands of nameless, faceless men scoping out Jeremy on the dating app. Well, technically a dating app, but obviously it was mostly for hookups. Which was the whole idea! Even if Honey was right and Jeremy might be into Max too, that wasn't the plan. Max had promised to help him navigate the app and take him to the Village.

"I should be shirtless, right?" Jeremy asked.

"Yeah." It was the truth, after all.

So Max watched Jeremy peel off the shirt, exposing his lean, tight little body. That Max wanted to run his hands over. Mmm, those dark pink nipples and scattering of ginger hair around them. Max wanted to bite and suck and see what kind of touch Jeremy liked.

Hair dusted Jeremy's freckled arms. There was another hint of ginger just above the waistband of his dark skinny jeans. He was slim, and his belly was soft. Max wanted to navigate that pale skin with his tongue. He wanted to hear what kind of sounds Jeremy would make as he got hard.

"Max?"

Blinking back to focus, Max said, "You look great." Also not a lie. When Jeremy rolled his eyes, Max said more forcefully, "Seriously.

You're hot. Here, give me your phone."

Keeping a lid on his desire and reminding himself to be a friend and not a creeper, Max took some pics, keeping Jeremy's face out of frame. "You wanna pose on the bed?"

Jeremy shook his head and put out his hand for the phone. "I'll look at these later. I don't even know if I'm going to..." He pulled on a green Henley, tugging at the sleeves. "Is this okay? Or should I dress up?"

"That's perfect." The forest green cotton hugged his slim body, and Max wanted to run his hand over Jeremy's chest. He didn't, obviously. Operation: Don't be a Freaking Creeper was in full effect.

Max added, "We'll go to Buddies. Buddies in Bad Times. It's a queer theater company, but they do events and club stuff too. It should be a mixed crowd—not just shirtless dudes looking to score. Sunday night is pretty chill. Less pressure."

Jeremy nodded tensely. "Okay." His shoulders were practically up around his ears.

"Hey, you don't have to do anything. We can just have fun. Hang out. You don't have to hook up with anyone."

"Right. I know." Jeremy fiddled with his glasses.

"Can you see okay?"

"It's fine. Just a little fuzzy compared to my newest prescription. But I'm not blind like I would be without them. Thanks again for helping me. You've been great. You don't have to do all this." He shoved his hands in his pockets, rocking on his socked feet.

"Well, 'all this' has been awesome. I like hanging with you. You're cool."

Jeremy rolled his eyes. "I am not cool."

"Are too. I'm cool, so I should know."

Jeremy laughed begrudgingly at that. "Okay."

They headed out—Jeremy wearing his new in-between boots and peacoat—and Max in a similar outfit, except he wore a casual red button-up over his jeans. They hopped on the subway and walked down to the Village from Bloor, not bothering to change lines to go one stop to Wellesley. It was just under the freezing mark, so crisp and a bit icy, but not too cold.

Buddies was at the south end of the Village and back toward Yonge Street where they'd gotten off the subway, but Max wanted to take Jeremy down Church Street through the heart of the action. Even though Toronto was queer-friendly all over, Church and Wellesley was the classic gay area. It was, like, historic and shit.

Glad Day was on the other side of Church as they headed south, and Max pointed to it. "Oldest queer bookstore in the world. It started in the seventies and used to be on Yonge. Now it has a cafe and bar area at the front. They do trivia nights and events. It's a cool spot."

Jeremy nodded, gazing around like a total tourist, but in an adorable way. There were groups of people on the sidewalks, some smoking outside bars and restaurants. Max motioned to Woody's across the street. "Woody's is famous too. Been around a long time, and it was on that show *Queer as Folk*. You ever watch it? Super white and not great on trans rep, but it has some good stuff. Some hot sex scenes."

"I've seen a lot of clips. I was afraid to stream it for real since my parents would check what I watched on Netflix and stuff. Somehow they never paid much attention to YouTube." He glanced around. "This is right where they filmed it. Justin going out for the first time. Meeting Brian."

"Yep. At least you're nineteen, so if you want to hook up with some thirty-year-old, you're allowed. Dunno if I recommend it, though."

Jeremy grinned. "I think Brian would say he was twenty-nine."

"Oh yeah, he definitely would." Max laughed. "That show is old, but some stuff holds up."

They walked on, the muffled music from a drag show in Crews & Tangos spilling out onto the street, laughter and shouts echoing. Jeremy gazed all around. "I should have come here months ago. It's all just…right here. In the open."

"Victoria's a small city, but it must have a queer scene?"

"Yeah, but I never got up the nerve."

Max loved the smile lighting up Jeremy's face as he watched two men holding hands pass by. Then Max stupidly blurted, "Are your parents really anti-gay? Is that why you were so nervous? Why you don't really talk to them?"

Of course, Jeremy's smile vanished, the lightness in his step disappearing. He shoved his hands in his coat pockets and looked down at the salty sidewalk. "They're not totally, but... It's complicated."

"Sorry. Shit, I'm an asshole. I shouldn't have brought that up. Curiosity got the better of me."

"It's okay."

"No. Forget I mentioned it, okay? Let's have fun. Turn right here. We should rub the ass for luck."

"Uh, what?"

They rounded the corner onto Alexander Street to find the bronze statue atop a thick square pedestal with a plaque explaining who Alexander Wood was and that he'd lived from 1772 to 1844. The guy in the statue was well dressed, with a hat and gloves in his hand, a walking stick, neat bow tie, and nice boots.

Max said, "He was pretty controversial. He was a magistrate and I guess there were rumors he was gay. When he was investigating an attack on a woman, he inspected men's dicks looking for a scratch that was supposed to be the smoking gun."

Jeremy dropped his gaze from the statue to Max, eyes widening. "Uh, what?"

"Come around the other side." Max led the way around the statue to the plaque on the back side of the pedestal. A plaque that depicted Wood on his knees checking out a soldier's junk. The soldier's pants were down, so his bare ass was there in bronze. And compared to the rest of the plaque and statue itself, it *gleamed*.

"That's..." Jeremy motioned with a gloved hand. "Not what I expected."

"Pretty weird, huh?"

"Do I have to rub the ass?"

Max laughed. "Nope. Come on. Buddies is down here."

Not far down Alexander Street, the theater sat beside a parkette where a few people smoked. A poster out front advertised *O Blasphemous Night*. Inside, the space was divided into different sections, with the DJ playing holiday remixes in the main space that was like a small warehouse with a bar and an upstairs. Glittery decorations adorned every metal railing and Christmas disco balls reflected merrily.

Like Max had hoped, it was a mixed crowd. They'd checked their coats, and Jeremy had his hands in the pockets of his skinny jeans as he looked around nervously. A couple of girls made out by the staircase, and Jeremy smiled to himself as he watched them.

"You can relax here," Max said. "Be yourself."

"Yeah." Jeremy gave him a strangely sad little smile. "If only I knew who I was."

"Dude, that's the whole point of university. I mean, yes, also the book learning, but you're nineteen. You don't have to have everything figured out yet."

"I guess not. You do though."

Do I? "Come on, let's get a drink. This isn't supposed to be my therapy session."

"Just mine? We can take turns." Jeremy smiled, then put his hand on Max's forearm, his expression earnest. "But if you do want to talk about it, I'm happy to listen."

For a moment, Max was sorely tempted to unload it all on Jeremy and get his advice, but no. That would be a dick move. "Thanks," he said, just as seriously. They smiled softly at each other, and Max was very aware of the light pressure of Jeremy's hand. Then someone jostled them as a throng of people passed by, and Max realized they were standing there smiling at each other like goofs, and maybe this was what Honey was talking about.

He shook himself. "I'll get the first round. You want a beer or something else?"

"Well, only if it's craft beer."

Max laughed. "Rickard's coming right up."

He actually went with Moosehead since that's what Jeremy had offered him in his room. They drank their bottles and half-shouted a conversation about football as the music got louder, more people crowding the dance floor.

"Wanna dance?" Max asked. "I mean, I'm sure you're fascinated by the differences between the NFL and CFL, but you've humored me long enough."

"Dance?" Jeremy looked at the dance floor as though it was a pit of writhing snakes and not people having fun to a disco mix of "Hark! The Herald Angels Sing." The colored holiday lights reflected off Jeremy's wire glasses.

"We don't have to!" Max laughed, draining his bottle. "You ready for another?"

"Yes!" Jeremy seemed relieved. "My turn! I'll be back."

Max leaned on a railing and watched Jeremy weave through the crowd to the bar. The skinny jeans and Henley were a great look. Which apparently a dude at the bar agreed with, since he started hitting on Jeremy while they waited for the bartender.

He looked university age and had a cute smile. Decent bod. Shaggy hair. From a distance, didn't have a creepy vibe, which was good. He leaned in closer to Jeremy, and Max tensed. Whatever he said made Jeremy laugh.

And Max got even more tense.

This was messed up. Max should have been happy. Not jealous. Not tempted to march over there and shoulder in-between them at the bar. "Jesus," he muttered to himself. "Who's the creep now?"

If Jeremy was into this guy, that was great, and Max was going to get his shit together and not be a dick. *This is what I get for listening to Honey.* Because maybe—*maybe*—he'd let what Honey had said about Jeremy liking him go to his head. Get under his skin.

This wasn't the plan. The fairy godfather wasn't supposed to be jealous. This was a fun distraction. But he'd planned to go to law school since he was a kid, and now he wasn't sure of that either. Maybe he was shit at plans.

Max gulped his beer, hearing Honey's persistent voice in his head saying yesterday had been one big, long date. No, enough. He and Jeremy were new friends and that was all. He determinedly looked at the DJ—their Santa suit flapping open over a sparkly padded bra—and stopped spying.

Although... When he looked back—just to make sure Jeremy was still okay—Jeremy had his arms crossed and was shrugging tightly. He got the beers and said goodbye to the guy, who watched Jeremy go and then started talking to the person on his other side.

Jeremy handed Max the beer with a shouted, "Here you go!"

"Thanks!" He took a swig before saying, "So, he was cute."

"What?" After a brief deer vs. headlights moment, Jeremy shrugged. "Yeah. He was all right."

"You wanna talk to him more? Don't worry about me. Go on."

Something like panic pinched Jeremy's face. "Do I have to?"

"What? No!" Max slung an arm around him. "Not at all." He frowned. "Did he say something gross? Do I need to kick his ass?"

"No!" Jeremy laughed, sagging against Max. "He was really nice. Seriously, no ass-kicking required. But thanks."

Max squeezed him before forcing himself to let go. "Anytime. Come on. Let's dance. Or shuffle in place. Whatever."

They sipped their beers and danced, Jeremy's awkward shuffle slowly loosening up as Boney M came on. Christmas disco didn't get much better, and they laughed as a group in Santa hats started a dance-off. They clapped and cheered, and Max was pleased that Jeremy seemed to be having fun.

Yet not long after, Jeremy returned from the bathroom with tension in his hunched shoulders and his smile strained. Max asked, "What happened?" He glanced toward the stairs down to the bathrooms. "Do I need to kick someone's ass after all?"

Jeremy shook his head, but he still wasn't smiling that bright smile

Max had come to enjoy seeing. Max asked, "You had enough? It's getting really crowded. I could use some fresh air."

"Yeah?" Jeremy's face brightened hopefully. "You don't mind leaving?"

"Nah. Let's walk back to campus. You hungry? I could go for street meat."

Jeremy nodded happily, and they collected their coats. Outside, the night was crisp and covered with a fresh layer of white. Leaving the thudding bass behind was a relief, the snow blanketing the night in a peaceful muzzle. They hadn't brought hats, but there was mercifully no wind.

"There should be a hot dog stand not far," Max said as they headed up Yonge. He wanted to ask what had happened to upset Jeremy, but maybe he should let Jeremy bring it up himself if he wanted to.

They grabbed sausages and cans of pop, and Max couldn't help finding it adorable that Jeremy chose orange. After loading their buns with sauerkraut and ketchup and mustard—plus mayo for Max—they headed west on a side street and found a low concrete wall to perch on while they ate. The fresh snow was dry and easy to brush off. The concrete was freezing, but Max ignored that.

They were across from a row of new townhouses decorated with wreaths and white fairy lights. With no wind, it was nice sitting there eating their sausages in companionable silence, their pop cans sitting between them on the wall.

"Mmm. Spicy," Jeremy mumbled around a bite.

"Mmm," Max agreed, swallowing his mouthful and washing it down with root beer.

They sat for a while longer until they'd finished eating and their asses got too cold. After crushing their empty cans, Max dropped them into a recycling bin behind a dark restaurant. He burped, and Jeremy laughed, and then they had a quick burping contest because they were twelve.

Jeremy raised his hands. "I can't compete. You've got mad skills."

"Let me tell you, if there's one thing being on football teams for years has taught me, it's teamwork, strategy, and burping."

Back to an easy silence, they zigzagged along the shockingly quiet residential streets south of Bloor. Even after four years in Toronto, Max was still surprised by just how calm and still the city could be right downtown. True it was Sunday night, but they were only a block or two from a major road, and there was only the crunch of their boots on the snow and salt. Their breath clouded in white plumes.

They passed a townhouse with a sad string of blue lights on a tree. Max said, "I hate it when people only put lights halfway up. Either do the whole thing or forget it. Like, what, you don't have a ladder? Get a ladder, bro."

Jeremy chuckled. "I've never really thought about it, but you raise a good point. Does your family decorate?"

"Oh yeah. We're into it. And Christmas was my mom's fave. Only time of the year we'd go to mass except for weddings and funerals. It was for the carols, not gonna lie."

"Are you Catholic too?"

"Yeah, my dad's family is from Goa like my mom's. He was a baby when they moved here. Goa was colonized by the Portuguese, so big Catholic influence and a lot of Portuguese surnames like ours: Pimenta."

"Oh, I didn't know that."

"Yep. Those Europeans sure loved to colonize."

Jeremy grimaced. "They sure did."

Max wasn't sure he should bring it up, but curiosity won out. "So, are your parents really religious? Is that why it's been tense?"

Jeremy sighed, pushing up his glasses. "You'd think so, right? But that's the thing that confuses me most, I guess. They're not devout or anything. We were always a hundred percent Easter and Christmas Catholics, and not even then sometimes."

He was quiet for a few moments, and Max waited, walking beside him quietly.

Jeremy said, "And obviously there are Catholics who accept their queer kids. What I'm saying is that...I didn't see this coming. I don't remember them saying negative stuff about gay people when I was growing up. I think I'd remember that."

"Yeah."

"So it was like… Before I told them, I was nervous. Hard not to be, you know?"

"Totally. My dad and stepmother are liberal, but it was still nerve-wracking. Luckily for me, they were great. My whole family was. Meg had told me not to worry, but I still did. Hopefully your folks will come around, right?"

"Yeah. It's weird." Jeremy breathed deeply, his breath clouding, snow catching in his ginger hair as flurries drifted down. They walked by dark, sleeping houses. "It's not like they threw me out. They didn't call me names or tell me they think I'm disgusting. They didn't say they're ashamed. They didn't say much at all. That's the problem—there's just all this silence now. When we do talk, it's awkward. We never mention anything about me being gay. We never acknowledge how weird everything is. That I can't really talk to my brother. If they hate me, I wish they'd just say it. You know?"

"Right. Shit, I'm sorry."

"I feel like they don't know what to say, so they kinda...stopped talking."

"That's brutal."

"Is it?" Jeremy's face creased. "I feel like I shouldn't be upset. Like I should be grateful they didn't throw me out and cut me off. Some people get told horrible things. That must be worse."

"That doesn't mean the way your parents are treating you isn't terrible."

Shoulders sagging, Jeremy nodded. "I… Thank you. Thank you for saying that."

"It's the truth." The words felt empty. Max wanted so badly to fix it. But all the fairy godfathering in the world couldn't change how Jeremy's parents were reacting.

"Lesson learned: Keep your expectations extremely low so you can't be blindsided." Jeremy's shoulders were hunched, and the sadness in his voice had Max's chest tightening.

"No," Max said. "I mean, as much as that makes sense on one hand, I don't want that for you. You deserve better than low expectations."

Jeremy smiled faintly. "Thanks."

They walked in silence. Max had so many more questions about Jeremy's family and seriously—what the fuck was wrong with them? How could they be so cold to their son who was sweet and kind and funny and so scared?

He didn't want to push. Instead he asked, "How do your new boots feel?"

"Good! Barely had to break them in." Jeremy seemed relieved at the change of subject. "Thanks for the suggestion. I'd have felt even more awkward tonight without the new clothes."

"You weren't awkward."

Jeremy shot him an incredulous look. "Dude, come on. I was there."

Max laughed softly. "It wasn't that bad. You just need to get out of your own way. It comes across like…" Okay, how was Max going to phrase this? He fiddled with the zipper on his coat. "Are you sure you really *want* to hook up with a guy?"

"What, you think I'm straight or something?" Jeremy's face screwed up. "Trust me, I wouldn't have come out to my parents if I didn't like men."

"No, that's not what I mean. I'm just being nosy and wondering if you've considered if you're asexual or on that spectrum. Ace, demi, gray. There are variations."

A car went by, the headlights glaring on Jeremy's glasses for a moment, hiding his expression. "Why would you think that?"

"I'm just throwing it out there for consideration. Like, tonight when that dude was trying to get with you at the bar, you were leaning away from him and your arms were crossed."

"Really? I didn't realize."

"Maybe you just weren't into him, which is obviously fine. But I wondered if maybe the reason you're so freaked out is that you don't actually want this."

Gloved hands in his coat pockets, Jeremy said, "I have actually considered that before, but I don't think I'm asexual."

"Okay. It's cool if you are and cool if you aren't."

"I am attracted to men. In the bathroom tonight, there was this really hot guy at the urinal. I was thinking about how nice his shoulders were. Then he noticed." Jeremy hunched even more as they passed a mailbox and stopped at a quiet intersection.

There were only a few vehicles around, the roads covered in the fresh snow. But it was cold enough that it hadn't gotten slushy, which meant it wasn't icy like it had been Friday. Friday seemed like so long ago somehow.

After Jeremy didn't elaborate, Max asked quietly, "Was he an asshole or something?" If he had to go back to Buddies and deliver a beatdown, he would. Well, he'd want to. He hadn't actually ever been in a fight, tackles notwithstanding.

"No, but his dick was out. There it was—like, *right there*. He nodded to one of the stalls, and all I had to do was follow him. He didn't seem weird or anything. But I froze right up. I really want to have sex, but…"

"What?" Max honestly didn't get it since he'd always found sex fun and exciting. Rarely stressful. He waited as they passed by a house decked out in blinking icicle lights. When Jeremy didn't speak, Max said, "It's okay."

"I have so many fantasies, but when it's real, I can't do it. I… I don't feel safe."

The last confession was barely a whisper over the crunch of their boots. Max wanted to sling an arm over Jeremy's shoulders like he had before, but he wasn't sure it was the right thing to do now. Another thought occurred. "Did something happen in the past, or…?"

"No, nothing like that. No abuse or anything. I'm just a chicken."

Jeremy laughed sharply with a burst of white condensation in the air. "I'm a loser."

"You are not. It's normal to be nervous."

"Yeah, but I'm not just nervous. I'm a disaster! I want to get laid so bad, but when a guy hits on me, I freeze up and want to hide. I shouldn't get freaked out when a guy at a gay club wants to hook up in the bathroom."

"Says who?"

"Like, the world? That old show they filmed here. Instagram. Tik-Tok. YouTube. It feels like I'm supposed to want to be clubbing and screwing like it's nothing. It's not supposed to be such a big deal, and I'm terrified I'll mess it up and get laughed at."

Max said, "Well, a hookup's not going to laugh at you unless he's a total asshole."

"That's the thing—how do I know he's not? That first guy tonight seemed cool, but I doubt he wants to court me like I'm a Victorian maiden until I decide he's trustworthy."

Laughing, Max bumped Jeremy's shoulder. "It's not like you have to fuck a dude right away. Go out a few times. See if you click. It doesn't have to be all or nothing."

"And this mythical guy's going to patiently date me while he could be hooking up with a million men on apps? I've never even *kissed*."

Max stopped by a house that had multicolored lights strung up a tree—all the way to the top, thank you very much—oversized ornaments dangling from the barren branches. He took hold of Jeremy's shoulders. Blue, red, green, pink, and gold glowed over Jeremy's face, reflected in his glasses.

"You're building this up way too much. You need to get out of your own way. It doesn't have to be a big deal. I could kiss you right now."

Jeremy's eyes widened. His Adam's apple bobbed as he swallowed with an audible *gulp*. It was freaking adorable, and Max wanted to ruffle his hair and keep him safe from the world.

He also really, really wanted to kiss him.

Hey, he'd be doing Jeremy a favor. Taking this big, scary thing and bringing it down to earth where it belonged. But he wanted this too.

Slowly, Max ran his gloved hands across Jeremy's shoulders and up to frame his face. He hoped the leather wasn't too cold, but Jeremy didn't jerk away. He stood unmoving, lips parted, breathing shallowly, his eyes locked on Max's under his color-sparkled glasses.

"Do you want me to kiss you?" Max asked.

"Do you want to kiss *me*?"

"Yep."

Jeremy's eyes flicked down to Max's mouth and back up again. He breathed shallowly. "You're just being nice."

"Trust me, I'm not *that* nice. You're gorgeous. Of course I want to kiss you." He said it with a grin and a shrug, belying the thumping of his heart.

Leaning in a few inches, Jeremy licked his lips, and *Jesus* he was trying to kill Max. "Okay. Kiss me, please."

Max smiled at the politeness. Watching Jeremy carefully, he leaned down and pressed their mouths together. Their lips were dry and cold and so were their noses. Max tilted his head slightly, kissing Jeremy tenderly. No tongue, nothing forceful or sexy. Just sweet—although as Jeremy clutched Max's waist and let out a soft little sound, Max's dick came to life.

With a vengeance.

Jeremy's lips parted on a sigh, and Max couldn't resist sweeping his tongue inside, tasting meat and sauerkraut—which he surely tasted of too, so it wasn't bad—with a hint of sweet orange pop. Which was somehow perfect as Jeremy tentatively met Max's tongue with his own.

After a few more seconds, Max leaned back, trying not to show how much he was affected. Because it was just a little kiss, and there was zero reason his dick should be joining the party with that level of enthusiasm. Jeremy blinked up at him, and Max still cradled his cheeks.

"There," Max said hoarsely before clearing his throat. "Your first kiss is out of the way."

Jeremy stared breathlessly. He was still gripping Max's waist through the layer of his coat, and he licked his pink lips. *Shit*, Max's dick liked that a whole lot. Jeremy smiled—*beamed*—and Max let go of him. Well, he let go of his face and took hold of his shoulders instead. He didn't want Jeremy to feel rejected or anything.

It wasn't because he couldn't stop touching him.

He tried for a casual tone. "That wasn't so bad, right?"

"No," Jeremy whispered. He pushed up his snow-wet glasses. "Not bad at all. Not scary."

Max wanted to tell him that now he just needed to find someone cool who'd go slow with him. Someone he trusted.

Someone like me.

Because it made sense, right? Max couldn't rely on some random dude to take care of Jeremy the way he needed. The way he deserved. Max wanted to help him have fun and figure out what he liked. Did Jeremy have sensitive nipples? Would he like ass play? Getting fucked? Doing the fucking? Blow jobs, rimming?

He could imagine Jeremy naked and spread under him, his freckled skin flushed and that pink mouth open on a moan—

Max's lungs seized, his balls tight and his dick rock hard now. Jeremy still stared up at him, and Max swore it was raw hunger he saw on Jeremy's flushed face, in his parted lips and soft panting breaths. He wanted to offer Jeremy more. He'd promise to go slow and make it so good for him. Shit, he wanted to *beg* Jeremy for more—to let Max teach him.

Stepping back took all his willpower. Jeremy had only just been to his first gay bar. He'd just been kissed for the very first time. He was lonely and vulnerable, and the way he was looking at Max, he'd probably do anything Max asked.

Which was exactly why Max said with a smile, "We'd better keep walking."

Ugh, why was Honey always right?

Max wanted Jeremy—there was no question now. No room for

denial. He wanted him, but he had to let Jeremy sleep on his first kiss. Max had to figure out law school and his life—he wasn't looking for a boyfriend or commitment. This wasn't the plan.

Staying strong, Max started talking. They went back and forth about nothing in particular, randomly getting on the subject of the best holiday specials, agreeing Rudolph and the Grinch were tops. Max loved hearing Jeremy laugh and thrilled at the heat of his sneaked glances as they crossed the sleepy city. No reason he and Jeremy couldn't have fun together, but he wouldn't rush it.

Even if his lips still tingled from that kiss.

Chapter Five

I T WAS THE middle of the night, but Jeremy sent the text anyway.

He'd tried sleeping, but it was no use. He'd told himself he'd feel better once he sent the message, but now the knot in his stomach was a clenched fist squeezing. Hard. He stared at his phone, willing Max to respond even though it was seriously the middle of the night and Max was surely asleep—or pissed to be woken if his ringer was on.

Shit. Why had Jeremy pressed send? Could you take back a text? He jabbed at the options as if his phone would suddenly have a magic button along with "Forward" and "Copy" that said "Recall the Stupid Text You Just Sent the Guy Who Actually Kissed You With His Lips."

Cringing, he cleaned his glasses with the hem of his old tee, then put them on to reread his message.

Thanks for being so cool. Sorry I'm such a drama queen about this stuff. But I had a great time.

At least he'd refrained from adding, *"Especially when you kissed me!!! With your lips!!!"*

There was so much he wanted to say, and it was all probably deeply uncool. Now he was extra anxious that he'd wrecked Max's sleep. But no typing reply bubble appeared, so maybe Max was out for the count and it was okay. Hmm. Could Jeremy somehow get Max's phone and delete the text before he woke up?

He groaned aloud in his empty room. "Sure. You'll just break into his apartment, sneak into his room, hold his phone to his face to open it, and delete the text. Then sneak out. All without waking Max or his linebacker roommate. Or quarterback? Whatever kind of 'back' he is. Sure. Sounds great. Easy. Because you live in a wacky rom-com. And you pick locks now or something."

The bubble. The bubble was happening! Jeremy nearly dropped his phone, shooting to his feet, the duvet twisting around his ankle and almost bringing him down. Pacing, he held his breath, dreading and anticipating Max's response in equal measure. Was he mad? Was he going to tell Jeremy he was sick of his whiny shit? Was he—

You have nothing to be sorry for. Chill. :)

Jeremy exhaled and climbed back under the covers. He was relieved for a moment, but then the worry returned with a vengeance. He couldn't tell if the "chill" was annoyed or not. He hoped not, but... Was the smiley face ironic? He tapped out a reply.

Okay. Hope I didn't wake you.

He waited again, jiggling his foot so hard the duvet half slid onto the floor. He yanked it back up over him. Max replied quickly.

Nah. Couldn't sleep. You neither, I guess?

Seriously, how was he supposed to sleep when Max had kissed him? Kissed! With his amazing lips! They'd *kissed*. And Jeremy reminded himself for the hundredth time that it hadn't been real. A real kiss was when someone wanted to kiss you because they liked you, not when someone kissed you because you were a nervous wreck and they felt sorry for you.

Studying for my last two exams.

Obviously a lie, but whatever. It was better than admitting he was thinking of how Max had cupped his cheeks, his big hands so gentle as he'd looked down into Jeremy's eyes. Then his gaze had flicked to Jeremy's mouth and back up, and it was like all the air in the world had been sucked out. *Whooosh.*

Because it had seemed like Max had *wanted* him. Not just being nice, but like there was some invisible current between them that made Jeremy's skin tingle and his head spin and heart sing.

And then Max had leaned down and pressed their lips together, and Jeremy's knees had actually gone weak. He'd clung to Max like they were standing on ice again. And their mouths had opened, and Max had kissed Jeremy a little harder. Deeper.

Max's five-o'clock shadow had scratched Jeremy's face, and he touched his smooth skin now as if he could still feel it. Max had cradled his head, and they'd shared breath and a little spit, and it was as perfect a first kiss as he could have hoped for. He'd felt safe tucked against Max's body even though they'd been standing right in the open on the street.

If you're tired, you're better off getting some sleep and studying tomorrow than pulling an all-nighter. That's what Honey always says. He's annoyingly right about stuff.

Jeremy smiled in the darkness of his room.

Yeah, he's probably right. I just can't sleep, I guess. Feel guilty.

As soon as he sent it, regret flooded him. Why had he admitted that? Max's response came quickly:

For what? And don't say nothing.

Jeremy had to smile a little at that. He typed back:

You went to all that trouble to take me out and I froze.

The reply bubble appeared. Then disappeared and reappeared. Jeremy's heart thudded as he waited. Then Max replied with:

Dude, it's cool. Didn't we talk about this already? You're good.

They *had* talked about it, Max had made him feel better, then Max had *kissed him oh my GOD*. And yet, Jeremy's brain still circled back. It did that a lot when he was trying to sleep, replaying mortifying moments from years ago like they were yesterday. In this case, he supposed it was. His dad had always said—

Inhaling sharply, Jeremy squeezed his eyes shut, the sudden surge of emotion too much. He couldn't think about his family right now. He gratefully read the new message from Max:

Should have started you with the app instead of a bar. Sexting might be easier for you at first.

"Sexting?" Jeremy exclaimed. "Are you freaking kidding me?" He replied:

I'll be even more painfully awkward, I assure you.

Max came back with:

You've gotta start somewhere. It's not hard, I promise. ;)

His heart skipped as he read and reread the text. It was true he had to start somewhere, but wasn't that kiss a start? Even if it hadn't been real. He wrote back:

I would be the worst sexter in history.

Max replied:

Worse than Genghis Khan? Because I hear that dude had no game.

Jeremy burst out laughing, the knot in his stomach relaxing. Before he could respond, Max added:

Do you want to try it? I'll give you pointers. Up to you, obvs.

Heart in his throat, he stared at the screen. He didn't want to try it with a stranger. He wanted to try it with Max. Which was kind of what Max was offering, right? Even if he meant he'd help Jeremy practice. His thumbs shook as he typed back:

Okay.

There was a pause as the bubbles appeared. Then came:

Just talk about what you like. Exchange dick pics if he's into it. Here, I'll show you.

Wait. What? Show him? Was Max going to send a dick pic? *Whoa. Holy shit.*

What had to be every single drop of blood in Jeremy's body flooded south as he instantly went hard. A picture of Max's cock would be better than porn. But another text came. No pic.

Hey. You look hot. What's the dirtiest thing you've ever thought of doing with a guy?

Jeremy's breath caught. He'd never considered that question before, but his brain supplied an answer immediately because his brain was a jerk. His dick throbbed as that particular fantasy filled his head. There was no way in hell Jeremy was going to reply that he'd imagined being rimmed. The idea of being licked *there* turned him on big time for some reason.

It probably wasn't even that dirty! Max would roll his eyes at how tame it was. Jeremy tapped out a response.

I'm sorry. I know you're trying to help, but I just can't.

He was about to add a thank you since he didn't want to seem ungrateful when his phone buzzed. He yelped and fumbled it, glad the cheap rug by the bed was enough to break the fall. He scooped it up and stared at the screen. Max was calling him. Sitting up in bed, he swiped to answer.

"Um...hello?" Jeremy couldn't remember the last time he'd actually used his phone as a phone. Like, to talk. Out loud.

"Hey," Max said in that rumbling baritone that ensured Jeremy's erection wasn't going anywhere. "Are you okay? I'm sorry. I didn't mean to pressure you."

"No, you didn't!"

"I think I did. This stuff comes easy for me." He laughed. "I've always had a dirty mind."

Jeremy laughed nervously, very aware of how hard he was. "I'm not a prude. I mean, I'm a virgin, and I'm clearly not good at saying stuff out loud—or typing it, I guess. But I'm not... It's not that I don't think things. Or...like them."

Max teased, "You telling me you have a dirty mind, Cherry?"

His childhood nickname took on a whole new meaning when Max said it, and that low, sexy tone made him tingle. "I think so? I mean, what I think is dirty might be stupidly naive, but I've had plenty of thoughts."

Max was silent for long enough that Jeremy lifted the phone away from his face to make sure they hadn't been disconnected. Had he said something wrong? "Um, hello?"

"I'm here." He was silent again before asking, "Do you trust me?"

Jeremy frowned at the serious tone. He didn't have to think about it. "Yes. You helped me after I fell when you could have just laughed like everyone else. But I could tell you were different. I knew I was safe with you."

Max exhaled loudly. "That's... Thank you." He half-laughed. "Honestly, that's one of the nicest things anyone has ever said about me."

"Oh! Well, it's true. I knew you'd take care of me. And you've been so great." Resting back against his pillows, Jeremy looked at Doug's almost-empty side of the room, the streetlights slanting a golden glow across the bare wall through the blinds. "I feel like I finally have a friend here."

"You do. A hundred and ten percent. I like you. You're cool."

I'm cool! He tried to sound like he actually was, since Jeremy knew he was extremely uncool and was usually okay with that. "Thanks. You too."

"Look—" Max exhaled noisily. "No pressure, okay? But do you want me to help you? With this whole sex thing."

Jeremy opened and closed his mouth. Did Max mean what he thought he meant? "Uh…" How could he be expected to make words when his brain was dribbling out of his ears?

"I'll show you the basics. Friends with benefits. No big deal."

Friends. With. Benefits. This was definitely a thing people did. "You'd do that for me?"

"Sure." Max chuckled. "It would be for me too. I could use the stress release. You'd be doing me a favor. If you're into it, we can have fun. Like I said, no pressure. I just thought if you're comfortable with me, it could be the perfect way to get your feet wet. Not to mention your dick."

Jeremy choked out a laugh. "Um, I, uh…"

"We can go slow."

"But I'm a neurotic mess."

"You're adorable. Trust me."

And he did. He really did. Yeah, he'd only known Max a few days, but… Flashes of memory played out—Max's strong arm secure around him as they slid their way to res, Max's encouraging smile dimpling his cheeks, the furrow between his brows as he listened to Jeremy talk about his parents, the warm press of his hand on Jeremy's cheek as he leaned down to give him his first kiss.

"I do," Jeremy said, reminding himself sternly that the kiss didn't mean anything. Friends with benefits, that was all. "I trust you. I want…" *I want you.* God, he did.

He let himself admit that he wanted Max Pimenta more than he'd ever wanted anyone, including Canucks player Brock Boeser, who'd gotten him interested in hockey. Well, in watching Brock Boeser play hockey, at least. But forget him. Because Max Pimenta was sexy and sweet and *real*. Jeremy was listening to him breathe.

Screwing up his courage, he said, "I want you to teach me." His throat was dry. "Please," he added hoarsely.

"Okay." Max sounded hoarse himself. He cleared his throat. "We can experiment. For science."

"Right. It's kind of our duty or something. Should I ask you what's the dirtiest thing you've ever thought of doing with a guy?" Jeremy had meant it as a joke, but he wasn't sure it had come out that way. At all.

"Mmm." And wow, that one, drawn-out syllable made Jeremy so hot. Max said, "You want to start with phone sex? It's not that different from jerking off alone."

Heart thumping and balls tingling, Jeremy had to beg to differ. "Oh my God," he whispered.

Max chuckled. "You're by yourself. No one can see you. I can't see you. I bet you could get hard in no time."

"Duh. I've been hard for, like, ten minutes." Holy shit. He just said that out loud.

Now Max laughed, and Jeremy loved that sound. Max asked, "What did the trick?"

"I'm not telling!" His face was so hot that he knew he was bright red. But Max was right—no one could see him.

The laughter was gone from Max's low voice. "Tell me."

A shiver raced down Jeremy's spine, and he rubbed his dick through his flannel PJ bottoms. Was he really doing this? Was he actually going to have phone sex?

"Jeremy—"

"When you mentioned dick pics," he blurted before Max could give him another out, which he could tell he was going to do from the gentle way Max had said his name.

"Mmm. It made you hard? To think about seeing my dick?"

"Uh-huh."

"You're touching yourself now, aren't you?"

Jeremy actually looked down, his hand freezing where he rubbed himself through his PJs. "Yes."

"You naked?"

He shook his head before realizing Max couldn't see him. And shit, there really was something exciting about that—hearing Max's gravelly voice in his ear but being completely alone. Safe. He answered, "No."

"Get naked."

Jeremy almost dropped the phone again as he kicked the duvet away and tore off his old T-shirt and PJs. He could have put the phone on speaker, but he liked the intimacy of Max's voice right in his ear. Just for him.

But is he enjoying it too? Is he just being nice?

"I am now," Jeremy said. "Are… Are you?"

"Hell yeah. Wanna see?"

"I…" He opened and closed his mouth. "You're going to…"

"Want to see how hard my cock is for you?"

Jeremy could only gasp and grip the base of his shaft to stop from coming. "Yes."

"Gimme a minute. Stop touching yourself."

He whipped his hand back. "Are you sure you can't see me?"

Max laughed. "I promise I can't. But here. You can look at me."

Jeremy lowered his phone and tapped the incoming text with a shaky finger. And then there it was, glowing in the darkness. Max's cock in all its glory, the camera looking down at it. Cut. Long and rigid and curving a bit to the left. The head flushed. Max's hand around the base, pubes trimmed. Dark hair dusted his thighs, looking black against his brown skin.

It took a minute for the murmuring noise to penetrate the rush of blood in Jeremy's ears. He put the phone back to his ear. "I'm here! Sorry."

"S'okay." Max had a smile in his voice. "Baby's first dick pic, huh? Whaddya think?"

"It's amazing. You're—" He had to clear his throat. "Your dick looks like…"

"Like what?" Max coaxed.

"I want to touch it. I wish you were here, but also I'm…"

"You're nervous? That's okay. Just touch yourself. That's all you need to do. You've done that before, right?"

A burst of laughter cut through his nerves. "Are you kidding? A million times."

"Me too. So what does yours look like?"

Jeremy had begun to stroke himself but froze up. "Um, I don't want to. I mean, I know you sent me a pic, so I should send one back, but…"

"Shh. No. You're good. I meant tell me what your junk looks like. I assume the curtains match the drapes?"

"Oh!" He relaxed back against his pillows. "Yeah. Red hair every-where."

"Mmm. Nice."

Jeremy wasn't so sure but wasn't going to bring up the teasing he'd received in elementary school. "And I'm, uh, cut too. I'm not huge or anything, but decent, I guess."

"I bet your dick is gorgeous. You're touching it now?"

He stroked himself, rubbing the precum already leaking from the tip down over his shaft. "Yeah."

"Where else do you touch yourself when you jerk off?"

Jeremy tensed again. "Um…"

"It's okay. Do you want me to talk? I like talking, in case you haven't noticed."

He huffed out a laugh. "Yeah."

"Get some lube," Max ordered. "Put me on speaker so you can use both hands."

He did, placing the phone on his pillow so Max's voice was still a low command in his ear. He could tell Max was on speaker now too.

Jeremy slicked his cock with the tube of lube he'd bought at Shoppers along with the unused condoms. He hadn't been able to look the cashier in the eye even though she surely didn't care. He ran a hand over his chest, teasing his nipples without even stopping to think about it.

"Spread your legs for me."

Jeremy did, a moan the only noise he made. Words were suddenly too much. He couldn't believe he was actually doing this, but it was too exciting to stop. He was alone and safe. Safe with Max.

"You ever fuck yourself with your fingers?"

He moaned again, thinking of his rimming fantasy. He'd experimentally squeezed a finger into his ass a few times, but it had hurt. He managed, "A little."

"Mmm. Bet your ass is so tight. Your legs are open for me, right? Nice and slutty while you jerk off?"

"Yes," he gasped. His legs were bent, his knees wide as he stroked himself.

"Fuck, I bet you look amazing. When you're ready, I wanna see you like this. Wanna see you come. Are you close?"

"*Yes.*" Jeremy's head was thrown back, his back and neck arched, his glasses crooked. He couldn't imagine letting anyone see him like this. But he didn't want to stop. Couldn't. He wanted to come. Max's voice in his ear had lust bursting through his veins, his whole body flushed hot as he strained.

"Reach down with your other hand and rub behind your balls. You know the spot?"

All it took was one firm stroke on his taint and Jeremy's orgasm went off like a grenade. He shook and gasped and probably swore, not even sure of what he was saying as he came hard enough to see stars behind his eyelids. The pleasure burned so intensely his whole body jerked, and he painted his chest and belly with jizz.

He could barely breathe, Max's urgent growl in his ear asking, "Fuck, are you covered in cum?"

"Yes." Chest heaving, Jeremy focused on Max. He could hear the slap of Max jerking himself, and it made his toes curl, aftershocks shivering through him. Max was thinking of *Jeremy.* "I came so hard, Max. It's all over me."

"Oh, fuck!" Max was panting, wet slaps echoing. "I bet you're dripping with it."

"Is it weird if I taste it?" Jeremy slid his finger through a splat on his belly.

Max practically shouted, then begged, "Eat it. Eat your cum for me. Let me hear you."

Jeremy hadn't meant that to be a sexy question, but apparently it was judging by Max's harsh panting and groans. So Jeremy lifted his finger and noisily sucked it by the microphone. He'd tasted his jizz before out of curiosity, and it was still the same—salty and bitter.

But it was making Max come, and excitement skittered over Jeremy's flushed skin as he sucked as loudly as he could through Max's shouted orgasm and moans. He'd actually made Max come.

Well, Max had technically made himself come, just like Jeremy had. But they'd been together. In the darkness of his room in the middle of the night, it felt forbidden and dirty and liberating in a way Jeremy had never experienced.

They breathed hard, and Jeremy whispered, "I didn't know it could be like that."

"Mmm." Max sounded drowsy now. "It sure can. And there's so much more where that came from. If you want it."

Oh, he wanted it. Because he did trust Max. And a new sensation was thrumming through him, one that took a minute to recognize. Confidence. Because last week, Jeremy would have never thought he'd be bold enough for what they'd just done. But with Max? He wanted more.

"Tomorrow?" he asked.

"Yep." Max yawned. "Now we sleep. We earned it."

"Wait. You never told me the dirtiest thing you've ever thought of doing with a guy."

Max laughed. "I don't want to freak you out. Ask me another time."

Whoa. How dirty *was* it? Maybe Jeremy shouldn't get ahead of himself with this newfound confidence. Was Max into golden showers? Was he—

"Now you're spinning out trying to guess what it is."

"Accurate."

Max laughed again. "I promise I'll tell you another time. Now sleep. See you tomorrow."

"Wait! Did… Did I do okay?"

"Baby, that was the sound of an A-plus orgasm. You aced it."

"Okay. Thanks." He grinned in the darkness, his heart swelling at the way Max had said that, low and sweet. *Baby.*

They hung up, and Jeremy stared at the line of streetlight across the ceiling. Who needed Christmas presents when he had this?

Of course, that thought immediately conjured his family, along with worry and hurt. And he had to remember Max would surely be leaving campus any day now. But that was fine. They could pick up in January, right? Jeremy wasn't going to worry about that now.

Now, he was going to sleep, tired and sated from the most incredible orgasm of his life. He was doing this. Max was giving him sex lessons, and he wasn't going to let himself freak out and get in his own way like always. Eyes heavy, he grinned. Maybe he'd live to regret it, but at least he wouldn't die a virgin.

Chapter Six

T-MINUS THIRTY-THREE MINUTES. Approximately. Not that Max was counting or anything.

He paced another circuit of the bushes on the small lawn outside Jeremy's building, squinting in the brief glare of afternoon sun before gray clouds closed in again. Jeremy had said he'd be back by three at the latest, but hopefully he'd appear down the block any minute now.

Max looked, but the sidewalk was empty except for a girl dragging a cheap suitcase. It was Tuesday, and campus was already pretty empty even though exams went for several more days. Jeremy and Meg still had one Wednesday—Meg's Arthurian legend lit exam also serving as Max's excuse for not going back to Pinevale sooner. They had bus tickets for Thursday morning.

Which meant Max had less than forty-eight hours to hang with Jeremy. After their phone call, Jeremy had needed to study for today's exam. Now that should be just about over, even if he needed all the time allotted, and they could hang for a few hours before he hit the books again.

In the meantime, Max was crawling out of his freaking skin.

He couldn't remember being this anxious to see someone again. He'd told Jeremy they'd have fun and it would be no big deal. Hearing Jeremy's breathy little moans on the phone had been a *ton* of fun, but Max couldn't deny that seeing him again felt like a bigger deal than he'd planned. A bigger deal than he wanted it to be.

Man, when Jeremy had asked if it was weird to taste his own jizz? Max tingled all over again just remembering. He circled the snow-dusted shrubbery, the grass sodden and slushy under his boots, making squelching noises. He'd been casual when Jeremy had suggested meeting at his dorm. He hadn't expected Monday to *draaaaag* so epically and had ignored Honey's knowing smirks. It had been stupidly hard not to text Jeremy just to say hey.

Max's heart slammed his ribcage as Jeremy turned the corner, his red hair like a beacon. He was still a block away, and Max could tell when Jeremy noticed him. Aside from lifting his hand in a wave, his slim body stuttered, and as he got closer, he was smiling broadly.

Fuck, he was gorgeous.

Max met him on the walkway by the door. "Nice glasses."

Stopping a few feet away, Jeremy touched the new black frames. "Thanks. I like them. It's nice to be able to see clearly again."

They stared at each other, and Max realized it was his turn to talk. "They look great." Then they were looking at each other again and would it be pushy to kiss him? Instead, Max asked, "How'd it go?"

"Good, I think. Glad it's over."

"Now we can celebrate. Until you have to study more. But you're almost done and soon you'll officially be on vacation." As soon as he said it, the nagging unease tugged at him. He hated thinking of Jeremy spending Christmas alone. But it would be way too much to invite him to Pinevale. Too fast. Right?

Fuuuuuuck.

Max felt like his head was in the spin cycle on the ancient washing machine he and Honey shared with the upstairs neighbors that clunked way too loudly. And now he was just staring at Jeremy. Time to get his shit together. Take charge.

"You hungry, or do you wanna hang, or do you want to study now and for me leave you the hell alone?" He laughed, but it didn't feel funny.

"Let's hang. I need a break before I switch to chem. I'm good for food for a bit. Unless you're hungry?"

"Nah, let's chill for while." Max nodded to the door and followed Jeremy inside.

In his room, they took off their coats and boots, and Jeremy ducked out to use the bathroom down the hall. Max paced the narrow room while he was gone, ordering himself to get a grip. He was supposed to be the experienced one here.

He sat on Jeremy's bed, leaning casually on the wall under the poster of the periodic table. Jeremy's pillow was to the right, and under no circumstances was he going to lean over and sniff it. Jesus Christ, he was the captain of the football team—or had been. He'd hooked up with plenty of guys. He was not a freaking pillow sniffer.

But he itched to do it. To smell and touch and taste. Like Jeremy was a drug and he'd gotten a little hit on the phone, and now he was jonesing for the real thing. Maybe it was because he'd had to wait all day Monday and now into Tuesday that it was building up. He just needed it, and then it would be out of his system. Then he could stop acting like *he* was the horny virgin.

Jeremy returned and kicked off the flip-flops he'd put on to go piss, clocking Max on his bed with a smile and lick of his lips that did nothing to improve Max's situation. Jeremy asked, "You want a drink?"

He shook his head. "I want you." Playing games wasn't his style, so enough small talk.

"Oh." Adam's apple bobbing adorably, Jeremy stepped closer to the bed.

"Are you still into experimenting? If you're not, it's cool. We can just talk." It would lead to the most epic blue balls of his life, but Max had to make sure Jeremy was game.

"I'm into it," Jeremy said softly, *thank God.* "I'm just nervous. I wish it was dark."

"I get it. Although you're way too pretty for the dark. You know how they say to picture everyone else naked when you're nervous? You've seen my dick already, so you've got the upper hand."

He laughed, flushing pink. "I guess that's true."

"Can I kiss you again?"

"Uh-huh." Jeremy nodded. "So we're gonna…" He waved his hand between them.

"We can do as little or as much we want. We can see what happens." Max gave him a little smile. "C'mere, Cherry."

Breathing deeply, Jeremy climbed onto the bed, sitting beside Max, both their backs against the wall.

Max traced a finger over Jeremy's lips. "You have a nice mouth."

"So do you."

They met halfway, kissing slowly at first. Max wanted to haul Jeremy over his lap and suck his tongue, but he let Jeremy set the pace. They opened their mouths, tongues stroking and tasting, and instead of orange pop, it was coffee and chocolate lingering this time.

Leaning back, Jeremy sucked in a breath and smiled shakily. "Been thinking about this nonstop."

Max tutted. "Thought you were studying."

"Well, I was. And thinking about this every other second." His hazel eyes gleamed, and Max loved the ginger in his eyelashes from this close.

"Do you wanna just kiss?" Max ducked to suck on Jeremy's neck.

"No," Jeremy breathed, tilting his head.

"C'mere." Max eased Jeremy over his lap so Jeremy was straddling him. They were both hard, and Max stroked Jeremy's denim-clad hips and thighs.

They kissed harder now. Deeper. Tongues exploring as Jeremy rocked his hips and moaned. Max could have gripped Jeremy against him until they both came in their jeans, but he encouraged him to rock and set the pace, to do what felt good for him.

They were panting now, and Max was into having Jeremy in his lap. Could imagine his dick buried in Jeremy's tight ass. He liked being ridden, and it was good even with layers of clothes between them.

Though soon the itch for bare skin was too much, and Max slid his hands up under Jeremy's sweater, breaking their wet kisses to mumble,

"Okay?"

Jeremy nodded, his pink lips spit-slick and parted. After a moment, he leaned back and pulled off his gray sweater, tossing it aside.

"Oh, fuck yeah," Max said, spreading his hands over Jeremy's bare back and going right for his nipples with his mouth. He sucked and teased with his teeth, Jeremy's moaning gasps music to his ears. Jeremy clung to Max's shoulders, his hips rocking, dick hard against Max's.

"God, please," Jeremy begged, one hand tangling in Max's wavy hair.

"Can I suck you?"

"Seriously?" Jeremy blinked down at him, his new glasses actually fogging as he panted.

"Hell yes. Wouldn't suggest it otherwise." He ran his fingers up and down Jeremy's hard shaft where it strained against his jeans. "I guess if you'd never kissed before the other night, no one's ever had your cock in their mouth?"

After exhaling a shuddery breath, Jeremy shook his head. "I told you I'm a virgin."

Max quirked a smile. "I know, but some people define that as penetration. Trust me—I went to Catholic school. I've heard some bullshit. My friend Becky still proclaimed she was a virgin even though she and her boyfriend went down on each other all the time. And this one douche in my class tried to convince his girlfriend she'd still be a virgin if she took it up the ass. As if it was all about the vagina."

Jeremy laughed. "There are definitely issues with that theory."

"Indeed. So…" Max rubbed Jeremy harder through his jeans, and Jeremy rocked and moaned before turning pink. "You like that, huh?" Max teased. He went back to the light caresses of his fingertips, leaning in to whisper at Jeremy's ear. "I bet you'll like it even more when I get your cock in my mouth. It's gonna be warm and wet, and it's incredible how tight lips can feel. Bet I can make you beg."

Jeremy gasped, nodding. "Please. God." He arched his hips, clearly trying for more contact with Max's hand.

Max had to kiss him, and he captured Jeremy's parted lips, slipping his tongue inside and exploring as Jeremy moaned low in his throat and dug his fingers into Max's shoulders. Max went back to Jeremy's ear, licking the shell of it. He loved that he could actually feel the heat of Jeremy's blush.

He whispered, "It's okay, baby. I won't make you beg. I can't wait to taste you. I jerked off this morning thinking about sucking you." The words had escaped without him stopping to think, but they were the truth, so what the hell. "Thought about how hot you'll look when I make you blush all over. I want you naked."

He'd also thought about how much he wanted to fuck Jeremy's virgin ass, but he managed to keep that to himself. All in good time. There was so much to explore…

"You really want me?"

Jeremy's question had barely been a whisper, but it made Max's heart hurt as though it had been an anguished shout. He took Jeremy's face in his hands, looking at him intently. "Yes. We wouldn't be here if I didn't want you." He grinned, trying to make a joke of it because staring into Jeremy's hazel eyes, sharing his breath with their bodies close, suddenly felt too intense. "I may be a good Samaritan, but I'm not *that* charitable."

Jeremy laughed and pushed his glasses up on his nose. "Okay. It's just surreal. You know?"

"I get it." He took Jeremy's hand, guiding it between them and over his prick straining in his jeans. "You can feel it yourself. I want you. Trust little Max. He doesn't lie."

Huffing out another laugh, Jeremy scooted back so there was more room between them. "Can I see? Is that weird?"

"Nothing you want is weird." Max freed his erection, giving himself a hard stroke. "How's it look compared to the pic?"

"Incredible. Looked great in the picture too." Grinning, Jeremy reached down to tentatively circle his fingertip over the leaking tip of Max's dick. He watched, apparently transfixed. Max thrust his hips, and

Jeremy wrapped his palm around Max's shaft.

"You wanna make me come before I suck you?" Max asked. He was torn between dropping to his knees and burying his face in Jeremy's crotch and chasing his own climax, which was suddenly barreling toward him.

"Yes," Jeremy breathed. He was still holding Max's shaft, his gaze fixed on the dick in his hand like he couldn't believe it was real.

"It's real, and it's spectacular," Max said, quoting that *Seinfeld* rerun with the chick from *Desperate Housewives*, which Meg had watched obsessively on her mom's DVD player when they were kids.

Jeremy laughed so loudly he snorted. Max wasn't sure he got the reference but supposed he didn't need to. "It is," Jeremy agreed. Tentatively, he ran his hand up and down Max's shaft.

"That feels good. Get that lube." He waited while Jeremy quickly grabbed it from a drawer and sat back over his knees. "You don't need much. Just—"

"Shit!" Jeremy stared at the huge squirt of lube on his right palm that was already dripping down to his wrist.

"It's okay." Max chuckled, rubbing a soothing palm up and down Jeremy's back. "Just get your hand back on me."

"Sorry." Jeremy shook his head, still staring at the mess of lube. "Sorry," he repeated. "I'm such a klutz."

"Dude, you can soak me in lube for all I care. Squeeze the rest of the bottle over my head. Whatever. Just touch me. Because, in case you forgot, I'm rock hard for you. And I need you to get me off. The sooner you do that, the sooner I'm gonna suck your cock."

Jeremy pressed his lips together, inhaling sharply. "I'm going to come in my pants if you keep talking like that."

Max grinned and pulled his head down for a rough kiss, biting at Jeremy's lip before he hissed, "You'll come when I blow you and not a second before. Trust me, it'll be worth the wait."

"Uh-huh!" Jeremy nodded again, reaching for Max's dick.

Max leaned back against the wall, loving the sight of Jeremy working him. He wanted to lick the freckles scattered over Jeremy's knuckles. "Mmm, that's good. Harder. You won't hurt me. You know what it feels like when you get yourself off. You know what you like. I probably like it too. I'll tell you if I don't."

With another nod, Jeremy stroked Max's cock more forcefully. Faster. Then slow. Teased the head with a twist of his hand and his clever thumb. His gaze was locked on his work, the pink tip of his tongue poking from between his lips in concentration.

Fuck, he's beautiful.

"That's good," Max murmured.

"Okay." With his free hand, Jeremy tentatively snaked under Max's sweatshirt. He circled one nipple, then squeezed.

Max arched his back. "Oh, yeah." He tugged the cotton off over his head and tossed it wherever. He clenched his hands in the sheets, letting this be Jeremy's time to explore him. "You like that?" he asked. "You touch your nipples when you make yourself come?"

"Yeah." Jeremy continued jerking Max while he teased and rubbed Max's nipples, sending zaps of electricity straight down.

Max lifted his hips to tug his jeans and underwear lower. "Touch my balls."

Jeremy shifted Max's lubed shaft to his left hand and explored lower with his right. He caressed softly. "Like this?"

"Mmm, more." Max breathed harder. He choked down a plea for Jeremy to suck his balls. That might be too much. "Yeah, like that. Bit harder..."

Whatever Jeremy lacked in finesse, he made up for in concentration and enthusiasm. It didn't take long for Max to thump his head back, gasping. "I'm gonna come. Don't stop."

Jeremy stroked him hard with his right hand again. "Please come now so I can too."

Max's orgasm burst out of him along with a belly-deep laugh. He laughed through the burn of sweet, intense pleasure, his hips twitching as he spilled. When he was done, he pulled Jeremy's head down for a long kiss.

"You did good," he mumbled against Jeremy's lips.

"Thank you."

Max opened his eyes. "Did you come in your pants?"

"Almost." He laughed and sat up.

"But you didn't. Good boy." Max had to kiss him again before flopping back against the periodic table. "Fuck. I needed that." His eyes were heavy, and he let them close for a second. He idly stroked Jeremy's back.

It was the wet smacking noise, barely audible, that had Max opening his eyes again. His usual drowsy, post-orgasm haze evaporated in a heartbeat.

Jeremy was licking Max's cum off his fingers.

"Oh my fucking God," Max muttered.

Brows meeting, Jeremy met his gaze, his jizz-splattered hand hovering by his mouth. "Is this weird?"

"Not weird," Max managed, his throat dry with fresh lust. "You like it? You like how I taste?"

"I think so?" Jeremy slowly sucked his index finger into his mouth like he was conducting a science experiment.

Max found himself laughing again. He'd had his fair share of good sex, but he couldn't remember laughing this much during it. He stroked Jeremy's hair. Couldn't remember feelings this...tender. It wasn't a bad thing. In fact, it was pretty great.

He said, "You don't have to like it, for the record. Some guys don't swallow to cut their risk of STIs."

Jeremy frowned again as he eyed the remaining jizz on his hand. "Don't studies show oral transmission risk is really low? And I got the HPV vaccine."

"Me too. I mean, there's herpes and probably a few others, but for me, it's an acceptable risk. Cum really gets me off. But obviously it's your decision. I was tested recently if that helps put your mind at ease."

Jeremy nodded, then licked another drop of milky jizz from a finger.

"It's different from mine. Not in a bad way. Like, less bitter or something."

"Do you like tasting yours?"

Ducking his head, Jeremy shrugged. "Sometimes."

"Me too." He took Jeremy's hand and licked up the rest of his own jizz. It was thick on his tongue when he kissed Jeremy hard and deep. Jeremy moaned into his mouth, his tongue meeting Max's eagerly. "Maybe you like it dirty too, hmm?" Max whispered. "Should I suck you now? I'm going to swallow every drop."

"Please. I need to come really, really badly. I—" He faltered, then nodded. "I'm ready."

Max didn't torture him any longer. He urged Jeremy off his lap and dropped to his knees on the floor—the thin little rug doing jack shit, his knee protesting. He ignored it as he unfastened Jeremy's fly and pushed his legs open, getting his ass right on the edge of the mattress, jeans down under his hips.

While he wanted him completely naked, he worried Jeremy would feel too exposed. For a second, he let himself press his face to Jeremy's briefs, loving how damp the cotton was where his hard dick was leaking. He tugged the cotton down to release a nice-sized cock and balls, wasting no time in swallowing him almost to the root. Ginger hair tickled his nose.

Jeremy cried out, his legs kicking and hands grasping at the crumpled duvet. His head flew back, spine arching. Max sucked his thick cock while he reached for Jeremy's hands, bringing them to his own head. He wanted those innocent hazel eyes on him, and Jeremy met his gaze.

Slurping and licking, he kept eye contact. Mouth open and chest rising and falling quickly, Jeremy tangled his fingers in Max's hair and moaned as Max sucked him.

"I'm going to come already," Jeremy gasped.

While Max should have planned it better so that Jeremy's first blow job lasted longer, he sucked harder, nodding. Desperate to taste him, knowing he was the first person to have this, he rolled Jeremy's balls in his hand, and that was all it took. Shit, Max hadn't even had time for nipple play, but whatever—his mouth was flooded as Jeremy emptied, shaking and gasping.

Max eased him through it, milking him until he could tell it was too much. He nuzzled at Jeremy's balls, rubbing his face on the wiry ginger hair before kissing his way up Jeremy's splayed body. Max shoved to his feet—*shut up, stupid knee*—and they rolled and tangled on the narrow bed.

"Is it always that good?" Jeremy asked sleepily, his lashes fanned over his flushed, freckled cheeks. He snuggled close. They both had their junk hanging out, but Max yanked the duvet over them.

"Sometimes," Max lied. The truth that he'd never been this turned on in his whole damn life was far too new. Not only new—a little scary, which made him feel childish to admit.

The warning signs had been flashing, alarms blaring, and now he had to admit this thing with Jeremy was building like a snowball barreling downhill. Now he just had to figure out how far he was going to let them ride before putting on the brakes.

"WHAT'S GOT YOUR dick in a twist?"

Max had to laugh before shrugging. "It's nothing."

Meg only watched him as she sipped her latte as they left the cafe.

Max sighed. "It's this guy."

Her thick eyebrows shot up. "Someone's finally stormed that beach? Do tell. Not that I don't appreciate you buying me a good-luck coffee before my exam, but—" She jerked to a stop at the curb and yelled to the bike rider who sped past, "Watch it! You're supposed to stop at red lights!" She shook her head, sandy brown ponytail swaying as she rolled her blue eyes. "Fucking people."

Meg took another sip as they crossed the street. "You were saying?"

She wiped foam from her upper lip. Her light cheeks were rosy in the cold, which made Max think of Jeremy.

Focus. "No one's storming the beach. It's nothing like that. He's a first year. Just a kid." *I'm only helping him out. Friends with benefits!* "He fell on some ice, and I gave him a hand. Anyway, he seemed a little...lost. I figured it couldn't hurt to be nice, and we're friends now." That was true enough.

Suddenly, all he could think about was how Jeremy's whole face changed when he *really* smiled—his cheeks creased and eyes crinkling under his glasses, the flash of his white teeth and how his nose scrunched up a bit.

All he could think about was when he'd kiss that face again.

"Ah. Didn't realize you had a new project."

Max rolled his eyes and rubbed his face, wiping away the smile that had automatically tugged his lips when he thought of Jeremy's grin. "He's not a 'project.' What's so bad about helping people when I can?"

"There's nothing bad about it. Josh Singh would still have a unibrow and be wearing floods if you hadn't stepped in. How's he doing, by the way?"

"Seems good. Finishing at Queens this year, and he's engaged to his girlfriend."

"Cool. So what's the prob with your new protégé?"

"He came out to his family in the summer and it went pretty badly. Hasn't really talked to them much in months. He's from Victoria, so he'll be on campus alone over the holidays. I was just thinking about how much that would suck."

Meg's mouth drew down. "Shit. It really would. Poor kid. Are you going to invite him to come home with us?"

And there it was, the idea that had been silently looping around his brain, building up steam. "I should, right?" Hell, it was technically *Meg's* suggestion.

"Mom and Dad won't mind. There's plenty of room."

"Yeah. They won't."

It still gave him a pang, the easy way Meg called Max's father "dad." She'd been younger when their parents got together, so maybe that was it. Max had always called Meg's mom her given name, Valerie. He'd already had a mom, and he was probably too old to start calling her anything different now. He wasn't even sure he wanted to.

Shaking off the vague, bittersweet memories of his mom, he refocused and asked Meg, "You wouldn't mind?"

"Nope. The more the merrier. If he's just a friend, they won't be weird about it. You remember that torturous Thanksgiving weekend when I brought Craig home?"

"Ugh, Craig. I forgot about that guy."

"I wish I could." She gave a full-body shudder. "He sucked. But it was so awkward. Suddenly they were Puritans and giving us 'The Talk' about how inappropriate it would be to 'engage in sexual activity' in the family home. As if we didn't masturbate there for years."

Max snorted. "Very true." He'd never dated anyone seriously enough to bring them home for a visit. But maybe Dad and Valerie's house rules could be just what he and Jeremy needed to slow down. The choice about law school loomed, and even though he was very tempted to distract himself with Jeremy, was that fair?

"Like, what did they think was going to happen? I was going to go down on Craig at the dinner table post-turkey and pre-pumpkin pie?"

"You do enjoy a palate cleanser."

"Let's just say I would have had plenty of room for dessert."

"*Oof.* Savage." Max's mind whirled. "But yeah, Jeremy and I are just friends." Though he had to admit he could already envision more between them. He could see them in a real relationship.

But was that the lust talking? Was that his desperation to focus on something shiny and new instead of dealing with the life-changing choice he had to make? The last thing he wanted to do was lead Jeremy on.

At a stoplight, Meg tapped her phone, and Max struggled to corral his thoughts. Maybe the responsible plan would be to cool things down between them while making sure Jeremy wouldn't be alone over the holidays. He wanted to make sure Jeremy didn't feel pressured, so it would be good for them have a breather over Christmas. Just be friends and not get in too deep.

So to speak.

What was the harm in extending the invite? Jeremy might say no, but Max would be eaten alive by guilt if he didn't at least ask. The thought of him stuck in the empty dorm for weeks made Max's stomach swoop with nausea, his chest going hollow with a horrible ache. It would be so *lonely*.

Jeremy was simply too good to be lonely like that.

"I'm going to ask him."

"Cool." Meg frowned as she put away her phone. "Are you sure you're okay?" She took his arm with her rainbow mitt. "LSATs?"

"No. They're taking their sweet time." He stopped on the sidewalk before the building housing Meg's exam. "Break a clavicle."

Meg waved, grinning at their old joke, which had come about when he'd told her to break a leg before playing in a school concert and she'd tripped backstage and cracked her violin and collarbone.

Max wandered the campus, walking salted paths and passing the spot where Jeremy had wiped out. When Max had leaned over him, his first thought had been that even in the darkness, Jeremy was a beautiful boy.

He realized he was grinning like a fool to himself as he strolled. Man, when was the last time he'd been so into a guy? He honestly couldn't remember it ever being quite this intense. Was this deflection?

Max headed up toward Bloor, mind still gnawing over the issue. Okay, he'd decided to invite Jeremy for the holidays. That part of the plan was settled. And even though Max had surprisingly strong feelings for him, it was clearly far too soon to introduce Jeremy to his family as a boyfriend or anything so official.

Since he'd never actually brought anyone he was seeing home for so much as dinner, let alone weeks at Christmas, his dad and Valerie would undoubtedly be embarrassing about it. Max cringed. They'd mean well, but their enthusiasm could be a lot. If Jeremy agreed to come, they should definitely hit pause on messing around. It would be much easier for everyone to simply be friends.

Besides, Max had a ton on his plate with deciding about law school. He'd been in limbo waiting for the results, but even if they came in before Christmas, he should take the holidays to really consider it. He'd worked toward law school for almost as long as he could remember, and he had to figure out what he was doing one way or the other before he threw even more of a wrench into the plan. Even if the Jeremy-shaped wrench was so damn kissable...

This made sense, right? He jogged across Bloor as the walk signal counted down. Hit pause on sex over the holidays and just be friends. In January, they could re-evaluate.

Besides, Jeremy was a frosh. This was his time to be experimenting and having fun. He might want to date around. Why shouldn't he now that Max had hopefully given him some confidence and helped him rip off the Band-Aid? It would be selfish to stand in the way, no matter how much he gritted his teeth at the thought of Jeremy with another guy. That wasn't his call.

If they went home to the farm for Christmas strictly as friends, it would be the perfect time to put on the brakes so they could both take a step back. It made sense to take a breather, didn't it? This snowball was careening downhill way too fast.

Sure, it was a rush knowing he was the first to touch Jeremy, but it was more than that. That Jeremy felt safe with him satisfied Max in a way he hadn't known he craved. It was addictive, and he had to make sure he didn't get ahead of himself and end up hurting Jeremy somehow. He was the older, experienced one. He had to be sure he did the right thing.

First times were intense and setting boundaries would be best for both of them. This way, Jeremy wouldn't be alone, Max could get his head on straight, and they'd have a nice, wholesome family Christmas on the farm.

He reached home and sat on a rusty deckchair on the porch, wanting to get this done, his thumbs flying.

Hey. Hope studying is going well. Don't want to bug you, but I had an idea. Do you want to come home to Pinevale with me for the holidays? I'd be pretty bummed hanging on campus alone in your shoes. Or new boots.

He paused and re-read, deleting the weak boot joke before continuing.

No pressure or anything. If you want to come, it's probably best to hit pause on sex stuff until January. My dad and Valerie are old-fashioned and have dumb rules. And we just met, so it's not like we're a couple at this point. Is it cool with you to take a breather on messing around? We shouldn't rush into anything anyway.

Taking a deep breath, he sent it. Then waited. And waited. And waited.

Shivering, he was just about to give up and escape inside when the reply bubbles wobbled. To his surprise, his heart raced. He really, really wanted Jeremy to say yes. And maybe this was partly a distraction from his law school conundrum, but he loved the idea of spending as much time with Jeremy as possible.

The bubbles appeared and disappeared, appeared and disappeared. Then nothing. Max paced the creaky porch. Maybe Jeremy had gotten distracted. Or maybe he wasn't sure what to say. It definitely fit his MO to overthink a response. Max almost sent another message saying: *Just a yes or no will do the trick, dude.* He smiled, imagining Jeremy overthinking *that* text too.

Then the response came:

Hey! Are you sure? That would be awesome if it's okay with your family. I don't want to impose. Re: taking a break with the other stuff until January, that makes sense. Totally cool with me! ☺

Max frowned. He didn't want Jeremy to be *too* cool with taking a break. Then he groaned aloud, muttering, "This is what you wanted, Maxwell. This is the new plan." He typed back:

Cool. I'll get you a bus ticket for Thursday morning and you can pay me back whenever. Now get back to studying. I'll text you the details. Crush that last exam, Cherry.

There. Max had no clue if he was going to stick to his law-school plan or go for being a teacher or maybe something else altogether. But at least he had the next couple of weeks figured out.

Chapter Seven

Totally cool with me! ☺

DRAGGING HIS CARRY-ON suitcase along the empty sidewalk in the lingering early morning darkness, Jeremy cringed for the zillionth time at his emoticon of lies. Not to mention the exclamation mark. He'd wanted to seem chill, and of course had failed in the dorkiest fashion possible.

Well, the smiley face wasn't a *lie*. Sure, the thought of no more sex with Max in itself wasn't happy-making, but Jeremy was thrilled to be going home with him for Christmas. So it *was* totally cool with him.

As he crossed St. George and headed south to the bus station, he huffed. He'd talked himself through this loop of embarrassment and justification repeatedly, obsessing over the text exchange to the point where he was amazed he hadn't answered "☺" for every question on his last exam.

"Everything's cool. Be cool," he reminded himself.

And it was! Exclamation mark! He was spending more time with Max than he could have dreamed. This wasn't Max blowing him off. It wasn't a rejection, even though Jeremy's anxious brain had circled around that drain too many times.

When the first text had lit up his silenced phone, he'd sat there at his desk reading it over and over, not sure how to feel. Thrilled on one hand, but with a nagging pulse of hurt.

Hooking up with Max had been surreal and incredible, and a voice that sounded way too much like his mother's had hissed that he should have known not to get ahead of himself. That Max didn't really want him. That he was bored of Jeremy's virgin nerves and awkwardness. Max was way out of his league.

"If he wanted to blow me off, the last thing he'd do is invite me home with him," Jeremy reminded himself once again. And it was true! It made perfect sense that they cool off the sex lessons. It wouldn't exactly be appropriate in his family's house. It wasn't a rejection even if it had felt like one at first.

Because seriously, Max wouldn't invite him home for *weeks* if he didn't like him. At least as a friend. Maybe more. And Max was right—they shouldn't rush into anything. It was smart to take a step back and get to know each other.

On impulse, Jeremy said good morning to a woman in UGGs who was waiting for her leashed black Labrador to finish pooping. She was clearly wearing PJs under her coat. After a moment where she seemed surprised he was talking to her, she smiled and said good morning back.

That hadn't been so hard. The people in Toronto seemed so remote compared to where he was from, but they were just like anyone else. This city wasn't so scary.

Especially now that he had a true friend. A friend who just might be more.

"And we just met, so it's not like we're a couple at this point."

Those three words—*at this point*—echoed through not only his head, but his soul. Which was incredibly cheesy, but the fact that this friendship with Max might lead to a real relationship was beyond exciting.

In January, when they *unpaused* the more-than-friends part, he and Max might become a couple. Not that Max had said that per se. But Jeremy had analysed it up, down, and around, and the implication in those three words was clear. They *might* be a couple at some point. Not at *this* point, but at *some* point it was infinitely possible.

It was all Jeremy could do not to skip down the wide sidewalks of

University Avenue past the sleepy row of hospitals all decorated for the season. As much as he was dying to throw himself at Max and beg to be fucked, it would be worth waiting for.

Especially if they ended up a real couple. He knew he shouldn't get his hopes up and just be glad Max was his friend. But the thought of Max as his actual boyfriend had him humming "Joy to the World" as he turned down Edward Street.

Soon, Jeremy peered down the long lines snaking along the bus station's outdoor platforms. The roof made the early morning even gloomier, and he passed the first few bays without spotting Max. His stomach knotted, but he reminded himself that he wasn't late. The bus wasn't leaving until eight a.m., and it wasn't even seven-thirty.

There were a couple of buses in the bays, one loading a slow-moving line of passengers. He checked the bus's LCD display just in case, but it said Windsor. He exhaled and carried on. The next bay was empty, but the line was already long. He hurried on and—there!

His stomach swooped as Max waved from halfway down the line, his face lighting up. As he waved back, Jeremy sternly reminded himself that, no, Max's face did not "light up." He was just smiling. Being friendly. Showing off his dimples.

"Hey!" Max said as Jeremy joined him. Then he stepped closer and leaned down before suddenly jerking back and painting on another smile. He lightly punched Jeremy's shoulder. "How's it going?"

"Great!"

Was he going to kiss me? It seemed like he was going to kiss me. No. I probably imagined it. It's the bus fumes. We're officially paused. And we're not a "we" yet.

"Great!" Max echoed.

They smiled and nodded at each other, and Jeremy tugged on the edge of his new woolen toque. "Are you sure your family's okay with me tagging along?"

"Absolutely. The more the merrier." Max nodded again. "You'll probably be bored. We're not very exciting."

"I won't be! I'm not very exciting either."

Max chuckled, his cheeks dimpling, and Jeremy's heart soared even though that was against protocol. Seeing Max again in person, the urge to climb him like a tree thrummed like a revving motor.

It was like when you were hungry, but you didn't realize just how starving until you had a bite of food. And then you were *ravenous* and you wanted to shove everything in your mouth. Which made Jeremy think of his dick in Max's mouth, which was a dangerous train of thought. They were just friends now.

Thirteen days until January first. Max hadn't said if they were staying for New Year's Eve or coming back to the city. So maybe it would be a bit longer than thirteen days. If they came back for New Year's, did that mean they could *unpause* a day early?

"You good?" Max asked.

"Yep!" Just needed to stop obsessing. "Thanks again," Jeremy said. "I don't need excitement. I'm just happy to be with you." He quickly added, "And your family. I mean I'll be happy to be with them too. I—" He forced himself to stop rambling. "Thank you."

Max smiled softly. "Anytime."

Jeremy ordered himself not to read into the smile. "It really is generous of you all." Even if nothing more ever happened with Max, he would always be grateful. He hadn't let himself think about how awful Christmas would be alone. "I'm so glad I'm not staying on campus."

"Yeah. That would be grim. We'll have fun in Pinevale, even if it's PG-rated."

As much as that would be torture on one hand, it really was for the best. Max had done more than enough for him already, and Jeremy didn't want him to feel obliged. If he wasn't careful, his crush would spiral out of control. Falling in love with Max wasn't part of the deal. Even if maybe, at some point, one day, maybe even in January...

Max's sister appeared with a box of Timbits and a tray of double-doubles, and after introductions, they sipped the hot coffee and ate the donuts, which were still warm. Meg talked about her exams, and Jeremy was happy to listen. She was friendly and had a warmth to her that was similar to Max's. Jeremy could imagine she was one of those people who could talk to anyone and not feel nervous.

He plucked one of the powdered donuts from the box, and mmm, the jam center of the little ball of dough was sweet and perfect. As Meg rambled on about King Arthur and how gay he and Lancelot were, Max was smiling at Jeremy.

"You've got..." He'd put his gloves back on, and he bit the tip of the index finger to slide his hand free, his coffee still in his other hand. With his bare fingers, he brushed the corner of Jeremy's mouth, and Jeremy was *very glad* his new parka went to mid-thigh. "Icing sugar," Max murmured. Their gazes locked, and Jeremy's heart thumped.

"So, yeah, totally want to bang each other," Meg said. Max whipped his hand back, and Jeremy forced his eyes to her. Meg smiled cheerfully. "Arthur and Lancelot."

"Right, yes," Jeremy nodded. "And, um, what about Guinevere? Did she..." He tried to think of a way to end that question.

"Enjoy watching? Definitely. I have some threesome theories. Not that I came up with that, obviously. But my term essay in the new year will be about sex and Arthurian society." She nudged Max. "Admit it. Law school will be boring AF compared to English lit."

Max gulped from his coffee cup. "Yeah." He laughed, but it was strained. Meg frowned, but then the bus rumbled into the bay, engine whining. They shuffled along and boarded, and soon enough they were on their way. Until they weren't.

"If there's a hell, it's sitting in traffic," Max grumbled.

Looking out the window of the packed bus at the multiple lanes of traffic crawling along, Jeremy chuckled. He had to admit he was enjoying every moment of his thigh pressing against Max's in the confines of the packed Greyhound's seats, which even Jeremy noticed seemed smaller than ever, especially with the people sitting in front of them putting their seats back. Meg sat a few rows up squished in with an old lady.

"Sorry it's taking so long," Max added.

"It's not your fault there's a closed lane." As far as Jeremy could see, the 400 northbound was a parking lot, and they didn't seem any closer to where the bottleneck actually was. "Trust me, it'll be worth sitting in traffic all day not to be stuck alone."

Max smiled. "I'm glad you're coming. It'll be fun. We're big on Christmas."

"I bet it'll be nice on a maple syrup farm with the trees and snow."

"It's peak winter wonderland. We've never really been into the religious part of the holiday, but lights and decorations and cookies and all that? Hell yeah."

"Didn't you say you went to Catholic school?"

"Yeah, but just because that school board has a better rep in our area. In Ontario, there's the public school board and the Catholic one, and you can go to either for free. So it's not a big religious statement like it would be paying for a private school. I mean, my parents were both Catholic and I was baptized and all that. I went through the motions, mostly for my grandparents. My mom's parents were really into it, especially after she died. They've passed away now."

"I'm sorry."

"It's okay." Max shifted with an exasperated sigh, his thigh pressing harder against Jeremy's. "Sorry. I swear seats get smaller as most of us get bigger."

"Uh-huh!" Whole leg tingling from the contact, Jeremy willed himself not to pop a boner.

"Wanna watch a movie?" At Jeremy's nod, Max stood and grabbed his tablet from his duffel in the overhead. He logged into the wifi and passed Jeremy one of his earbuds before propping the tablet on his meaty thigh.

They went with a brainless action movie, and Jeremy was glad there wasn't a ton of plot he had to pay attention to. Their legs were still pressed together, and now their shoulders too as Jeremy leaned in a bit to see the screen.

Oh my God, he smells amazing.

There was that faint whiff of coconut. Jeremy wanted to rub himself all over Max. Wanted to climb over his lap the way he had in his room and kiss him until he couldn't breathe. It was like a genie had escaped its bottle and every nerve ending felt like a live wire. Could you die from being horny?

Because Jeremy had thought he was horny before, but now?

He gulped from his water bottle and reminded himself that he needed to keep it in his pants until after the holidays. He and Max were currently just friends. Although it would be amazing if said friend sucked him off again, Jeremy couldn't deny it.

He shifted in his seat remembering the incredible sensations. He'd fantasized and jerked off, but the real thing was...wow. The pressure and wet heat felt better than he'd imagined.

He'd given a hand job and received a blow job. Tick and tick. Jeremy was pretty sure the first time wasn't supposed to be that incredible, but maybe good things *came* to those who waited. He snorted at his own corny pun.

"What?" Max asked with a puzzled smile.

Jeremy blinked at the screen, where a car was screeching around the corner of a narrow European cobblestone street. "Oh, just how unrealistic movies can be."

"Yeah, the torque would be way too much."

"Yep." Jeremy had no clue about cars, but that sounded reasonable.

Max watched more of the movie as the bus crawled along while Jeremy tried to refrain from humping Max's leg on the Greyhound. He stared blankly at the screen, replaying the sex they'd had on a loop in his mind.

They'd dozed on Jeremy's tiny bed, and Max hadn't minded that he drooled on his chest. Then they'd ordered pizza, played a hilariously bad football game online, and had orgasms again. That time they'd started making out before Max had taken their shafts in his big hand and rubbed them off together before he left Jeremy to study because they were both annoyingly responsible.

Being next to Max again, Jeremy was dying to kiss him. He'd gone from his first kiss to shared orgasms to just being friends again so quickly his head was spinning. Honestly, he still felt like a virgin. There was so much more he was dying to explore.

He'd always thought of his virginity in terms of being penetrated. Probably because of what society made him think and also because that's what he fantasized about the most. What would it be like if Max fucked him? He'd touched Max's cock, and maybe he'd imagined a few times since what it would be like to have it inside him.

Maybe a few dozen times. Or a hundred. Whatever.

It would hurt, no question. Jeremy had fingered himself but never had the guts to try anything bigger. Yeah, it would hurt, but he could imagine how good it would feel eventually. How Max would be gentle at first, but maybe eventually he'd fuck Jeremy with more force. Bend him over and take him hard, stretch him open with his dick and have control—

Jeremy's face burned, and he looked out the window, glad his new parka was balled on his lap. Max nudged his arm, and when Jeremy reluctantly looked at him, Max gave him a knowing smile.

He popped out Jeremy's earbud and leaned in to whisper, "If it's any consolation, I'm horny too."

Jeremy gaped, and Max laughed, taking out his own earbud. Jeremy glanced around them, but the other passengers didn't seem to be paying attention. "Did I say it out loud?"

"You don't need to," Max murmured. He lifted his hand from his lap as though he was going to touch Jeremy's knee or thigh before seeming to remember himself. "But my dad and stepmother are weirdly uptight about some stuff. Meg brought her old boyfriend home for Thanksgiving once and it was hellishly awkward. And since we just met last week, it's way too soon to subject you to that. If they think we're only friends, they'll be chill."

"Right. Makes sense." Jeremy tried to play it cool. "And in January, we can…"

Max popped an eyebrow. "See what happens. Pick up where we left off if we want."

Why wouldn't we want to?? Jeremy breathed through the surge of panic as he nodded.

Max's playful expression tightened. "I've got some stuff to figure out in the meantime."

Concern replaced Jeremy's nagging anxiety. "Did you get your LSAT results?"

"Not yet. But I don't know—" He broke off, shaking his head. "You don't need to worry about this."

"I don't mind. I want to hear it. Really."

But Max smiled, popped his earbud back in, and returned to the movie. Jeremy didn't press, although he was eager to help Max with whatever problems he might have. Maybe Max would confide in him another day.

Where his leg pressed against Max's was like being on fire, and Jeremy willed the traffic to start moving already. At least it was good practice for being close to Max without having anything more than friendship on offer.

He attempted to concentrate on the dumb movie, the bus crawling forward before jerking to a stop, the brakes on and off and back on again.

HANGING BACK WITH his little rolling suitcase on the sidewalk by the Barrie bus station, Jeremy watched Max and Meg greet their parents with big hugs and kisses. Max had assured Jeremy he was welcome, but he hoped he wasn't totally intruding on their family Christmas. He'd been so excited to spend more time with Max that he hadn't really thought about it.

The wind gusted with a bitter bite, and Jeremy zipped up his parka to his chin, trying not to think of the stiff, short hugs he'd exchanged with his parents at the end of August. They were on the cruise now—the first day at sea. Dad had emailed a copy of the itinerary and emergency numbers the same way he had last spring when he and Mom had spent a weekend at a B&B in Tofino. Jeremy tried to tell himself it was proof that nothing had changed, not really.

Max's stepmother, a small woman in her mid-forties or so with a blond ponytail and a bright smile, said in a perky voice, "You must be Jeremy! I'm Valerie." She walked toward him.

Jeremy extended his hand, but Valerie opened her arms and gave him a hug. For a moment, Jeremy stood frozen before hugging her back. She actually smelled like apple pie, or maybe it was maple syrup? It was incredibly wholesome, whatever it was, and he hugged her gratefully.

She stepped back, adjusting her red woolen toque, matching mittens on her hands. "Sorry, I'm a hugger. We don't stand on ceremony in the Nadeau-Pimenta household. This is John."

Max's father stuck out his gloved hand, pumping Jeremy's enthusiastically. He looked a bit older than his wife—in his early fifties, Jeremy guessed. He was stocky and a few inches shorter than Max, his hairline receding and smile big and gleaming white. "Greetings, young man! Merry Christmas and happy Hanukkah and joyous Festivus."

"You forgot Kwanza," Meg noted.

"Oh, yes! And happy Kwanza. We never met a holiday we didn't like."

Meg asked Jeremy, "Did you know Canada has a national tartan day? It's in April. He legit made us wear plaid that day every year."

"And you loved it," John said. As Meg and Max opened their mouths in unison to likely protest, he cut them off and said, "Let's get moving. Only fifteen minutes for the parking."

They hurried down the street, which ended a block away at a lake. Jeremy shuddered in the icy blast. "It's so much colder here!"

They all laughed. Meg said, "Oh yeah, Barrie and Pinevale might only be an hour or two north of Toronto, but it's a whole different world up here."

"Welcome to the snow belt!" Valerie chirped.

Jeremy volunteered to sit in the middle in the SUV, and he buckled his seatbelt securely, keeping his arms folded so he didn't take up too much room. His right foot was against Max's left, and he angled his knees inward so he was touching as little of Max as possible. Because an erection wouldn't make a great first impression on the Nadeau-Pimenta household.

As Valerie drove them back up to the 400, which had finally cleared, she asked Max about Honey and the guys, and they chatted about his friends' plans for the holidays. Jeremy realized after a few minutes that Meg was eyeing him. He smiled hesitantly.

She smiled back, but her gaze was assessing. "You comfy?"

"Uh-huh!"

"You seem a little tense."

"No, I'm good. Just don't want to squish you."

"Don't worry about it. I'm not very breakable, I assure you."

Valerie asked, "Okay? Is it too cold? Too hot?"

"Or just right?" John added.

"Just right," Max and Meg chorused, like it was an old joke or something.

Jeremy stayed quiet as the family caught up with each other. They turned off toward Pinevale, and there was definitely way more snow than the slushy remnants in the city. Here, it was banked up along the sides of the road where plows had rumbled through.

"And…any other news?" John asked.

A strange silence filled the SUV. The radio was down low, and a faint, tinny carol played. Jeremy thought it was "Deck the Halls." Yes, there was the "*Fa-la-la-la-la, la-la-la-la.*" A second before Max spoke, Jeremy realized what John had been asking.

"Not yet." Max was tense beside Jeremy. "There's some processing delay. They sent an email saying they might not post the results until after Christmas."

Valerie tutted. "Oh, that's frustrating, sweetheart."

"But we know you aced it," John said.

"We know you did your best," Valerie added, which made Jeremy like her even more.

"Of course!" John agreed.

Max shrugged, a jerky motion. "I guess we'll see."

Meg rolled her eyes. "As if you don't crush every exam you've ever taken."

"Shut up," Max muttered.

Should Jeremy pat his arm? Leg? What would a normal person who didn't want to hump him do? He wasn't sure, so he kept his hands in his lap. He also couldn't help but wonder if there really was a delay on the results. There was something about the way Max usually tried to change the subject when law school came up. Probably just nerves.

Valerie slowed and turned into a laneway with a big, red wooden sign at the entrance. In black script, it read: *Nadeau Family Farms.* The lane curved for a few kilometers through endless trees that Jeremy assumed were all maples. The snow would probably be up to his knees. For a second, he thought there was a strange single-rope fence before realizing it was a line of blue plastic tubing strung horizontally along the trees.

"It's beautiful," Jeremy said.

"Thank you!" Valerie beamed at him in the rear-view mirror, her eyes crinkling. "I was born here, and my family's been producing syrup for almost half a century."

Meg sighed dramatically. "Are you seriously going to give him the full tourist spiel? Also, you were born in the hospital, not on the hearth in the middle of a blizzard like Mamy and Papy were pioneers."

Valerie blew a raspberry and they all laughed. "As I was saying before I was so rudely interrupted by my darling daughter, this is my family's pride and joy. We have fifty-five acres of maple bush here near the shores of Georgian Bay."

"Wow. The tubes are for the syrup?" Jeremy asked.

"Yep," Valerie said. "We operate thirty-four hundred taps during the season. These pipelines bring the sap to two collection points, where we transfer the sap to our sugar house in our tanker that holds four thousand liters."

Jeremy asked, "How many liters of sap do the trees, uh, leak?"

"Oh, thousands a day. Keeps us hopping in the season."

Meg jumped in, using a TV reporter type of voice. "The season can begin as early as February, but typically it's March."

"And how do you determine that, Meg?" Max asked, holding his fist to his mouth like a microphone.

"Well, Max, that all depends on Mother Nature. And we all know what a fickle bitch she can be."

"Language!" John and Valerie scolded in unison.

Ignoring them, Meg added, "Frosty nights and thawing days get that sap running so farmers know it's time to 'tap that.' The season typically lasts four to six weeks, although it can be shorter."

"I see what you did there." Max gave a fake laugh. "Very punny."

Meg laughed falsely. "You know I can never resist a pun, Max."

"Are you two done?" Valerie asked, although she was smiling. "Jeremy, I'm sorry for boring you with syrup talk."

"No, you're not! I'd love to learn more."

Max and Meg groaned, and Max said, "You asked for it, Cherry."

"Wait, what? Cherry?" Meg's brows drew close.

"Oh, a dumb nickname I can never seem to shake," Jeremy said. "My little brother Sean couldn't pronounce my name at first. Called me Cherry."

"Aww. Bless him." Valerie slowed, and around a bend a clearing with buildings came into view. "Here we are. Home sweet home." She pulled up to a freestanding garage and shut off the engine.

"It looks like a postcard," Jeremy said, peering at the brick farmhouse, two stories with a covered porch in front, red shutters, and a yellow door. Snow covered the gable roof, smoke curling from the chimney.

"You really don't have to work so hard to butter them up," Meg said. "They're easy."

Jeremy cringed. Did he sound like a suck-up? He was momentarily speechless, and Max snapped, "*Meg!*" as John and Valerie protested.

The SUV door open and one leg out, Meg's smirk vanished. "I was just kidding. Honestly." She touched Jeremy's arm. "Sorry."

"It's okay," he said. "It really does look like a postcard to me."

"*Thank you,*" Valerie said emphatically. "That's a wonderful compliment."

They all climbed out, and Jeremy knew his cheeks were flaming and wished he could dial down the redness. A thin layer of snow crunched under his new heavy boots, the area in front of the garage cleared.

Max came around the SUV and murmured, "You didn't say anything wrong. Meg's just being a brat."

Valerie pointed to a red barn on the right. "That's the sugar house over there. We've got a little storefront inside it. Those big doors on the front swing open."

Jeremy nodded, listening to Valerie as John opened the back of the vehicle. Jeremy grabbed his suitcase and put it on the ground, but Max snatched it up and said, "Better to carry it so the wheels don't get all snowy and then puddle on the floor inside."

"Oh, sorry! I can do it."

"It's cool. I got it." Max winked.

And *shit,* that wink made Jeremy's knees weak. He supposed it was normal to be so affected since it had only been a couple of days since they'd—

Nope, don't think about what we did on Tuesday. It's in the past. That was then, this is now.

Now he was with Max's family at their Christmas postcard farm, the scent of burning wood sweet and fresh in the air. Fresh garlands with red berries adorned the porch railings along with lights, a fresh wreath with tartan ribbons on the yellow door. The porch creaked as the family stamped their boots and Valerie said, "Kick the brick!"

"Mom, you know we're way old enough now that you don't have to remind us," Meg groused as she kicked the brick wall of the house beside the door, knocking off any remaining snow from the treads of her boots.

"I know, but it makes your mother happy," Valerie replied. "When you were a little girl—"

"Meg, how old do you think you'll have to be before your mom stops telling that story?" Max asked in his announcer voice. His hands were full of luggage, or else he'd probably have done the fake microphone again.

"Well, Max, I suspect I'll have to be dead."

John opened the door, shaking his head. "That's not funny."

"Sorry, Dad," she said, the smirk returned. She told Jeremy, "Long story short, I was so used to kicking the brick here at home that I did it everywhere, and one time I kicked a glass door and somehow broke it. I maintain that if a seven-year-old can crack your door, it's time for a new one."

Jeremy dutifully kicked the brick when it was his turn, inhaling deeply as he entered the house. Something cinnamon-sweet was baking, and a Christmas tree seemed to vibrate with fresh pine scent. They all took their boots off inside the foyer, a tile floor covered in three mats. Boots were lined beside the closet and coats hung inside it. Valerie and John stepped into moccasin-style slippers.

Valerie called, "Dad! We're home."

"I'm not deaf yet," came a growly response. Jeremy tried not to laugh, but the others did cheerfully. He assumed this was Valerie's father, who Max had mentioned still lived on the farm.

John said, "You kids remember we've got the last holiday open house on Saturday, so there's lots to do in the meantime."

Jeremy expected Meg and Max to grumble and give their parents a hard time, but they readily agreed, apparently done with their teasing routine. "Can I help?" he asked. "That sounds really fun."

"You sure can, hon." Valerie motioned up the staircase on the left and said to Max, "I'll give Jeremy the tour while you take those bags up." She motioned to a living area to the right. "Welcome! You can see we're all ready for the holidays."

That was an understatement if ever he'd heard one. Along with a massive, still-undecorated fresh tree, the source of the pine scent, stockings hung from the fireplace's stone mantel, holiday candles and a Christmas village on top. Long ribbons were hung on the narrow dividing wall leading to a dining room, Christmas cards pinned to the crepe. Jeremy didn't even know that many people still sent old-fashioned cards. Maybe his parents just didn't have as many friends.

The thought of them off on the cruise and the house in Victoria dark and empty and undecorated hurt more than Jeremy wanted it to.

The fireplace was in the corner to the left of the tree, a TV above the mantel. Three love seats bracketed the hearth and a square wooden coffee table with its own holiday centerpiece of holly and ivy. A large rug carpeted most of the living room, and it was thick beneath Jeremy's socked feet.

The cream walls were decorated with dozens of framed family photos. Jeremy was eager to examine the pics of younger Max, but followed as Valerie led him past the solid dining table into the kitchen, where a thin man with wispy gray hair was taking out a tray of golden pinwheel pastries from the oven.

"Got it?" Valerie asked.

"'Course I do," he grumbled. He dropped the tray on the gas stove top with a clatter, the Santa-themed oven mitts comically big on him. Valerie and John shared a look but said nothing. She went and kissed the man's papery cheek.

The kitchen had clearly been remodeled, with a big island and white cabinets that gleamed. The marble countertop along the wall under a small window was cluttered with the baking ingredients, a spray of flour over the wood floor.

"This is Jeremy. Max's friend."

"Oh, you mean you didn't pick him up on the street corner? Of course he's Max's friend." Extending his hand, he said, "I'm Pierre." At the last second he realized he was still wearing the oven mitts and took them off to reveal gnarled fingers.

Jeremy shook his hand, which felt dry and bumpy but had a surprisingly crushing grip. "Very nice to meet you, sir. Thank you for having me."

"Well, why wouldn't we?" He wheezed a laugh and went back to his cookies, picking up a spatula to transfer them to a wire rack.

Jeremy followed Valerie and John out of the kitchen and down a passageway that looked very new. They explained that they'd had a sitting room converted into a bedroom and en suite bathroom for Valerie's father, passing the closed door and heading back to the main living area.

"It's a really nice house."

"Thank you, Jeremy." Valerie gave him a smile. "What a polite young man you are."

"Max said your parents are away? Where did they go?" John asked.

"Oh, they're on a cruise in Hawaii."

"You chose rural Ontario over Hawaii? You need to give your head a shake!" John exclaimed with a hearty laugh.

Max appeared, glaring. "*Dad.*"

"It's okay," Jeremy said, trying to laugh along. "I wasn't actually invited to Hawaii." He quickly added, "My parents are paying for res and my tuition. I can't expect more. It's only fair they get to treat themselves and my little brother. They're meeting up with my mom's old friend who lives in the States, and she has kids my brother's age, so it all works out well. I had a late exam, so I couldn't go anyway…"

He trailed off, aware of the awkward silence and pitying expressions.

"It's okay. It's not like they kicked me out or told me they hate me. It's all very civil." He winced internally as he said the soulless word.

"Civil," Valerie echoed. "My goodness." Her face pinched before she forced a bright smile. "Lucky for us we get the pleasure of your company. And another helping hand for Saturday!"

Jeremy nodded eagerly. Anything to get off the subject of his parents. "What's the event?"

She answered, "We do three Saturday open houses leading up to the holidays and promote it with a Christmas tree farm not too far from here. Joint flyers and ads encouraging folks to visit us both and make a full day of it. We coordinate to make sure we have different activities. Oh, John, did you ask Hunter if they need more syrup for this weekend for their flavored coffee and hot chocolate?"

"Let me text him now." John pulled out his phone.

In a conspiratorial half-whisper, Valerie said, "The tree farmer has a young lover who's done such a wonderful job promoting the business."

Meg hopped off the last stair, coming down from upstairs. "He's probably, like, twenty-five now. Super hot if you're into twinks. Nick Spini was such a grumpy fucker before Hunter came along. Super hot if you're into lumberjack daddies."

Lips thin, Valerie's nostrils flared as her eyes narrowed. "Megan."

Meg shrugged, trying not to grin. "Am I wrong, Mom?"

Valerie opened her mouth, then snapped it shut. "Fine," she muttered. "You're not wrong, but *language*."

John, who seemed to be happily ignoring the whole exchange, glanced up from his phone. "They're running low. Max, can you run over a few cans this afternoon? Then we can decorate the tree."

"Cool," Max agreed. "Jer, let me show you your room."

The stairs creaked under them, another fresh garland and golden fairy lights wrapped around the banister. The upstairs hallway was narrow, the floor uneven.

"They renovated downstairs first, as you can tell," Max said. "That's the master at the end of the hall, and they have their own bathroom. We're stuck with the ancient one that's the second door on the right. Meg's up on the left, this is you, and this is me across the hall." He motioned to the first room on the right.

Jeremy couldn't stop the spark of excitement at sleeping so close to Max. *Maybe we can just... No! We can't. Only friends! No benefits! At least not until January.*

"Great, thanks. Um…" He cast about for something to say and stupidly landed on, "Is there really a delay on the LSAT results?"

Max bristled. "You think I'm lying?"

"No!" Jeremy floundered. "I just thought… Well, maybe you didn't want to talk about it because you're not happy with how you did."

Rubbing his face, Max sighed. "Sorry. Don't know why I got so defensive. It's not you." He briefly squeezed Jeremy's shoulder. "It really is delayed."

Jeremy itched to soothe him, but a hug was probably way too much. Instead, he tentatively took hold of Max's arm. "Whatever happens, it'll be okay."

Max exhaled sharply. "Yeah. I… Thank you. I needed to hear that."

Jeremy smiled, and his hand was still on Max's arm, and maybe hugging him wouldn't be too weird? Friends hugged. He could make it one of those back-slapping bro hugs. But the moment stretched out too long, and he had to drop his hand. They stared at each other, and Jeremy fiddled with his new glasses.

"I should run that errand," Max said, jerking his thumb toward the stairs.

"Right. Yep. I'll unpack or whatever."

Max nodded, but at the top of the staircase, he spun back. "Or if you want to come with me, you can see more of the area."

"Sure." He tried hard to hit a casual tone. "That would be cool."

Jeremy practically skipped after him, the *fa-la-la-la-la* on the radio earlier echoing in his head.

Chapter Eight

ONE KISS WOULDN'T hurt.

Max scoffed at himself as he turned Valerie's old pickup onto the main road under a gray sky. One kiss would be a disaster because there was no way it wouldn't turn into more. Way more. He fiddled with the radio, settling on the rock station playing Tragically Hip. Jeremy gazed out the window from the passenger seat, apparently engrossed in the snowy forest and the odd house they passed.

It wasn't supposed to be this hard.

He'd known Jeremy barely a week. It should be easier to hit the pause button. He'd had casual sex before. He'd had friends-with-benefits arrangements that had come and gone for whatever reason.

He hadn't struggled with the kind of desire that had been simmering all day being with Jeremy, threatening to boil over. It wasn't just that he wanted to suck and fuck. He wanted to hold Jeremy and feel him close. He could kiss him for hours, teasing out sweet little whimpers…

He wanted Jeremy to take off his seatbelt and slide across the bench seat to tuck up under his arm. He'd gotten it in his head that Jeremy smelled and tasted like cherries, which was obviously not true. He even knew it for a fact, but he longed for it anyway. He wanted to make Jeremy smile—which was totally something he was allowed to do.

The problem was that Jeremy's smile made Max want to lean over and catch his mouth in a kiss.

He had to admit he really liked that he was the only guy Jeremy had ever kissed. Although for all he knew, he wasn't anymore. Jeremy might have gone out last night and hooked up. He might have gone on the app and invited some rando to his room. It was none of Max's business.

"You okay?" Jeremy asked.

Max realized he was gripping the steering wheel like it was about to be ripped from his hands. He forced a laugh and unclenched. "Yep. Thought there was a patch of ice."

After another minute of silence, the radio station transitioning to Led Zeppelin, Jeremy said, "Your family's great. And I'm not sure I've seen a house more Christmassy in my life."

Max laughed. "I did warn you."

"You did," Jeremy agreed with a smile. "So what's the story with the guys who run this Christmas tree farm?"

"Nick Spini and his 'young lover' were quite the scandal a few years back. Not only an age difference, but Nick is a total daddy. Like, a kinky daddy. As Meg said, they're both hot. Tongues were wagging, but Pinevale's also the most boring place ever, so it was the first exciting thing that happened since a Boston Pizza opened."

"People are okay with them being gay?"

"Yep. I'm sure there are some people secretly disapproving because they're joyless dipshits, but the farm has done better than ever since Hunter moved in and ramped up the marketing and stuff. Nick was alone for a long time after his partner died, out there with his dog hiding from the world."

"Wow. That's so sad. How did they meet?"

Max grinned. "Nick got roped into playing Santa at the old mall, and Hunter was his elf. Not gonna lie, my imagination went pretty wild on that one. I bet it was naughty and damn nice."

Jeremy looked a little scandalized, which was *adorable*. He laughed. "That's...yeah, that's..." His voice dropped to a whisper. "Kinda hot."

Max tore his eyes back to the road. "Anyway, they seem really happy."

"That's great." Jeremy pulled his phone from his pocket as it vibrated with a low *buzz* and sucked in a little breath when he looked at the screen.

"Okay?"

"Yeah. My dad texted from a port. I guess it's the first time they've had a signal. Just checking in and saying they're having a good time."

"Right. Very…civil."

Jeremy was quiet, and from the corner of his eye, Max watched him staring at the message. Max turned down the screeching guitar on the radio. "Sorry. You okay?"

After a long exhale, Jeremy said, "Yeah. It is, though. Civil. Polite. Not like my parents would ever be *rude*—they hate that. But I looked at that text and part of me was hoping it would say they love me the way I am and everything'll be okay. That everything will go back to normal. I—"

Jeremy broke off and stared out the window, his knee jiggling as he fidgeted. "Part of me was relieved they went on this cruise because it took me going home for Christmas out of the equation. Because I'm afraid they would have told me not to come."

Max gripped the steering wheel again as he slowed for the tree farm. He had a lot of choice words for the Rourkes, but he wouldn't do Jeremy any favors by calling his parents selfish assholes. That would make Max feel better, but this wasn't about him. He asked, "What about summer?"

"I don't know. We haven't talked about it. I assume I'm going home, but I guess I could register for a couple of classes and stay on campus. Assuming they'll still be paying my tuition and res. Or I'll have to get a loan." He shifted restlessly. "That'll be a lot of debt."

It was like Max could see the anxiety gathering force like a tornado about to touch down. "Don't think about that right now. Valerie would tell you not to borrow trouble, and she's right. Whatever happens, you'll figure it out. For now, your dad texted you and that means he was thinking about you. So you should reply. Focus on what you can control right now. You don't know exactly what the other team's strategy is, so think about yours."

"Are you going to start talking about touchdowns and tackles?"

Max laughed as he turned into the drive, passing under a huge banner advertising the holiday open house. "I might!" He was relieved to see a little smile tugging on Jeremy's lips. "We have to take this one game at a time. Leave it all on the field."

"Give a hundred and ten percent?"

"Now you're getting it. There are no easy games at this level. Put pressure on the defense. Make plays on both sides of the ball. Go out there and execute."

"Aye-aye, captain." Jeremy gave him a salute.

Max saluted back and they burst out laughing. He navigated the winding, snow-covered drive. The snowbanks here from the plow were even higher than at home. "You want help with what to text back?"

"I'm just going to go with a 'Have fun! I'm at a Christmas tree farm.' Then send a pic?"

"I like it. Show them you're not sitting around feeling ashamed of yourself, waiting for their crumbs. There's a great spot where you can see the trees into the distance. I'm sure Nick won't mind."

"Awesome."

They reached the farm and parked. Ella the beagle raced over to investigate, snow flying up from her paws. She reached Jeremy first, and he crouched, murmuring a greeting as her tail wagged violently.

Jeremy started petting the dog, and damn if Max didn't want to pet him. Jeremy's toque was still in the truck, and his ginger hair was gorgeous. Max looked down at his head, fingers itching to comb through.

"Ignore her!" Nick called, striding over from the barn past the rustic chalet house with big windows. Both the barn and house were decorated for the holidays with fresh garlands and wreaths and tons of lights. Max bit back a laugh as Nick got closer. Nick wore his typical plaid work wear—plus an extremely uncharacteristic pink toque with a wobbling pom-pom.

Hunter came out of the house, zipping up his jacket and pulling a hat over his blond hair. "Why would they ignore the cutest dog in the world?"

Nick looked like he wanted to argue—which seemed to be his usual expression in Max's limited experience—but grunted. He extended his hand to Max, and damn, he really was a big daddy lumberjack. Max was pretty big himself, but Nick had this intimidating aura. Even with the hat.

They made introductions, and Hunter was his usual smiling, energetic self. He and Nick seemed like polar opposites, but Max supposed that was what made them work. Hmm. Were he and Jeremy opposites? Maybe a little. Jeremy was anxious and unsure and pocket-sized. Max—

He realized everyone was staring at him. "Hmm? Sorry, Ella's just too adorable for me to concentrate on anything else. Aren't you?" He crouched to pet her, and she eagerly soaked up the affection like a dry sponge.

"Don't encourage her," Nick grumbled. "You'd think we ignored her all day." He scratched his salt and pepper beard. Max stood and squinted at the toque Nick was wearing. Was the pink wool threaded with...glitter?

Nick frowned, then yanked off the hat with a muttered curse, shooting Hunter a death glare. Hunter grinned, his blue eyes gleaming with amusement. Nick said to Max, "Thanks for the syrup. Your folks need any more greenery?"

"Nope, we're good. I love the hat by the way."

"It suits him, right?" Hunter asked with pretend innocence.

"It matches the green plaid," Jeremy offered with real innocence that made Max want to kiss him all over again.

"That's what I said!" Hunter exclaimed. He drew Nick's face down and pressed a kiss to his bearded cheek. "See?"

Shaking his head and clearly fighting a smile, Nick marched back to the barn, Ella on his heels. Hunter snickered. "I gave it to him as a gag last Christmas, but the inside is super soft, and he secretly loves it."

Max held out his fist, and Hunter bumped it.

"Let me grab the syrup from you."

"Also, do you mind if we walk over and get a few pics of the farm? Jeremy needs some Insta shots."

"No prob. Want me to show you around?"

Of course they did, and Hunter took them to all the best spots for pictures. It was cold and the snow was deep, but the wind was mellow. Jeremy's cheeks were pink by the time they returned to the truck, and while he quickly replied to his dad's text, Max stared at him biting his lip in concentration.

Maybe if Max just gave in and kissed him one more time, he'd get it out of his system...

They headed for home, Jeremy's glasses fogging up as the truck's heat kicked in. He took them off and wiped them on his scarf before digging a crumpled tissue out of his pocket.

"That was great. I've never... We saw lots of couples on Church Street and stuff, but it was cool seeing two guys who actually live together." He shook his head. "That's dumb."

"It's not."

"I mean, obviously plenty of same-sex couples live together."

"Right. But there's knowing that and seeing it for yourself."

Jeremy nodded eagerly. "Exactly. You get it. It's all been so theoretical for me. Then I met you." He ducked his head, cleaning his glasses so vigorously the tissue ripped. He put on his glasses and kept his gaze on the road ahead. "I don't just mean...what we did together. Meeting you has expanded my world so much in, like, a week. Thank you."

For a moment, Max couldn't breathe and he sure as hell couldn't speak as he turned onto the narrow highway. He wanted to tell Jeremy that it had been the best surprise and there was so much more he wanted to show him.

Not just sex—he wanted to take him to all the Instagramable places, and all the queer places where they could be themselves and see themselves, and show him...everything. More than that, he wanted to discover new places together.

But would they even be living in the same city next year? He'd applied to law school in Toronto, but also Kingston, Halifax, Ottawa, Calgary, and Vancouver. Depending on his LSAT results, he might not even be accepted. He might not even want to go.

This was exactly why they needed to hit pause. Max had to decide what he wanted before getting carried away with a sexy, adorable new guy.

He cleared his throat. "No prob. Anytime."

"HAVE A GOOD time?"

Max whipped around to find Meg closing his door. She leaned against it, head tilted and arms crossed, a too-innocent smile on her face. He said, "Yeah. Sure. Hunter says hi."

Her smile didn't alter. "You guys were gone for a while."

"Yeah, they showed Jeremy around."

Her arms dropped and so did the smile. "Dude, come on. You said you weren't fucking him!"

"I'm not! We went to the Spini farm to drop off the syrup, and they gave us a little tour for Jeremy. We didn't do anything else." It was the truth, after all. He waited with hands on his hips.

Meg's gaze narrowed. "Okay. You seem to be telling the truth."

He huffed. "You and your 'tell.'" It still bugged that she wouldn't tell him what it was.

"You're the one with the tell when you lie. Don't hate the player, hate the game. So let's say I believe you that this excursion was all business. But you want to fuck him. And you already have."

"No, I haven't." Depending on one's definition of the word. Max turned back to his duffel, emptying it into the laundry basket in the corner.

"Did you bring anything that doesn't need to be washed?"

"Of course not."

"Me either, to be fair. Also? You're lying."

He held out his hands in protest, running over every movement he'd made. What the hell gave it away?

Meg went on. "I mean, the way you two were eye-fucking this morning at the bus station, even the old lady behind us was like, get a room."

"We're not—" He tossed his toilet bag onto the bed and zipped his empty duffel, kicking it into the corner by the closet. "Fine, we had a little friends-with-benefits thing going on, but just for a few days. I told him about the house rules, and we both agreed to put on the brakes. He's a nice kid. Are you going to narc? Would you rather he spent Christmas alone in res?"

She curled her lip. "Obviously not. What kind of asshole do you take me for? Also, Mom and Dad wouldn't throw him out, so throttle back on the drama. They're just uptight about us sleeping in the same bed with someone at home. Even though we're supposed to be adults, it's their house, so whatever. You and Jeremy are still allowed to be dating. You're staying in separate rooms, so why are you being weird about this?"

"Because I'm not supposed to like him this much!" Max shout-whispered.

Meg grinned triumphantly but kept her voice down. "I knew it."

"Yeah, yeah."

She frowned. "So what's the prob? He seems really sweet. Kinda nerdy, so not your usual type, but nothing wrong with that."

"I was just going to do a little fairy godfathering. Help him find his way since he came out pretty recently and doesn't really have any friends at school yet." Obviously Max wasn't going to betray Jeremy's trust and tell Meg about the virgin stuff. "I'm not supposed to be falling for him."

"Why not?"

"Because that's not the plan." But did he even want that plan?

"I know law school will be busy, but I'm pretty sure you can still date during it."

Law school was the last thing he wanted to get into. "I've just had everything laid out for so long and now…"

She smiled, her tone teasing. "You know, it's okay for Captain Max to not have every little thing figured out. You can call an audible."

"Changing the play at the last minute doesn't always go well."

I promised Mom at her funeral I'd be a lawyer just like her.

But do I actually want to be a lawyer? Would I rather be a teacher? Or something else?

Will Mom understand?

Meg said, "But sometimes you get a touchdown."

"Kids!" Valerie called from downstairs. "Tree time!"

It was a relief to put aside the swirl of conflicting emotions, the little whispers fading. They met Jeremy in the hall coming out of the bathroom and went down. Max inhaled the delicious smell coming from the kitchen with relish as Jeremy asked, "Wow. What is that?"

"Papy's maple bourbon apple cider," Max answered. "It's our tradition for tree-trimming."

Papy came into the living room with a tray of steaming mugs, his shuffling steps steady enough, though Valerie and his dad looked like they wanted to grab the tray from him. But he set it on the coffee table himself with a groan as he stooped, then went to get the pastries.

They all took a mug, and Max warmed his hands around it, blowing on the steaming cider. His dad stoked the fire with a shower of sparks, and Valerie unpacked the old boxes of decorations, unwinding neatly twined bundles of golden fairy lights.

Jeremy exclaimed, "Oh!" as he gulped a mouthful of cider. "Is that alcoholic?"

"Of course," Papy said as he shuffled back in with a plate stacked high with pets-de-soeur pastries.

"We're French-Canadian," Meg said. "Booze, maple, Catholic guilt. The three major food groups."

Jeremy laughed. "What's the fourth?"

"Hmm." Meg said, "Papy, what do you think?"

"Tourtière."

"Not poutine?" Max teased, knowing Papy wasn't a fan.

Papy glared as he got settled on his spot on the middle love seat. "Meat pie is better and you know it."

Max grinned and took a bite of buttery pastry. "Mmm. Papy, this is amazing."

He shrugged but looked pleased. "Your mamy's recipe is the best. Simple."

Mouth full, Meg mumbled, "Mmm. Butter, brown sugar, maple. Doesn't get better."

Dad stood and clapped his hands. "All right, this tree won't decorate itself."

"It's your job to put on the lights while we watch," Max noted.

"Funny guy." But Dad didn't argue, methodically looping the strands of lights around the tree. Beyond the tree through the front window, the afternoon was already getting dark. The colored Christmas lights on the barn and house were on a timer, and sure enough they soon flipped on.

Kneeling on the area rug, Max unpacked decorations, one of the cardboard boxes so old and ratty that one of the flaps ripped right off when he gently tried to unfold it.

Sitting beside Papy, Jeremy sipped his cider, his cheeks a little rosy. He was quiet, listening to them all tease each other, but he was smiling. When he caught Max's gaze, he whispered, "What? Is there something on my face?" He swiped at his mouth.

"No, you're good." Max bent his head to examine the ornaments, unwrapping glass balls from ancient tissue paper.

"Done!" Dad proclaimed. He flopped onto one of the love seats. "Tinsel is your job, kids."

Meg had the long red and green metallic garlands ready to go, and Max helped her loop them around the tree. They had to redo one of them three times before they achieved the perfect even coverage.

"Wanna help us hang the ornaments?" Max asked Jeremy.

"Are you sure?"

"Of course!" Valerie exclaimed, passing him a box. "Get in there."

Meg, Max, and Jeremy went to work while the others drank and ate and pointed out where they should hang things so there were no bare patches. Hanging a dangling silver ornament, Jeremy leaned into the tree and inhaled deeply.

"It smells amazing. Now I see why people get real trees."

"Have you never had a real tree before?" Valerie asked, her eyebrows raised.

"Nope. My mom says it's too messy and a fire hazard."

Valerie said, "Well, yes, but it's *tradition*. Also, we need more cider."

Papy started rocking the way he did when he was going to heave himself up to standing, so Max quickly said, "I'll get it!"

"I'll help you," Jeremy offered, following Max into the kitchen. His phone buzzed, and he pulled it out. "Oh!"

"Did your dad reply?" Inhaling the sweet, spicy deliciousness, Max stirred the pot of cider that'd been left on a low simmer.

"No, it's… I didn't realize—oh! Holy shit." Jeremy slapped a hand over his mouth and glanced back toward the living room.

Laughing, Max asked, "What?"

Jeremy murmured, "When I unpacked, I looked at that dating app. I was just curious to see if there was anyone else around here using it. I didn't want to hook up with someone!"

Max worked hard on keeping his smile in place. "It's okay, dude. You're allowed to want to hook up." Which was absolutely true. There was zero reason Max should have the ladle in a death grip. "Usually have to go to Barrie, but once in a while there'll be 'straight' guys in the sticks on the down-low who wanna get busy in their pickup."

"Wow." Jeremy seemed legitimately shocked, which was adorable. "I didn't even realize anyone could see my profile."

"Probably have to opt-out in the settings." It was all Max could do not to snatch the phone away and delete the app, which would definitely be a dick move for a fairy godfather. He shouldn't discourage Jeremy if this was what he wanted. He was free to explore and have fun. "So who is it?" He couldn't resist adding, "Can't imagine there's anyone really worth seeing around here."

Jeremy held up his phone. "Um, 'Upbeat-underscore-drummer-underscore_guy.' He lives near Barrie."

"Which username did you go with?"

"Oh, just a variation on my Insta. Had to add an extra underscore or something."

"Cool, cool, cool. So, what do you think of him?" Max stirred the cider roughly, the ladle clattering on the sides of the pot and hot liquid splashing the stove.

"Looks…nice? He's showing his face. Kinda hipster, I guess? Shaggy hair and a beard. Around our age. Not sure how he can really tell, but he says I look cute."

He's right. "Clearly has good taste." Max reminded himself this had been the initial idea when he'd taken Jeremy under his wing. Here was the fairy godfathering he'd intended. The responsible, unselfish thing to do was encourage Jeremy, not hold him back.

The words actually hurt his dry throat as he said, "Ask him if he wants to meet for coffee," before he could change his mind. Because it would be selfish. Fairy godparents weren't supposed to cock block.

"Uh… Really?" Jeremy blinked at him, his forehead furrowed. "You want me to go out with him?"

"Well, you're totally free to." Which wasn't exactly answering the question. "I have to go into Barrie tomorrow for Christmas shopping. I can drop you off and pick you up or whatever." He shifted from foot to foot as he stirred, Jeremy's quiet gaze prickling his skin.

"Is that… You want me to?"

Max focused on a cheery tone. "Up to you, obviously."

Jeremy was quiet for a few beats. "I guess I should?"

"Sure, why not?" Max's brain had a bunch of loud suggestions as to why not, and he brutally smothered them. "There's a cool games cafe in Barrie. Tell him to meet you there around eleven."

And if he can't make it, oh well!

"Okay." Jeremy didn't sound too thrilled but tapped his phone and waited.

"And don't feel bad if he says no. He might be busy, or maybe just wants a hookup and not a date, or—"

"He just said yes." Jeremy gaped at the screen. "I guess I'm doing this."

"If you want to." *Say you don't want to.*

"Well, I can't cancel now. I'm the one who asked him out."

"Right." Because Max had suggested it—because he was a *complete fucking idiot.*

"I don't want to hurt his feelings."

Max's frustrated confusion dissipated in a swell of affection for Jeremy. "No. Of course not." Jeremy was right—this guy didn't deserve to be jerked around. "It's one morning date. Doesn't have to be a big deal."

"Yeah." Jeremy smiled weakly. "This is the kind of thing people do all the time, right?"

"Totally. You should go and have fun." He tried very hard to mean it. Jeremy deserved to have these experiences. A good friend and fairy godfather wouldn't hold him back.

"Are *you* hooking up while we're here in Pinevale? Like, with guys in pickup trucks or whatever?"

"No." Max laughed. "Been there, done that."

"Oh," Jeremy whispered, his face going red. "I guess I should too?"

Over my dead body. Gripping the ladle, Max took a calming breath and was honest. "No, I don't think that's your speed. And that's okay. But you were looking at the app for a reason."

"I told you I was just curious!"

"*Exactly.* You're nineteen. You're living away from home for the first time. Of course you're curious. It's okay to be curious. I support your curiosity."

Jeremy looked dubious. "Thank you."

Lifting the pot in two hands, Max headed toward the living room, needing this awkward AF conversation to be over. What was done was done. Jeremy was going on a date.

Yay.

He held the pot while Jeremy ladled out seconds for everyone, then returned it to the stove. Back by the tree, he and Jeremy decorated in silence while Dad, Meg, Papy, and Valerie had a spirited debate about the Maple Leafs' defense or lack thereof.

As he went up on tiptoes to hang a glass snowflake around the side of the tree facing the window, Jeremy whispered to Max, "I'm going to get drunk soon." He made this adorable little giggle that said the bourbon might have already gone to his head. His smile faded. "I can't believe I'm going on a date with someone I've never met." He bit his lip. "But you think I should, right?"

"Absolutely." Max clinked their mugs together, forcing a smile. He tried very hard not to think about how he'd just pushed Jeremy into a date with another guy, and he definitely didn't think about how if they kissed now, it would taste just like Christmas.

Chapter Nine

I N THE CAFE'S vestibule, Jeremy hid next to a massive, fake potted
plant, waiting for his glasses to de-fog.

Well, he wasn't *hiding*. He was gathering his courage. To go on a
date with a complete stranger. He glanced back through the glass door,
spotting Max's truck turning onto the main road. It was wild to think
that Max had been a complete stranger only a week ago. Maybe this
drummer guy would be just as awesome.

So why was Jeremy hoping he wasn't?

He rolled his eyes mentally. *Gee, I wonder why.* But Max seemed to
want him to go on this date. Or did he? Honestly, Jeremy wasn't sure.
He'd stared at the ceiling half the night replaying the bizarre conversation in the kitchen.

If they were only pausing things between them, why would Max
want him to meet up with another guy? Maybe Max *was* actually done
with Jeremy and just hadn't had the balls to tell him. But why would he
invite him home? Was Jeremy *that* pathetic? He sure hoped not.

He supposed if he was being fair, they'd agreed they were only
friends for the next couple of weeks. They were both free to do whatever—or whomever—they wanted. But maybe Jeremy wasn't as mature or
evolved or cool as other people, because he absolutely hated the idea of
Max dating anyone else.

Hated. It.

And he felt like Max didn't like it either? On the way to the cafe,

Max's smiles had been so tight and quick that it seemed he wasn't happy at all with the idea of Jeremy seeing someone else.

He crushed the bloom of sweet happiness and hope. Max was helping him out and being a friend, but was he really going to end up as Jeremy's *boyfriend*? He'd made it seem like they'd pick up where they left off in January, but Jeremy needed to keep his expectations realistic. Max was way out of his league.

He was lucky he'd been able to touch and taste and learn, and that Max and his family had been so generous. Wishful thinking about the future wouldn't get him anywhere. He needed to be an adult and go on this date. Even if all he wanted to do was run after Max's truck and never look back, he'd agreed to meet this guy and couldn't stand him up.

Where he lurked, he couldn't really see the cafe, which spread out to his right after the narrow entrance. So he figured he couldn't be seen either and took another minute to calm his nerves. It was fine.

Upbeat_drummer_guy probably went on dates all the time. This wasn't a big deal. Jeremy needed to chill already. Now that he and Max had fooled around, this was supposed to be easier.

Yeah. Not so much.

He groaned to himself. Thinking about fooling around with Max was dangerous. When he hadn't been obsessively replaying the kitchen conversation the night before, he'd fantasized about Max creeping across the hall and surprising him. Which had obviously led to jerking off as silently as he could.

Now that he'd kissed and touched Max for real—had experienced the wet heat of his mouth on his dick—getting himself off had felt disappointingly hollow. Even though he'd come hard remembering shooting into Max's mouth, having Max so close but so far was torture.

Annnd if he didn't stop thinking about it immediately, he was going to pop a boner in the cafe entrance at eleven o'clock in the morning like a huge perv. Not that there was a good time of day to have a throbbing erection in a cafe.

He banished all thoughts of Max and erections and forced himself to walk into the cafe and look for Upbeat_drummer_guy, whose name he realized he didn't know yet. Shit. He should have asked. What an idiot. He was terrible at this. He should turn around and—

Upbeat_drummer_guy was waving to him from a table near the back. Jeremy waved back, then dropped his hand. Had he looked too enthusiastic? Dorky?

What would Max do?

Taking a deep breath, he passed by various groups of people playing board games and laughing loudly and joined his date at the table, shaking his hand and learning his name was Levi. Jeremy hung his coat on a nearby rack. He hadn't brought his Blundstone knockoffs, so was in his clunky boots. But considering how much snow there was in Barrie, he certainly wasn't alone. He resisted the urge to peek under the table to see what Levi was wearing.

Levi looked like his pic: white, shaggy brown hair, beard. He wore a plaid shirt and jeans, so was maybe a little hipsterish. Jeremy had gone with his new pink sweater and usual jeans. He adjusted his glasses and tried not to fidget as Levi went to the counter for a refill on his coffee and to get Jeremy a cappuccino.

"I've never been here before," Levi said when he returned, setting down their cups. "It's cool. You come here a lot?"

"No, actually. This is my first time." Jeremy willed himself not to blush, his words conjuring a bunch of other thoughts. "I'm spending the holidays with a friend and his family. He recommended it."

"He lives in Barrie?"

"No, near Pinevale. They have a maple syrup farm. It's really cool. If you like maple syrup. Which I guess most people do? But maybe not." Oh God. He needed to stop talking.

Levi smiled. "It would be un-Canadian to not like maple syrup."

"Yes!" Jeremy agreed too loudly. "Um, so, yeah. They have this maple syrup farm. There's an open house tomorrow, actually. It's called Nadeau Farms if you want to check it out." Wait, had he just accidentally asked Levi on another date? "I mean, you're probably not into face painting and maple candies."

"Actually, my nieces would love it, and I need somewhere to take them tomorrow. Sounds very wholesome."

"Uh-huh. Great!" His mind spun. *Say something. Something not completely pathetic.* "Sorry. I'm really nervous."

Chuckling, Levi said, "I kinda picked up on that. Let's play something. Any suggestions? I'm not much of a gamer, but these look cool." He motioned to the bookcases lining the cafe's interior wall that were stuffed with board games.

Jeremy wanted to crawl under the table. "I'm sorry. We can go somewhere else."

"No, that's not what I meant. I'm not really into video games." He laughed. "That's a lie. The problem is I get completely obsessed with them and it takes over my life. I need to just say no to video games. Monopoly, I can handle." He squeezed Jeremy's arm, his hand lingering for a moment. "This was a great suggestion."

"Oh. Okay." Jeremy didn't know how to feel. Levi seemed nice, so that was good, right? He was supposed to want to go on dates, so here he was. "I guess we could try something a little more advanced than passing GO and collecting two hundred dollars."

"Sure," Levi agreed easily, pushing back his chair. They slowly scanned a nearby shelf, and Levi said, "There are a ton of games I've never even heard of."

"We definitely live in the golden age of board games. This one's supposed to be really good." He went on tiptoes and strained to snag Dead of Winter from a high shelf.

Laughing, Levi easily grabbed it since he was a few inches taller. "This one?" He eyed the box. "Zombies? Let's do it."

They settled in, sipping coffee while they played. It was slow going at first, with lots of referencing the instructions, but they got the hang of it eventually. It was fun that it was a cooperative game so they could work together.

Their knees bumped occasionally under the table, and they laughed and strategized, and Jeremy was relieved he hadn't had to give his life story and talk about his family. He just said he wasn't going all the way back to Victoria for the holidays. He asked Levi about drumming and learned he played in a local band and was attending college in Barrie for mechanics.

They chatted and tried to save the world from zombies, and eventually had sandwiches and pints of beer. Jeremy thought he was doing okay on this date after all. But did he want to kiss Levi? While Levi pondered his next move, stroking his beard absently, Jeremy tried to imagine making out with him. It wasn't that it would be bad, but...

It wouldn't be Max.

An ache filled him, and he told himself this longing was ridiculous. It was his turn, and he tried to focus on the moves he could make and what would be best for their characters.

"Hey, do you know that guy?"

Jeremy turned in his chair to follow Levi's gaze—and blinked in surprise to see Max on the far side of the cafe whipping his head down. "That's my friend," Jeremy said. "I guess he's done his shopping."

"Sure he's not your bodyguard? He's been watching us pretty closely."

A thrill sang through Jeremy, and he tamped it down, forcing a laugh. "He knew I was nervous, so he's probably just being..." What, exactly? Jeremy waved his hand, unable to think of the right word.

"Hmm. Okay. Do you need to get going, or..."

"No, I'm sure it's fine. Let's finish the game." He glanced back over his shoulder, but Max was engrossed in his phone.

They played on until Levi said, "Okay. This has been fun, but it feels like I'm the third wheel here."

Jeremy whirled his head back from peeking at Max again to face Levi guiltily. "I just wanted to make sure he was still good over there and didn't want to leave or anything. I'm sorry." He cringed. "I'm a terrible date. I have no idea what I'm doing."

Levi softened with a sigh. "It's okay. Are you sure you two are only friends? Because you can't keep your eyes off each other."

"Really? We only met a week ago. Although he did give me my first kiss. And blow job." *Did I just say that out loud? Oh my God.* "But we're just friends!"

"Your first...ah, okay." Levi laughed. "I dunno, man. Because he looks jealous as hell." He raised his hands. "Look, it's cool. I'm not about to get in the middle of whatever this is."

"I don't blame you." Jeremy shook his head. "I'm so confused." He took off his glasses and cleaned them on his soft sweater, which only made a smear worse. Head down as he tried a napkin on the lens, he sighed. "You seem great, but I really like Max." It was the truth and there was no point fighting it.

"Fair enough. It's too bad, because you're damn cute."

Feeling his face go hot, Jeremy put his glasses back on. "Um, thank you."

"I'm pretty sure Max shares this opinion."

"What? No." Jeremy shrugged and fiddled with the crust of his sandwich. "He's so out of my league. Look at him! Literally captain of the football team and a senior. I'm a skinny frosh with no friends. I mean, I only met him because I wiped out on some ice and he took pity on me."

Levi laughed. "Ouch. But I'm not getting pity. His vibe is more like he's wanting to punch me and haul you off over his shoulder."

"No way. He's the one who pulled the plug on teaching me. Or put it on pause. We're paused."

"Teaching you?"

"Forget it." Why on Earth had he brought that up?

"Ah. Got it."

"Anyway, back to the game. So, our food stocks are really low. I think we should go to the grocery store, although there's a pretty high risk to making that move."

But Levi would not be deterred. "So your friend Max over there was giving you *private* lessons?"

Tips of his ears burning, Jeremy nodded. "But now we're staying with his family, so it's all on hold. Because of the house rules and because it would just be weird. Which was fine with me because it's only a couple of weeks until January, and then we can…pick up again. But he encouraged me to meet with you, so maybe he doesn't actually want me? I'm not sure. It's so confusing."

Levi frowned. "Sounds like he's playing games with you."

"No, it's not like that."

"Hmm. Maybe you should teach *him* a lesson in not taking you for granted." He beckoned Jeremy closer. "Here, I'll tell you a secret."

Not sure what to expect, Jeremy leaned in across the table. Levi whispered, "He's watching us right now. I bet if I touch your hair or something, steam's going to come out of his ears." Winking, he barely touched Jeremy's head. "Probably looks like I'm going to kiss you from where he's sitting—oh shit, I'm good. He's coming over. Don't look. Laugh like I'm amazingly funny."

Jeremy sat frozen, trying to laugh, his heart thumping. Max was coming over?

Then Max was there, looming beside the table, opening his mouth to say something before snapping it shut. He tried again and said, "Uh… Hi."

"Hi," Jeremy replied warily. "Are you okay?"

Max's face was flushed, and he looked mortified. "Yeah. Sorry to interrupt. I was… Hi! I'm Max." He extended his hand to Levi, who half stood and shook it, offering his name before sitting again. Max cleared his throat. "Just wanted to make sure everything's okay."

Jeremy shifted uncomfortably. On one hand if Max was actually jealous that was incredible—but on the other, he was being kind of a jerk for coming over. Maybe he just wanted to make sure Jeremy didn't need rescuing? Which made him feel warm and gooey. And maybe Jeremy *should* make him jealous.

"Yeah, we're great. This is a fun game. Zombies and stuff."

"Cool." Max rocked on his heels. "Cool, cool, cool, cool."

Levi said, "I've got to run. I didn't think coffee would last this long, but time flies when you have great company." He shot Jeremy a wink. "Talk soon? I'll see you tomorrow."

Tomorrow? Jeremy managed, "That would be cool. Thanks for a great game."

"Tomorrow?" Max echoed.

"Yeah, that maple syrup thing sounds fun. Perfect for my nieces. I'll see you both then."

Jeremy pushed his chair back and gave Levi the world's awkwardest hug because a handshake didn't feel right. "It really was good to meet you."

"Follow my lead tomorrow," Levi whispered. "It'll be fun."

Max was staring daggers at Levi's retreating back. Frustration surged, because that really *had* been rude of him to butt in, and Jeremy had already been a terrible enough date to someone who deserved better.

"Why'd you interrupt?"

Max shrugged. "I was done shopping, and I figured I'd check in to see how things were going. You weren't even supposed to know I was there."

"I didn't, but Levi noticed you staring."

Max laughed uneasily. "My bad. I wasn't trying to…"

"What?"

"Dunno."

Crossing his arms, Jeremy tried to laugh it off. "You were the one who wanted me to come on this date in the first place."

But Max didn't laugh. "Not exactly. I was encouraging you. I thought it would be good practice. I thought you wanted to date."

Jeremy didn't know what the right answer was. "I feel like I'm supposed to. You said we're just friends now, right? That's what you said."

"Yeah. That's what I said." He rubbed his face. "You're right. I'm being an asshole. Sorry. I shouldn't have barged in on your date. He seems cool."

But he's not you. "Yeah, he's laid-back. He's a drummer in a band."

"And you scored a second date!" Max held up his palm. "Your fairy godfather is very proud."

Jeremy didn't leave him hanging for the high five, even though *triumphant* wasn't one of the many emotions swirling around his gut in a big ball of anxiety. If Levi was right and Max was jealous, why didn't Max just say that? Jeremy wanted to ask, but he couldn't get the words past his tongue. The fear of humiliating himself was too strong.

If he said it out loud and Max denied it—or worse, laughed at him—it would crush him. Maybe Jeremy was a coward, but the last thing he wanted for Christmas was a broken heart.

MACAULAY CULKIN SLAPPED his cheeks on the big TV over the crackling fire, and they all laughed. Jeremy finished most of his third slice of pizza and picked at the crust idly. He half watched the movie, his socked feet curled under him on the couch and knee pressing Max's thigh comfortably through the layers of their jeans.

Was Max manspreading on purpose so they could touch? Or was Jeremy reading way too much into it? Probably the latter. They sat on the love seat closest to the tree, and the pine scent filled his nose. Under it were faint notes of coconut, and Jeremy wished he could lean to his right and nuzzle Max's thick waves.

The phone rang in the kitchen—an old rotary one that had likely been attached to the wall for many decades and had apparently been put back up after the reno. Taking the empty pizza box and a few plates, Valerie hopped up to answer.

Jeremy had the ridiculous thought that maybe it was his mother calling, and he stamped down the sudden bloom of hope. His parents didn't have the number. They didn't even know Max or his family existed. It was hard to believe Jeremy hadn't either until the past week. He had to remember that. Remember that this was all new and very likely transitory.

Valerie called, "John! It's your parents. On speaker phone."

Everyone laughed, and Jeremy smiled. "Is this a thing?"

John pushed up from the other end of the couch. "Yep. They'll talk over each other and the dogs will be barking, and it'll be chaos." He smiled fondly and shrugged. "Parents."

A swift punch of loss hitched Jeremy's breath as he nodded. He stared at the TV, one of the crooks falling down the stairs with a huge shout and sound effects. His hand rested on his curled leg, and his breath stuttered again when Max covered it with his own, tugging it down hidden between them, although Meg definitely noticed. Max still watched the TV, laughing, but he rubbed Jeremy's knuckles with his thumb reassuringly until John returned and told Max it was his turn.

When Max came back and told Meg she was up, he flopped down on the love seat. He folded his hands in his lap, and Jeremy tried not to miss that small touch Max had bestowed. Papy didn't get up to talk with his in-laws, but shouted greetings, his feet up on an ottoman.

When Meg returned with Valerie, they paused the TV and everyone laughed about something to do with aunties and uncles that Jeremy didn't quite follow. He didn't mind, though. It was nice just being with a family, even if it wasn't his.

"The monthly phone call is always stellar when they're in Goa," Meg said.

"The airing of grievances is next level," Max agreed. He added to Jeremy, "They winter in Goa now. They have a house near the beach. It's amazing. We all went a few Christmases ago. Dad and Valerie are going for a few weeks in January."

Valerie asked John, "Think they'll try to make you and your sisters go to confession?"

John laughed. "My father will probably try." To Jeremy, he said, "When I was a teenager, my dad packed me and my three sisters into the car and drove us to church in Scarborough. Marched us inside and stood there with his arms crossed while we went into the confessional one after the other. I was last, and I told the priest my father was making me do it and I had nothing to say. The poor priest shook his head and asked, 'How many more of you are there?'"

Jeremy laughed. "Did you just sit there in silence for a few minutes?"

"Nah, we talked about the holes in the Habs' offense. Father Rossi didn't think prayer would be enough to get past the first round of the playoffs. He was right."

They cleaned up the rest of the plates, and Jeremy jumped up to help. In the kitchen, Valerie asked, "Can one of you take out the composting, please?" She took a green bucket from under the sink and plunked it on the counter by the back door.

"Max can do it," Meg said.

Of course, he replied, "You can do it."

"No. You can." She tossed a mini pine cone at him from a holiday potpourri in a bowl on the kitchen island.

Max tossed one back. "You."

"You."

"You."

They pelted each other back and forth, and Jeremy laughed, missing Sean. Valerie heaved a dramatic sigh.

"How old are you two?"

Meg shrugged. "We'll never be too old to throw sh—stuff at each other." To punctuate her point, she aimed a cinnamon stick at Max. "You do it."

"I'll do it!" Jeremy offered, sticking his socked feet into the big pair of rubber Crocs sitting by the door, which he assumed were used for this very purpose. He opened the main door and unlatched the glass screen door.

Max came around the island with a smile. "No, I'll do it. Go sit down."

"I've got it!" Jeremy was pleased to be helping, and he grabbed the green bucket.

"Thank you, and careful, hon," Valerie called. "It might be slippery."

The back porch wasn't covered and hadn't been cleared that day, but it was only a few steps. Jeremy crossed to the composter, dumped the bucket, and then closed it with a flourish.

Too much of a flourish, as he momentarily lost his balance, shuffling backwards. On cue, the worn Crocs slid out from under him as he wiped out, landing on his ass on the snowy porch.

Again, seriously?!

"Shit!" Max bolted outside, dropping to his knees before Jeremy. "Are you okay?"

"Uh-huh! Just the clumsiest person ever." His face burned, and he tried to push himself up, still holding the bucket.

"Oh my goodness!" Valerie exclaimed from the doorway. "Are you hurt? John, you were supposed to salt the back porch!"

Max's hands were strong on Jeremy's waist as he lifted him to his feet—and almost off them. "Your tailbone okay?"

"Yeah." It smarted, but the snow had cushioned his fall a bit, he thought. He looked down. "You're in your socks," he said to Max. Max's feet must have been freezing, but he ignored him, leading Jeremy back into the kitchen, where the rest of the family crowded around.

"I'm fine!" Jeremy insisted.

Meg took the bucket from him. "Are you sure?"

Pierre said, "It'll put hair on your chest."

Jeremy had to laugh. "I don't have much, so that's good."

"Papy thinks everything unpleasant puts hair on your chest," Max said, rubbing Jeremy's arm.

Valerie shook her head. "I'm so sorry. We can take you to the ER to get checked out."

"Honestly, I didn't fall that hard." Jeremy waved off more concern from Valerie and John, who clearly felt guilty.

"All right. You boys change out of those wet clothes." Valerie shooed them upstairs.

Along with Max's wet feet, the knees of his jeans were damp. Jeremy's butt had taken the brunt of it, but his socks had gotten a little wet too. He flipped on the light in the guest room, surprised when Max followed him in.

"Seriously, I'm fine."

Max's brow was furrowed. "You're sure it doesn't hurt too much?"

"Positive." Jeremy bent to peel off his socks and couldn't hide a wince. Before he knew what was happening, Max was on his knees, his hands steadying on Jeremy's hips.

"Lift," he instructed, tapping one of Jeremy's feet.

Jeremy did as he was told, holding on to Max's shoulders as Max gently removed his socks and rubbed his cold feet one after the other. His hands were so big, and it felt damn good. Way, way too good. Then those hands were on Jeremy's fly, and Max was peeling down his jeans, helping Jeremy step out of them.

In the perfect spot to see Jeremy's dick swell.

Max's breath caught audibly, and he peered up at Jeremy through thick lashes. His lips parted, and it felt like the air between them was suddenly electric. Heart thudding, Jeremy clutched his shoulders.

"I'm okay," he whispered hoarsely. "You don't need to worry." This was the part where he had to step back, but he was rooted to the floor.

Slowly, Max pushed to his feet, running his hands up the outside of Jeremy's thighs to rest on his hips again. He stared down, their eyes locked. "You sure?"

Jeremy could only nod.

Even more slowly, Max's hand slid around to brush Jeremy's ass over his boxer-briefs. "It doesn't hurt?"

Jeremy shook his head, swallowing thickly. Max's hand rested there against his butt, and he was dying to push back and rub against it. Beg for more contact. Even though they'd done way more, there was something so exciting about this light touch.

Slowly, Max slid that hand up Jeremy's back, a trail of heat in its wake, coming around his shoulder and stopping at his cheek. He traced one side of Jeremy's glasses, following the black frame. "At least these survived this time."

Trying to smile, Jeremy nodded. He made a little sound that was embarrassingly like a whimper. Max's breath was warm against his face, and Max licked his lips. He leaned down, his body pressing close—

"Jeremy, how are you doing?" Valerie called, her voice too close, the stairs creaking.

He and Max sprang apart, and Jeremy leapt for the bed, grabbing his PJ bottoms and yanking up the plaid flannel. Max dove across the hall into his room as Jeremy whipped off his sweatshirt and balled it on his lap to hide his erection. He curled his toes on the carpet reflexively.

"I'm great!" His voice was far too high and reedy.

Valerie appeared in the doorway, concern obvious on her face. "Really? I feel awful."

"Honestly, I'm totally okay. Are we going to watch the rest of the movie?"

"Absolutely. John's stirring the hot chocolate." She beckoned him. "Let's get comfy."

Fortunately, he'd gotten his body under control. Max joined them wearing his own PJs and fresh socks, and Valerie took his cheek and gave him a kiss. She squeezed Jeremy in a half hug, and they trooped downstairs.

Curled up on the love seat again, Jeremy sipped his milky, perfectly sweet hot chocolate next to Max—so close, but so, so far away.

Chapter Ten

THE EMAIL NOTIFICATION appeared at the top of the screen, hovering there for a few seconds before disappearing. Max's thumbs froze, his text to Honey half-finished.

LSAT results. This was it.

Squinting in the sunshine of a cold and crisp day that was perfect for the open house, Max slid his aviators back on and finished the text quickly before putting his phone away. Standing by the long narrow planter they'd set on two tables across from the barn, he packed down clean snow with a pair of nylon mitts fresh from the dryer.

Soon, kids would be lining up for maple taffy made by pouring hot syrup on the snow, but right now, Max's head spun. The doubts he'd been muffling—smothering—for months were finding their voice. Did he really want to be a lawyer?

"Just look at the results," he muttered as he dumped another bucket of snow into the planter and packed it down. He was breathing hard for no good reason, the clouds of his breath puffing in and out.

He had to talk about this. It was like the words were climbing his throat and fighting to get out.

Meg was arranging hay bales in the back of the big wagon a neighbor had lent for the day for tours along the service roads through the maple bush. He could go over and spill everything knowing she wouldn't sugar-coat her opinion. But as much as he loved his sister, he didn't know if he could handle her honesty right now.

Papy was communing with the borrowed horses who would pull the wagon, and Max didn't want to bug him. Dad and Valerie bustled around the barn, its doors opened wide. He knew they'd be understanding, even though he was afraid of disappointing his dad. But was he ready to tell them? For fuck's sake, he didn't even know what he was telling them. And the open house was starting any minute.

Outside the barn, Jeremy poured syrup samples into tiny paper cups not much bigger than thimbles, setting them in neat rows on a table. It looked like he had them organized by variety, from the lightest to darkest, adjusting the cups by fractions so the rows were exact. He wore his new green toque and parka, and even from a distance, Max could see his cheeks were pink from the cold.

It was only when Jeremy glanced up and did a double take that Max realized he was staring across the wide parking area. That he was watching Jeremy organize with a big, dumb smile on his face. This was who he wanted to talk to. The knot of tension in his gut loosened.

Tentatively, Jeremy smiled back and gave him a little wave. Max beckoned him, meeting him halfway. "Can you help me get something from the house?"

"Sure." Jeremy fell into step beside him. "It's a perfect day, huh? The fresh snow last night looks amazing on the trees. Reminds me of Whistler, without the mountains. And it's mostly maple trees, so not really like Whistler at all. It's just the only place I've seen this much snow, I guess."

"Makes sense." Max had spent all morning trying not to think about kissing him—or dropping to his knees the way he had last night—but Jeremy was so cute when he talked like that, words tumbling out.

"The kids must love it. Lots of snowmen and stuff."

"It's not great packing snow right now—needs to be a little wetter. But yeah, when I was a kid, I still loved it. Any kind of snow can be shoved down your sister's collar."

Jeremy laughed. "I guess that's a brother's job." His smile flickered. "You must miss Sean."

"Yeah." He shrugged tightly. "But it looks like he's having fun." He pulled out his phone and displayed a picture of his brother grinning at the railing of a cruise ship. "My dad sent it. We're sending pictures back and forth now. Hopefully that's a good sign."

"Definitely. It's progress." Max took the steps onto the covered porch, stamping his boots. Maybe he shouldn't bother Jeremy with his shit. Jeremy had enough of his own. For all Max knew, he was busy texting Levi. He didn't need to deal with Max's not-even-quarter-life crisis.

"Are you going to see that guy again today?" Max kept his gaze down as he kicked the brick by the door. It didn't bother him. Well, it *shouldn't* bother him was more accurate.

Last night when Jeremy had slipped on the ice, Max had wanted to scoop him into his arms and not let go. He'd barely been able to control himself when Jeremy's hard-on had tented his boxer briefs. He could imagine the smooth curve of his dick springing up from ginger hair and had burned to swallow Jeremy to the root. Not just to satisfy his own lust, but to give comfort and release. To see Jeremy smile and hear him gasp and give him pleasure.

He realized Jeremy was taking a long time to answer and was about to apologize for being nosy. Max should focus on his own problems and stop interfering with Jeremy's. Not that having a guy interested was a *problem*. Max was supposed to be happy for him.

"I guess so?" Jeremy said. "He made it seem like he was going to come. Should I text him and confirm?"

"Nah. Don't want to look too eager." As soon as the words were out, Max cringed internally. That was bad advice. This wasn't how fairy godfathers were supposed to operate. Or friends, for that matter. He said, "But if you like him, you should text. Playing it cool has a time and a place, but there's nothing wrong with showing someone you're into them. Go for it."

"Well, he said he was coming, so I don't want to seem pushy. He's nice, but…"

Max was far too happy about that *but*. "No pressure, man." He pushed open the door, the bells on the wreath ringing merrily. They pulled off their boots, gloves, and hats, but kept their coats on. Now Max had to either spit it out or make up some excuse for bringing Jeremy to the house.

Jeremy looked to him expectantly. Max's phone felt like it was burning a hole in his jeans pocket now. "I, um…"

Ginger brows meeting, Jeremy asked, "Are you okay?" He only lightly touched Max's arm though his puffy coat, yet it still sent sparks to Max's dick. He realized this was the first guy he'd dated that had ever had this effect on him. He felt drunk with it.

Except we're not dating because I'm an idiot.

"Max?"

"Yeah. I don't know. I mean, yes. I'm fine."

His mind sputtered, ping-ponging between the LSAT results and the urge to sweep Jeremy into his arms and kiss him like nothing else mattered. Except he wasn't supposed to feel this strongly this fast.

He'd liked guys before. Had dated guys before. He'd never felt so out of control. This was exactly why he'd put on the brakes. The snowball hurtling downhill needed to slow its roll. He had enough to deal with.

Like that waiting email. He needed to rip off the Band-Aid already. Be a grownup and face it.

Jeremy's phone buzzed in his pocket. "Sorry, I—" He stared at the screen. "My mom."

"Take it, take it." Max slipped into the living room to give him privacy. Except Jeremy's mother was talking so loudly Max thought for a second it was on speaker.

"Where are you?"

"What?" Jeremy seemed instantly frazzled. "What's wrong?"

"*Where are you?* I saw the pictures you sent your father." She flung it like an accusation. "That doesn't look like Toronto."

Whoa. Max froze by the fireplace where he was going to sweep up the cold ashes from last night. He should go into the kitchen and stop listening, yet he couldn't seem to move.

"It's—it's not. I'm near Pinevale. It's a couple of hours north."

"Who are you with?"

Standing in the foyer, Jeremy's eyes met Max's across the living room. His Adam's apple bobbed. "A friend from school. I'm staying with his family for the holidays."

"Who is this friend?"

"His name's Max."

"And what kind of a *friend* is this?" She was shouting now.

Jeremy flinched. "Just a friend," he said, his voice cracking.

It was all Max could do not to march over, grab the phone, and tell Jeremy's mother where to go.

"Why didn't you tell us? You're supposed to be on campus!"

Opening his mouth, Jeremy closed it again as his mother shouted, going on a tear about honesty and earning trust. Max's blood pressure zoomed as he listened to her basically call Jeremy a liar, not letting him get a word in edgewise. Jeremy hunched in on himself, staring at the floor. When he glanced up at Max, he cringed, and Max could see the apology in the grimace.

Again, Max fought the urge to march over, take the phone, and tell her off. He wanted to shield Jeremy and yell at her for abandoning him. Instead, he mouthed, "*That's bullshit!*"

Eyes locked with Max's, Jeremy took a deep breath and stood up straighter, rolling his shoulders back. He cut off his mother. "Why shouldn't I spend the holidays with a friend? He's great and his family is great. You'd rather I be all alone in my dorm room for Christmas? Is that what you want, Mom? Is that supposed to be my punishment?"

His words hung in the air, a terrible silence following. Max held his breath.

A pained sort of whimper echoed from the phone. "No." Her voice was fainter now, but Max could still just make out the words. "I was worried. I worry about you. You might not believe that, but it's true."

Tears glistened in Jeremy's eyes. He pushed up his glasses and swiped. He whispered, "I'm fine, Mom. You don't need to worry."

She said something Max couldn't quite make out, and then there was silence, but Jeremy still held the phone to his ear. A few seconds later, a loud young voice exclaimed, "Cherry! It's me!"

Joy lit up Jeremy's beautiful face, and Max wanted to take a picture. Jeremy said, "Hey, Sean! I miss you so much. Are you having fun in Hawaii?"

Max finally moved, giving Jeremy a thumbs up and hurrying to the kitchen to finally give him privacy. He unzipped his coat and tugged at his scarf. There were a few of Papy's pastries left, and he ate one gratefully. It wasn't too long before Jeremy appeared.

"Sorry about that."

"Don't be." Max brushed pastry crumbs off his fingers. "You okay?"

"I think so." He smiled. "It was great to hear Sean's voice. He's having a blast."

"That's good. Your mom sounds…intense."

Jeremy grimaced. "That's one way to put it." He took off his glasses and rubbed his face. "She makes me so mad."

Max tugged Jeremy into a hug. Forget his own bullshit—Jeremy looked like he'd just been tackled by a linebacker. Max wanted him to be okay. He wanted to see that smile again. Jeremy sagged against him, his arms circling Max's waist, parka thick between them. He rested his head against Max's shoulder.

"Sometimes I almost hate her," he whispered. "But she's my mom."

Max stroked Jeremy's hair. "I'm sorry it's like this right now." He wanted to call her every name he could think of, but that wouldn't make Jeremy feel better. "I hope it'll change. I'm sure she was genuinely worried about you. I could be a serial killer for all she knows."

Jeremy laughed softly and lifted his head, slipping his glasses back on. "If you are, you're taking your time."

"Maybe that's my MO. Maybe my whole family's in on it. We're waiting for the right moment."

Jeremy widened his eyes. "What's really in those bottles of extra dark maple syrup?"

"You'll soon find out. The hard way." He laughed maniacally, and Jeremy giggled.

"Thank you. I feel better." He peered up at Max, their bodies still close.

Max cupped Jeremy's shoulders, rhythmically squeezing the puffy material. "Sorry I eavesdropped."

"No, when she's like that, I think people in the next postal code can hear."

Reluctantly, Max said, "We should get back out there. People will be arriving any minute."

"What did you need to get for the taffy?"

Max had to laugh sheepishly as he grabbed the box of Popsicle sticks and held them up.

Jeremy raised an eyebrow. "Should I take one side? I don't know if you can manage that on your own."

"I'll have you know this is a jumbo box."

"It does say it right there in black and yellow. Clearly a two-person job. Glad I'm here to help." He hesitated. "Someone might think you were trying to get me alone."

Car engines were rumbling outside, so there was no time to press his lips to the pretty blush on Jeremy's cheeks. But he had to get Jeremy alone soon. Rules or no rules. Plan or no plan. Why was he cockblocking himself? If they both wanted it, why not go for it?

They tugged on their boots and hurried out, and Max was about to suggest they sneak off later once the crowd had thinned when a voice rang out.

"Jeremy!"

Max bit back his groan. Levi had shown up as promised. Stupid reliable nice guy who was sexy to boot. Ugh. What had Max been thinking when he encouraged Jeremy to go on that coffee date? Now he had to smile and grit his teeth as Levi strode up and gave Jeremy a hug.

A hug!

Two pig-tailed little girls trailed Levi, and they waved at Max with cheery hellos. He couldn't exactly shove Levi into the nearest snowbank accidentally-on-purpose with the kids watching. Not that he should be shoving Levi at all. He grumbled to himself. Could they rewind and go back to a few minutes ago when Jeremy was safe and warm in his arms?

He avoided shaking Levi's hand, which was petty AF, and made his escape. Cars were streaming up the drive now, and he had to get the taffy going or Valerie would be pissed. Well, not so much angry as disappointed, which was somehow worse.

Max turned on the kerosene camp stove and put on a pot of syrup. He hurriedly dumped in the rest of the fresh snow, packing it down in the wooden planter. While he worked, he kept an eye on Jeremy and Levi. They'd brought the girls over to the face-painting station that Max's dad was manning with big smiles and his usual steady hand.

Levi and Jeremy were talking about something, and Levi kept touching Jeremy's arm. There was no need to be touching him that much. Definitely no need to be leaning so close. Jeremy could surely hear him fine.

What were they talking about? Why were they smiling so much?

Why am I such an idiot?

The sweet smell alerted Max just in time as he spun and snatched the bubbling pot off the camp stove. "Shit!" He grabbed the ancient candy thermometer that had been Mamy's. It was in Fahrenheit, and he could just make out the faded numbers. Two-fifty, which was at least ten degrees too hot, but oh well. The first batch would be a little crunchy rather than chewy.

He called out, "Who wants maple taffy!"

Soon, he was swamped with kids who took a Popsicle stick and lined up along the planter. Max poured the hot syrup in a line along the planter, the kids rolling their sticks in it to create a sort of lollipop. In the season, they'd do this with sap straight out of the trees, but it still worked well with syrup.

Max was busy with a steady stream of takers. When he turned back from the stove with a fresh pot, there was Jeremy—and Levi. And the nieces, who enthusiastically rolled their sticks. This batch was perfectly chewy, and they giggled in delight as they pulled at it with their teeth.

Max could only watch as Levi rolled up a ball of taffy and offered it to Jeremy, putting it right up to his mouth. Jeremy licked it, his pink tongue darting out, and *why had Max encouraged him to go on that stupid date?* Surely Levi and his nieces would leave soon.

Except they didn't.

An hour went by, the kids somehow not bored and Levi hanging on Jeremy's every word and sometimes hanging on his body, an arm around his shoulders or a squeeze of his biceps.

"Looks like Jeremy made a new friend."

Max bit back a groan. "Shut up, Meg." He fed the stove more kerosene, ignoring her and hoping she'd go away. Of course, she was standing there smiling placidly when he turned.

"What's the prob, big brother?"

"You know exactly what," he grumbled.

With a laugh that was a straight-up cackle, she said, "I sure do. You loooove him."

"*Meg.*"

"Okay, okay." She held up her hands in surrender. "Mom's going to give Papy a break and take out the next wagon tour. I'll do taffy if you want to take over the sugar house. Oh look, Jeremy and his hot date are heading in there."

Max cursed her under his breath, giving a bright smile to a nearing family as he passed them. Sure enough, Jeremy and Levi were in the sugar house, examining the boxes of maple sugar treats. Judging by the depleted stock, they'd sold quite a few.

"Hey folks!" There were about fifteen people milling around. "I'm happy to answer any questions you have, and I can tell you about our operation." In the silence, his gaze slid to Jeremy—and Levi, who slung his arm over Jeremy's shoulders and gave Max a bright smile.

"How many taps do you put in the trees?" Levi asked.

"We have um—" Max cleared his throat and gulped from his metal water bottle. "Sorry. Frog in my throat. I'm sure you all saw the tubing run along the trees as you drove in. When the sap starts running, probably in March, we'll put the taps back into the trees, and the syrup will travel through the tubes. We have thirty-four hundred taps."

Levi's niece asked, "Does it come out of the trees like this?" She motioned to the clear bottles of amber lined on the shelves.

"No, it's just sap when it comes out of the tree and finds its way here to the sugar house. He motioned to the metal equipment that dominated the space. "That's our evaporator, which is wood-fired. We cook the sap in there until it becomes the syrup you pour on your pancakes."

He answered more questions and sold some products from the little register. When that group moved on, he sighed in relief before realizing Levi and Jeremy were still there. And Levi was still way too handsy, leaning close and whispering something in Jeremy's ear near the evaporator.

Which Max was about to shove Levi into.

"You should go," Max blurted. Jeremy and Levi blinked at him in surprise. "We have a two-hour limit. To, uh, give other people a chance," Max added weakly, motioning to the new vehicles pulling in outside.

"Uncle Levi, I'm hungry for real food! I'll get a tummy ache if I eat more sugar."

Levi smiled at his nieces. "Burgers and fries? Don't tell your mom."

"Yay!" The girls jumped up and down.

"You want to come with us?" Levi asked Jeremy, whose face had flushed. Which was perfectly reasonable, Max reminded himself.

"No, I should stay and help."

This was the part where Max should have told him to go for lunch, but he couldn't seem to get the words out. Because he was an asshole.

"Sorry we stayed too long," Levi said to Max, offering his hand. "Good to see you again."

Max cringed inwardly. "No, it's cool. You can stay as long as you want." He shook Levi's hand.

"Burgers and fries!" One of the nieces exclaimed, and Levi ushered them out. At the door, he said, "Later, Jeremy." And winked. Because he was the worst even if he seemed disgustingly nice and reasonable.

Max unclenched. The guy was gone. Now he'd tell Jeremy what an idiot he'd been—except Jeremy was glaring at him. His stomach clenched.

"That was so rude!" Jeremy hissed as Valerie led a red-cheeked family into the sugar house. Shaking his head, he squeezed through the group, disappearing outside.

"Wait!" Max asked Valerie to take over and dashed out, speed-walking across the lot so he didn't draw attention. Jeremy neared the house. Cursing, Max followed him inside and yanked off his boots before sprinting up the stairs, taking them two at a time, Jeremy disappearing around the corner.

No doubt about it. He wanted Jeremy. The snowball was still careening down the hill. The snowball was a damn avalanche, and Max was done fighting it.

Chapter Eleven

JEREMY REACHED BEHIND him to close the bathroom door, hitting solid flesh instead. It was Max, and he crowded him inside and shut the door behind them. He pulled off his hat and gloves, tossing them on the counter. He still wore his coat.

"Look—"

"No, you look!" Jeremy clenched his jaw, frustration and embarrassment battling. Levi had only been trying to help him. "He's a nice guy, and you were totally rude."

"I was just—" Max huffed. "Rude. Yes." He held up his hands and let them drop. "I'm an asshole. I'm sorry."

Jeremy wasn't sure what to say. "That's it?" After the call with his mother, he was automatically in argument mode, expecting defensive justifications and lashing out.

Max rocked on the balls of his socked feet, looking agitated. He unzipped his coat and restlessly flicked the overhead light on and off even though sunlight streamed through the window at the far end of the small bathroom. "I really am sorry. I was out of line."

"No, I mean—you're just admitting it?" Jeremy had slung his parka on a hook in the foyer, and he fiddled with the sleeves of his sweater before crossing his arms.

Max frowned. "Would you rather I didn't?"

"No." He laughed awkwardly, and Max gave him a tentative smile that melted Jeremy's anger. "Not used to it, I guess." He bit his lip.

Screw it. "Are you jealous?"

The question hung in the air. Max was still by the closed door, and Jeremy had retreated to the end of the narrow bathroom by the toilet, the old claw-foot tub and shower to his right. He fiddled with the shower curtain as he waited for Max's answer. Levi had been so certain, but…

"Yes." Max gazed at him, his brown eyes focused on Jeremy like there was nothing else in the world. "I'm jealous as fuck."

Heart skipping, Jeremy kept his expression neutral, or so he hoped. "What if I was trying to make you jealous?"

Max's eyebrows shot up. "It worked. I hated seeing you with him. I don't want him touching you." He stepped closer. He cupped Jeremy's face and ran his hands down over his shoulders. "Truth is, I don't want anyone touching you. I want you all to myself."

Jeremy could barely resist throwing himself into Max's arms, but he held firm. He had to know his trust was warranted. "What if I say you can't have me?"

Inhaling sharply, Max stepped back and shoved his hands in his pockets. "Then I can't have you. Then I really did fuck up everything."

Warmth swelled in his chest, and Jeremy couldn't hide his grin. "Can we stop pretending we're just friends?"

In an exhaled rush, Max hauled Jeremy into his arms. Jeremy clung to his broad shoulders through his thick coat, his toes barely touching the worn tile floor.

The kiss was everything he'd imagined—hot and tender and absolutely consuming, Max's tongue invading his mouth. He tasted faintly of chocolate and mint, and Jeremy wondered if it was mint chocolate or chocolate and toothpaste or maybe gum. He met Max's tongue with his own, and Max hummed, seemingly in approval.

He'd never tasted or smelled or felt another person so intimately. It had been less than a week since they'd last kissed, and it felt like forever. Jeremy was almost frantic with need, on his tiptoes rubbing against Max. His cock ached, pressing against the fly of his jeans. He tried to hook a leg around Max, relief and joy taking a backseat to lust.

Max broke away with a grin, that dimpled flash of white teeth firing Jeremy's blood even hotter. Max tore off his coat and reached down to hoist up Jeremy, propping his ass on the edge of the sink. Jeremy wrapped his legs around Max, groaning as their erections thrust together through their jeans. Breathing hard, Max broke away.

"I'm supposed to be the experienced one here, but I screwed up that play big time."

"Are you going to start talking in football clichés again?" He slipped his hands under Max's sweater, stroking up to his nipples and making Max gasp. That gasp was fuel to the fire, Jeremy's confidence growing. Max *wanted* him. Max had been jealous! Jeremy boldly joked, "Because I might have to catch up with Levi if you do."

Max laughed. "Oh, I see how it is. Fine, I deserve that." He nipped Jeremy's ear, his fingers threading through his hair. "I was an idiot. I never wanted you to go on that date. I hated that you even opened the app."

"I really was just curious! Trust me, I don't want anyone else with my dream guy sleeping right across the hall."

Max groaned. "God, the last two nights were torture." He rubbed Jeremy's erection through his jeans. "Especially last night. Couldn't stop thinking about this. Getting my mouth on you."

Jeremy shuddered, arching into Max's touch. "I was dying for you to sneak over."

Max kissed him. Hard. When he broke the kiss, he whispered, "You have no idea how hot you are."

Jeremy opened and closed his mouth, and Max laughed. "You're going to argue with me, aren't you? Tell me you're not hot. You're so innocent, but you drive me crazy. You tease me with that tongue of yours. One flick and I'm thinking about blow jobs. Thinking of all the ways to break the stupid house rules."

Jeremy's dick swelled even more, his body tingling. "We shouldn't. I'm a guest."

"You want me to stop?" He rubbed Jeremy, bending to suck his neck.

"Don't you dare. Can you—" Jeremy broke off, suddenly shy.

"What? Anything you want, baby."

"Can you kiss me again?"

Max caressed Jeremy's cheek with his rough hand and pressed their lips together. This kiss was gentle at first. Dry and light. Their noses bumped, and Jeremy laughed softly. "Sorry. I still have no idea what I'm doing."

"Don't worry." Max traced Jeremy's cheekbone with his thumb. "I do." He grinned, then tilted Jeremy's head and kissed him harder.

Now it was wet again, the rasp of Max's stubble wonderful on Jeremy's skin. Jeremy was very much *being kissed,* and when Max slipped his tongue inside, he moaned and clutched at Max's thick arms. Being invaded like that turned him on big time, and he surrendered gratefully, gasping for air whenever he could.

Still kissing him, Max tipped him back on the sink, reaching down to push Jeremy's legs farther apart. Jeremy winced at the pressure on the fresh bruising on his butt.

"What?" Max blinked at him in the sunlight streaming through the yellow curtains on the small window. He bolted up to stand straight between Jeremy's splayed thighs. "Does it hurt?"

"A little. Don't worry about it." Jeremy tugged Max's sweater, but Max didn't budge.

"I'm totally going to worry about you being in pain. That's not good pain." He eased Jeremy back onto his feet.

"Please don't stop." Jeremy didn't care how much his bruised butt hurt.

"Oh, don't worry." A smile tugged on Max's full lips. "I'm not stopping. Wouldn't be cool of me to leave you in this state. You really need this, huh?" He rubbed Jeremy's straining cock slowly, the denim taut.

"Please." Jeremy arched his back, eager for more pressure on his dick. He'd come in his pants before, and right now he couldn't seem to care if it was embarrassing or not.

"I've got you. It's okay." Max ran his hand up, snagging the hem of Jeremy's sweater and pulling it over his head.

Jeremy lifted his arms, shivering as Max tossed the wool aside. Max's eyes roved over Jeremy's chest, his hands following. Jeremy almost cried out at the light touch. He was ticklish and squirmed.

Max smiled, his fingers dancing over Jeremy's ribs. "Sensitive, hmm?"

"Uh-huh. Please, just..."

"Just make you come?" He raised an eyebrow. At Jeremy's nod, he laughed softly, his fingers skimming Jeremy's skin. "I will. I want to find out what you like."

"This. I like this. All of it. Please."

Laughing again, Max bent and kissed him deeply. He nuzzled at Jeremy's cheek and dropped his head lower, sucking what would surely be a mark on his collarbone.

"We're not supposed to be doing this. Hurry up."

Max smiled against Jeremy's skin. "Everyone's busy out there. We can take a break."

When Max closed his mouth over Jeremy's nipple, Jeremy cried out. Flushing, he pressed his lips together. It was like all his nerve endings that weren't occupied with his dick had centered on his nipple, and there was an invisible chain between that nub of flesh and his balls.

Max lifted his head and sucked his own index finger, releasing it with a *pop* that had Jeremy helplessly humping the air with his hips. He was dying for friction on his cock.

"I wish I could hear you." Max circled Jeremy's other nipple with his wet finger before dropping his head again to lick and tease the first one. "But we. Should..." He nipped with his teeth. "Keep quiet. Just in case."

Jeremy had been pressing his lips together so hard it hurt, and he gasped for air, letting his mouth open. When he'd jerked off growing up, he'd typically had to be quiet. It'd been all muffled gasps and little cries drowned out by the shower or his face in his pillow. Somehow, having to be quiet with Max excited him even more than when he'd been able to be noisy in his dorm room.

Then Max dropped to his knees, and Jeremy had to muffle a moan. He thought of last night, and how turned on he'd been. Standing with Max—big and muscled and so masculine—kneeling at his feet was shockingly hot. He concentrated on not coming before his jeans were even undone.

"I guess if we're going to break the rules, we should make it worth our while," Jeremy whispered.

Max's chuckle was low, and it sent a shiver down Jeremy's spine. The shiver morphed into a full-body tremor as Max freed his cock and swallowed it. He hummed around it, the vibration making Jeremy gasp so loudly he clapped a hand over his own mouth.

Max only chuckled again, and it was all lips and tongue and spit and breath and perfection. Jeremy had to touch him, holding Max's head with both hands, careful not to pull his hair. Having Max's mouth on him again was everything he'd imagined. His balls were so tight. He wasn't going to last, but God, he wanted to.

He couldn't stop the thrust of his hips, and Max choked a bit. "Sorry!" Jeremy hissed, drawing back and releasing Max's head.

Max let go of the spit-wet shaft, breathing deeply. Eyes on Jeremy's, he traced his own lips with the head, licking the drops of pre-cum with a groan. Then he took Jeremy's hands and put them back on his head.

"Fuck my mouth. Hard as you want."

Those words almost made him come. "Oh, Jesus."

Breathing shallowly, his throat dry, Jeremy guided himself inside. Max closed his lips around him, nodding. Jeremy thrust an inch or two. He didn't want to hurt him, but Max nodded again, taking hold of Jeremy's hips in his open jeans, urging him on.

Jeremy barely found his rhythm before he shot his load, groaning way too loudly. Max swallowed and held him pinned to the sink by his hips, milking him until Jeremy's knees were about to give out and it was too much.

Max stood, looming over him and holding him close. He rubbed Jeremy's back and nuzzled his head, and Jeremy wanted to stay there forever, warm and sated and...*liked.*

"You like me, right?" Jeremy cringed. He'd said it out loud, hadn't he?

But Max didn't laugh at him. He drew back, his gaze serious. "I like you a ton. I'm sorry I put the brakes on. We can definitely stop pretending we're only friends." He grimaced. "Although if we tell my family, they'll just be so annoying about it. It's not you, it's a hundred percent them."

Jeremy laughed. "It's okay. It can be our little secret. We still have to obey the house rules anyway."

Max brushed their noses together. "I need to come first."

He stroked the bulge of Max's cock. "You want me to make you come?" It was a dumb question—*duh,* the answer was pretty obvious— but it gave Jeremy a thrill to ask it out loud.

"You don't have to."

"I want to." With a shuddery breath, Jeremy reached for Max's fly, backing him up to lean on the door. Max groaned.

"Then hell yes, baby. Make me come."

Max was rock hard when Jeremy sank to his knees and freed his cock. At eye level, it looked huge. Tentatively, Jeremy licked the leaking tip, savoring the bitter taste. Not because it tasted particularly good, but because it was Max. He'd fantasized about sucking cock more times than he could count, and now he had a meaty dick and big hairy balls inches from his mouth.

"You don't have to," Max murmured, smoothing a hand over Jeremy's head.

Jeremy pushed his glasses up his nose, meeting Max's gaze as he took him into his mouth. He sucked on the shaft, tasting warm skin as he moaned. *Finally.* He licked up and down and around, wrapping a hand around the base and twisting like he'd seen when he and Kara secretly watched porn on her laptop, giggling and curious.

Max must have had far better blow jobs, but he only gave praise. He caressed Jeremy's hair, whispering how good he was doing, reassuring him in murmurs and touches.

"That feels amazing. I love your mouth. You look so good with my cock in you."

Jeremy moaned around him, sucking harder. It was true—Max's cock was inside him. What would it be like in his ass? Jeremy was tempted to turn around on hands and knees and beg to be fucked, but he had to see this through. Had to know what it was like to have Max come inside him.

Max didn't thrust or push, giving Jeremy total control. He gasped and whimpered, clearly struggling to stay quiet. Clearly pushed to the edge by *Jeremy*. The heady burst of confidence had Jeremy taking him deeper, almost choking, breathing hard through his nose.

"Gonna come," Max whispered.

Jeremy sucked, his lips stretched and spit dribbling. Max seemed huge above him, his lips parted, throat working. He held Jeremy's head, fingers tightening as he released, thumping his head back against the door as he shook.

Swallowing desperately, Jeremy coughed but got most of it. He released Max's shaft with a wet smack, the last few drops of jizz spraying his hot cheeks.

"Jesus," Max breathed, running his thumb over Jeremy's wet lips and feeding him the stray drops. He lifted Jeremy to his feet and kissed him deeply, their tongues tangling. Jeremy was getting hard again, but he sagged against Max, content to rest in his arms.

"Max, you in there?" Papy's voice rang out, along with a thudding knock.

Adrenaline shot through Jeremy like a rocket as he and Max sprang apart. Jeremy had thought Papy couldn't climb the stairs, but apparently was mistaken. He stared at Max in horror, but Max doubled over laughing, smacking a hand over his mouth to muffle it.

When he was able, he said, "Yeah, Papy."

"Once you're finished in there, we need you back on taffy."

Oh God, did he know? Jeremy's head spun. *Please let him think Max is pooping.*

"Okay!" Max called back too loudly. After a few moments, he tried to smother more laughter.

Jeremy couldn't stop a laugh of his own, though guilt followed swiftly on its heels. He was a guest, and he should follow the house rules. He cleaned himself up quickly, face hot. "That can't happen again. We have to be good."

"Oh, we're good together." Behind him at the sink, Max circled Jeremy in his arms, nuzzling the back of his neck.

"Mmm." Jeremy leaned back before shaking his head and elbowing Max away, turning to face him. "Stop tempting me. We have to follow the rules. Your family has been so amazing to me. I don't want to disappoint them by breaking their trust."

Max sighed dramatically and whispered, "Okay, okay. We'll follow the Puritanical rules. At least for the rest of the day." He pressed his lips to Jeremy's forehead, the kiss so gentle that Jeremy's breath caught. "I'm sorry I was a jerk." He took Jeremy's hand.

"It's okay. Levi and I were trying to make you jealous, after all." Jeremy squeezed Max's fingers. "He had your number as soon as he saw you spying on our date."

"Guess I owe him a thank you," Max grumbled, a smile breaking through. "Come on. Let's go be good."

BEING GOOD WAS highly overrated.

Jeremy flipped onto his side, kicking at the tangled duvet restlessly. He should give in and jerk off again, but what if someone heard him? God, what if someone had heard him the night before? He replayed breakfast like a movie in his head, scouring his memory for hints from

Valerie, Meg, or John that they knew what he'd gotten up to.

Of course now he'd gotten up to far more than furtively jerking off. His stomach flipped, the giddy rush of memory not helping him drift off to sleep. He'd had Max in his mouth—more than that, he'd made him come. After so long of tying himself into knots and overthinking, with Max he could let go.

Except he couldn't because they weren't supposed to be hooking up. John and Valerie were so cool, and their rules about language and no sex in the house were cute somehow. Not overbearing and stressful, but...wholesome.

Jeremy's parents would surely have the same rule about no sex in the house—if they even let a boyfriend stay over. But it wouldn't be cute. It would be stressful and judgy and condemning. It made his stomach acidy to even think about Max meeting them, even though he knew it was stupid to get ahead of himself and worry about it.

He stared at the blur of gauzy curtains lit by the silver glow of the moon. There was a blind he could have pulled down, but he got freaked out trying to sleep in total darkness. There were no streetlights, and the moonlight reflecting on snow was soft and peaceful. Should have been perfect for falling asleep, but his brain wouldn't turn off.

Instead of replaying humiliating incidents from years ago like usual—how many times did he need to remember asking Jake Podowski if he'd had chicken pox when it was actually new, terrible acne—Jeremy thought about Max actually being his boyfriend.

But he only had fleeting visions of how awesome it would be: holding hands, doing things together, kissing and touching whenever they wanted. Mostly, he worried about what his parents would think. They'd struggled enough with the theoretical idea of Jeremy being gay. His mom's meltdown earlier didn't bode well for accepting a boyfriend.

He shifted onto his back, closing his eyes resolutely. Maybe if he quietly got off, he could lull himself to sleep. There was so much spank bank material that he didn't know where to start as he slipped his hand into his PJ bottoms and lightly touched himself.

And there it was. He zeroed in on the memory of the night before here in this room, Max's strong hand spread over Jeremy's ass. Resting there, not squeezing or pressing. Promising so much...

The guest room door *creeeeaked* open. Jeremy released his dick and lunged for his glasses, finding Max in the doorway in a tee and pajama bottoms, the silver glow of the moon outlining him. Jesus, he was *beautiful.* His breath rushed out as desire ignited.

Max motioned, clearly asking if he could come inside. Jeremy nodded. Maybe there was something he'd forgotten to say or ask, or maybe he just wanted to talk? Or maybe—

Jeremy's heart thumped as Max raised his eyebrows, nodding at the bed. Another question, and Jeremy nodded vigorously, removing his hand from his crotch and throwing open the duvet. He shivered at the cool air. A smile blooming on his gorgeous face, Max climbed in and pulled the duvet back over them both.

Not just climbed in—climbed on top of Jeremy, his muscled body pressing Jeremy into the mattress, covering him, deliciously warm and strong. They kissed until they were breathing hard in the silence, lips wet and tongues exploring.

"Hey," Max whispered, rubbing their noses together.

"Hey. Thought we were being good."

"I tried. It's after midnight, so we *were* good the rest of the day." He grinned before asking seriously, "Do you want me to go?"

No point in pretending. "No."

His smile returned full force, gleaming in the moonlight and making Jeremy's breath catch. "What do you want?"

"Everything." The word sounded raw. Desperate.

Max kissed him hard, then soft. "I know, baby." He nudged Jeremy's legs apart so he was completely between them, hard cocks meeting through flannel. "Patience," he murmured.

Jeremy didn't want to be patient. He needed more. Not just *more,* but... Free. He needed to be *free.* To be whole and complete. He wasn't sure why, but he tugged at his T-shirt and PJs. The cotton and flannel felt all wrong. Too constricting. He was panting, fingers clumsy as he squirmed under Max.

Brow furrowed, Max stilled Jeremy's hands. "It's okay."

Jeremy shook his head. "Please. I need…" He trusted Max. It felt right to be totally bare and vulnerable with him. To be seen. "Can we be naked?" It was probably stupid since they'd sucked each other's cocks, but being completely undressed together felt even more intimate somehow.

Nodding, Max helped him get the T-shirt off, then scooted back to peel off Jeremy's PJ bottoms and socks. He ran his palms up Jeremy's hairy shins, the rub making him shudder. Max was still dressed, the duvet around his shoulders. Jeremy was totally naked in the moonlight, legs spread, his hard dick curling up despite the cold.

And Max looked at him like he was precious, caressing his body with his hands. Jeremy was splayed, bared for Max, willing to do anything. More than willing—eager, verging on desperate. Desperate not only to come, but to *become*. For this to all be real and true and right.

"You're beautiful, you know that?" Max murmured.

"Me? I'm too small and scrawny. Look at *you!*"

Shaking his head, Max bent to kiss and nuzzle Jeremy's inner thighs and nose at his tingling balls. "You're not too anything. You're just right. Pocket-sized and perfect."

Max retreated, but only to rip off his PJs faster than Jeremy thought possible. His thick cock was hard between strong thighs when he knelt between Jeremy's legs again. His abs and chest were muscled and hairy, and he tweaked his own peaked nipples, shivering.

"Heating sucks in this old house." He pulled the duvet up over his shoulders again and settled back between Jeremy's thighs, both of them groaning softly. "This good?" Max asked.

Jeremy nodded. They were naked together and he felt wonderfully safe even though they were sneaking around and could only talk in whispers. "Always wondered what this would be like."

Max flattened a hand over Jeremy's chest and toyed with his nipple.

"Skin on skin?" He rocked their bodies together, rubbing legs and arms. "You like?"

"It's okay, I guess." Jeremy couldn't keep a straight face. He ran his calves over Max's, eager for friction. Under the duvet they were warm in their own little world, and Jeremy couldn't stop the words. "I want you to fuck me."

Max kissed him, groaning into his mouth before pulling back. "You want my cock inside you? Have you thought about it?"

Jeremy wasn't sure if he meant being fucked or his cock in particular. "Want you. Always wanted to be fucked. Now I trust you."

Pressing kisses to Jeremy's face, Max whispered, "Thank you." He eased back and met Jeremy's gaze. "Have you watched much porn?"

"Yeah. Especially since I came to school. When I was younger, I had to be really careful. But my mom's always read these romance novels. You know the big thick ones with, like, a shirtless pirate clutching a woman with big boobs? I'd sneak them when she was done. Fantasize about that. Being..." He swallowed hard. "Taken."

He swore Max's eyes gleamed dark with lust in the moonlight, a breath shuddering through him visibly. Max rolled his hard cock against Jeremy's. "You want to be ravished, hmm?"

Jeremy's silent laugh shook him, and Max grinned. Max kissed him playfully but deeply, his tongue commanding. Jeremy moaned into his mouth.

When Max broke the kiss, they both gasped in a breath. Max whispered against Jeremy's ear with another hot gust. "I want to fuck you so bad, but not here. Not when I can't hear you. But we can still explore. Okay?"

Jeremy nodded. "Will you..." He hoped Max couldn't see his blush.

"What, baby?" Max kissed his hot cheek. "You can say anything. Don't be afraid."

He cleared his dry throat. "Will you touch my ass?"

"Hell yes. You want to roll over for me? Let me see you."

Heart thumping, Jeremy stretched out on his stomach, propping his chin on his hands so his glasses weren't smooshed into the pillow. Chilly air raised goosebumps over his bare body as Max partly pulled back the duvet. He expected Max to touch him immediately, but the seconds ticked by, and when he glanced over his shoulder, Max was taking a long, slow look. Being examined was nerve-wracking and embarrassing, yet *thrilling*.

Max whistled softly, finally smoothing a hand over Jeremy's ass. "What a view." His touch was light as he explored, tracing his fingertips over the globes of Jeremy's butt and teasing his crack. Shivering, Jeremy wriggled, encouraging more pressure. He bit his lip as Max spread him open.

He realized the soft, wet noises were Max spitting into the crease of his ass, the light splats warm. Jeremy's hard cock was trapped against the mattress, and he was just about to squeeze his hand underneath when Max licked a long, firm stripe along the crease of his ass.

The cry was way, *way* too loud.

Jeremy gasped as it escaped his lips, and before he could apologize, Max's hand clapped over his mouth, his weight on Jeremy's back. They stayed like that for almost a minute, and Jeremy could feel Max's heart against him.

Silence.

No creaks of wood from the hallway, no curious or concerned footsteps or soft knocks or murmured questions.

Breath tickling Jeremy's ear, Max released his hand. "My bad. Should have warned you I'm going to eat your ass."

"Oh my God," Jeremy breathed. So many fantasies coming to life. "I've always wanted that."

"Yeah?"

He nodded. "Remember when you were teaching me about sexting? That's my answer. For the dirtiest thing I've imagined doing." He laughed awkwardly. "Probably really tame, I know."

"Not at all. Some people definitely are freaked out by it, which is totally fine. But you're into it? Want me to lick your ass?" Max kissed the back of Jeremy's neck. "You had a shower before bed, right?" He circled Jeremy's hole with a fingertip.

"Uh-huh!"

Taking his time, Max kissed down Jeremy's spine. When Jeremy had first seen rimming in porn, he'd gone from thinking it was kind of gross to getting hard from it instantly. Feeling Max spread his cheeks, warm breath on his hole, and then the wet, textured stroke of his tongue right *there* was incredible.

He wasn't going to be able to stay quiet.

Jeremy's dick was painfully hard. He whimpered and squirmed, the sensations of Max's wet, powerful tongue teasing him too much to take. His chest was tight, teeth digging into his lower lip. He reached down and tugged Max's left hand up to his mouth.

Max's chuckle against his ass was warm. "You need help not being loud, hmm?"

Jeremy nodded, sighing in relief as Max moved up and covered his mouth with his palm. On his belly, legs spread with Max on top of him, Jeremy felt pinned in the most amazing way. He'd never expected being held down to feel so good, but it *so* did. They were breaking the rules, and Jeremy had to be quiet, the forbidden aspect exciting him just as much as the sensation of Max's tongue had been.

Max eased him over so he could muffle Jeremy's moans with one hand while he went to town on his ass. Jeremy clutched at Max's arm, his knees up and hole exposed. Max drew back, and Jeremy could have screamed but whimpered against Max's damp palm instead.

"I know." Max slid his right middle finger into Jeremy's mouth. "Get it good and wet." Jeremy sucked Max's finger like it was his cock, and Max breathed deeply, fighting a smile. "You're a fast learner." He pulled his hand free and secured the duvet back over them with a rush of warmth.

"This'll be better with lube," Max murmured, "But it's too cold out there to get it."

With Max deliciously on top of him again, Jeremy clutched him. "Don't go anywhere. I can take it."

It was only a finger, and Jeremy had fingered himself before. But this was different. This was another man. *Max.* Jeremy was naked, his legs were open, and he was being penetrated. This was another person pressing inside him. This was *Max.*

In the midnight hush, their eyes were locked. Their ragged breath filled the night, soft enough no one else would hear, but all-encompassing in their secret, private world under the duvet.

Even with everything they'd done before, Jeremy had never felt intimacy like this. Max looked into his eyes, slowly rubbing his finger inside, all his attention fixed on him like Jeremy was the only thing that mattered.

"Imagine what'll it be like when it's my cock." Max's whisper was barely audible.

Jeremy's breath caught—he could imagine it vividly. It would be huge in comparison, and it would undoubtedly hurt no matter how much lube they used. He would feel like he was being split open, like it would never fit, while at the same time he would feel complete and perfect and *right*.

Max's brows met, and his finger stopped moving. "Does it hurt too much?"

"No!" Jeremy whispered, reaching down to grasp Max's wrist. "Don't stop. Please."

"But you look like you're going to cry."

"I'm just happy. Sorry."

A little smile tugged at Max's full lips. He kissed Jeremy tenderly and crooked his finger, rubbing against the perfect spot. Jeremy gasped, his dick twitching. He let go of Max's wrist, running his hands up over his bare, broad shoulders.

"Don't be sorry," Max murmured. He pressed little kisses to Jeremy's forehead and temples and cheeks, all the while stroking his prostate. It would feel smoother with lube, but Jeremy groaned in pleasure at the rawness of it, the catch and drag and blunt pressure.

"*Max.*" It was a whine, but Jeremy couldn't help it.

"I know, baby. Feel good? You want more?"

Jeremy nodded, watching avidly as Max edged back, the duvet slipping off his broad shoulders, and spit onto his index finger by Jeremy's hole, the middle digit still inside. Along with his own soft, panting breath, the only sound was the wet smacks of Max gathering spit.

It was the kind of thing some people might find gross, but Jeremy couldn't look away, his cock aching. The intimacy of it was weirdly beautiful. A week ago, he couldn't have imagined being this exposed with another person. Like he'd been peeled open. Raw and vulnerable. But as Max pushed in another finger, the stretch burning as he thrust and retreated, teased and tormented, Jeremy trusted him completely.

"You need to come, baby?"

"*Yes!*"

"Let me see you come." Max propped up on his elbow, still finger-fucking him. The pressure on Jeremy's prostate was almost too much. "Touch yourself. Get your hand on your cock."

Fumbling to stroke his neglected dick, Jeremy trembled all over, staring into Max's eyes in the moonlight as the orgasm exploded in a powerful rush. He tensed, back and neck arching, Max slapping his free hand over Jeremy's open mouth. Jeremy painted his stomach and chest with cum, trying to keep his eyes open to see the way Max watched him with parted lips and blown pupils.

When Jeremy was spent and panting, Max took his own hard cock in hand, jerking himself quickly and coming on Jeremy with harsh gasps. The white jizz combined with Jeremy's, and the sight made Jeremy's balls twitch.

Max kissed him messily, sighing into his mouth as he shifted them to their sides, sliding his meaty thigh between Jeremy's.

"I never knew fingering could be like that," Jeremy said before he even had a chance to second guess himself and overanalyze his words.

Max laughed softly, nuzzling his cheek. "Just wait. That's only the beginning."

Sweat-damp and sticky in Max's arms, Jeremy wanted desperately for that to be true.

Chapter Twelve

MAX WOKE AFTER seven with a raging hard-on despite the post-midnight sex. He was dying to sneak back into the guest room and plow Jeremy until neither of them could see—or walk—straight, but it still wasn't the right time or place.

He hadn't set his alarm, but he hurried out of bed like usual, the wooden floor nippy under his bare feet. He could smell the sizzle of meat—turkey bacon, probably—and could hear the murmur of Dad and Valerie talking downstairs. Meg's door was surprisingly open and her room empty, although she usually wasn't a morning person. Jeremy's door was closed, and Max grinned to himself as he went by into the hall bathroom.

Fuck, that had been *hot.*

He'd broken the rules with zero regrets. Hiding under the covers with Jeremy beneath him, eager and trusting... Max had never had sex like it before. He'd never been so ready to blow his load from rimming and fingering someone.

In the shower, he jerked himself, imagining what it would be like to fuck Jeremy with his cock instead of fingers. Max didn't want to hurt him, even though he knew a little pain was inevitable the first time.

The first time.

He knew it was dumb to get all caveman and possessive about fucking a virgin, but he couldn't deny the tingle in his balls and rush of *want* when he thought about being Jeremy's first in every way. He wanted to make it perfect. He wanted it to be the greatest first time in the history of first times. He wanted...

More than he'd ever wanted before.

Max stroked his shaft harder, spreading his legs and leaning one hand on the wet tile. Closing his eyes, he imagined pushing inside Jeremy, filling his body and kissing his sweet mouth. Showing him how good it could be, hearing him cry out in pleasure—

The water went freezing, and he yelped, dancing out of the spray and tripping onto the fuzzy bathmat. Cursing, he couldn't help but laugh as he reached back in to turn off the water. Damn ancient plumbing.

He wrapped a towel around his waist, his erection subsiding. He should get downstairs for breakfast anyway—it seemed to make Valerie so happy to feed them. Reluctant to leave the steamy warmth of the bathroom, he opened the door, bracing for the colder air.

Jeremy was right there in his PJs with his hand raised to knock, and they both jumped, then laughed. Jeremy said, "I wasn't sure if anyone was in there or if the door was just closed. My grandmother used to keep the bathroom door shut all the time because it was vulgar or..." His gaze traveled down Max's wet body. "Something."

Under the white towel around his waist, Max's cock roared back to life. With a playful smirk, he rubbed himself through the soft material. "Vulgar, hmm?"

Lips parted, Jeremy swallowed hard, his gaze locked on Max's groin before he looked up to meet his eyes. Jeremy opened and closed his mouth as though he was going to say something.

He looked left and right.

He pushed Max back into the bathroom with a surprisingly strong hand on his bare chest and locked the door behind him. His glasses fogged at the corners.

Hell yeah.

The rules were made to be broken, right? Max lifted his finger to his lips. "Shh." But as Jeremy took a deep breath and tugged Max's towel free with determination, it was Max who had to bite back a loud groan. "I've created a monster."

Instead of laughing, Jeremy hesitated, clutching the towel. "Is this too much? Am I too…" He motioned jerkily, the towel swaying.

"What?" Max hadn't had coffee yet, and he tried to figure out which nerve he'd struck. "Whatever problem your anxious brain is dreaming up, the answer's no. You're not too anything. You're just right."

Jeremy blew out a long breath. "Okay. I'm just afraid—" He shook his head. "Never mind." He fiddled with the towel before dropping it.

"Tell me what you're afraid of." Max drew him near and kissed him. Even Jeremy's morning breath was adorable.

"I dunno." Jeremy rolled his eyes. "That I'll get everything wrong. Be too needy. Too eager."

"Yeah, I hate it when a gorgeous, sweet, sexy guy wants my dick. Such a burden."

Ducking his head, Jeremy laughed. "Okay, okay." He looked up, pushing his glasses up his nose. "I want more than that too. Not that your dick isn't—I mean—" Rubbing his face, he mumbled, "This is why I shouldn't talk."

Max's heart had swelled, and all he could do was kiss Jeremy until they were gasping. "You should always talk," Max murmured. "You're way better at this than you think."

With a determined gleam, Jeremy dropped to his knees on the discarded towel, and Max wanted to shout to the moon. Or the sun, or wherever. Spreading his legs so he had a solid stance, Max stroked his straining cock from root to tip. "You want this?" he whispered.

Jeremy nodded hard, taking tight hold of Max's hips.

"You like it, hmm? Such a pretty little cock slut, aren't you?"

Breathing shallowly, Jeremy nodded again desperately. "Can I? Please?"

"Baby, I'm all yours."

Max had to grip the edge of the sink with his left hand, the hot suction of Jeremy's eager mouth making his knees weak already. He'd been close in the shower, and he was right back there in no time. Jeremy used his tongue more this time and though he was still learning, it was the hottest blow job Max could remember.

He threaded his fingers through Jeremy's gorgeous hair, the bed-head mess of it so adorable it made him smile. He bounced back and forth between the powerful current of desire and the soft, warm affection for Jeremy.

Seeing his cock disappear between Jeremy's red lips made his head spin. Jeremy had been licking and sucking with complete concentration, and now he gazed up at Max. Spit dribbled from his stretched mouth, his nostrils flaring. His glasses had cleared, and Max stared into his eyes, stroking his head.

"You're a natural," Max murmured. "I'm so proud of you."

Jeremy made a little moaning sound around Max's cock, and then Max was coming. Jeremy hung on to his hips, not letting him retreat, swallowing as much as he could. The pleasure burned so intensely Max's knees wobbled, but Jeremy held him up, his grip sure.

Max gasped as he spurted a last time, the semen dripping down Jeremy's chin as he pulled off to breathe. Max hauled him to his feet and kissed him deeply, tasting himself, Jeremy moaning into his mouth.

Jeremy was rock hard in his pajamas, and Max dropped to his knees to free him and swallow him down. Jeremy shook and whimpered, emptying down his throat almost immediately. Max swallowed it all, then stood and kissed him again. Both of their flavors mixed on their tongues, and Max held Jeremy tight against him.

The knock made them jump a mile. "Are you coming to breakfast?" Meg asked from the hallway.

Max and Jeremy stared at each other in frozen horror—then dissolved into helpless giggles. Max cleared his throat. "Coming."

That was certainly the truth.

"Merry Christmas, my brother!" Honey hopped out of the banged-up Yaris wearing a Santa hat and a grin. "We're ready to get our winter wonderland on." He waved his arm around at the fresh snow. It was cloudy, but they weren't calling for more accumulation until later.

There were a flurry of hugs and greetings, Dad and Valerie coming from the sugar house to say hello to Honey and Alicia, who was stunning in black leggings and tall boots, a form-fitting red coat, and matching lipstick. Her dark skin was flawless. Max had always joked with Honey that she was way out of his league, and Honey didn't even argue.

"I'm so glad you two could make it," Dad said.

"Sorry we had to miss the open house." Alicia gave Honey a sidelong look. "*Someone* needs to put things in his calendar, so we don't double book."

Honey shrugged. "You're not wrong, but now we get the whole place to ourselves." He slung an arm around Max. "You finally got me up here. I'm ready to dive into a vat of syrup or whatever it is you do for fun. Where's Meg?"

"Out with friends. You'll just have to tease her mercilessly next time."

"Oh, like she doesn't start it every time?" Honey made a *hmph* sound. "But here's my man Jeremy!" He strode off to the porch, where Jeremy had emerged, bundled up and smiling tentatively as though he was waiting to be the butt of a joke.

"Ohh," Alicia said softly. "*Cute.*" She elbowed Max playfully. "Not your usual type."

"We're just friends!" Max insisted way too quickly and with way too much vigor. He glanced at Dad and Valerie, who had been saying something to each other and hopefully hadn't been paying attention. Max was being ridiculous. He was supposed to be an adult. The house rule was only about sleeping with someone under their roof.

Valerie smiled like usual, the wrinkles around her eyes crinkling. "Come to the sugar house when you're ready and grab the camp stove.

You kids can make taffy." She and Max's dad headed back to work going through the remaining inventory.

Alicia's graceful, sculpted eyebrows met. "Sorry. I thought you were a thing? Honey was going on about how he's never seen you so into a guy. He was sure you two would be hooking up, down, and around the town. His words."

Max looked to the porch, where Honey was animatedly telling Jeremy some story. The hunch was gone from Jeremy's shoulders. His smile lit up his face, the music of his laughter carried on the wind.

"Uh…"

He turned back to Alicia. "Sorry. What?"

With a laugh, she drew a circle in the air near Max's face, her leather gloves sleek. "I see what he means. Your poker face needs work, son."

"Fine," he muttered. "We're hooking up." He didn't like how those words felt, though. "We're together."

Alicia frowned. "Then what's the prob with your folks? You're ashamed of him or something?"

"No!" He practically shouted it. "It's just so new. I wanted it to still only be ours. And my family can be so embarrassing. They'll be cringey and make a big deal about it. I don't usually bring guys home. Like, ever."

"So let them make a big deal. You may have been captain of the football team, but don't act like you're too cool."

"But we only met over a week ago. It might not go anywhere."

Again, Alicia circled her finger near Max's face. "It's going somewhere. So I suggest you go with it. When I met Honey, I thought it would be one night and done. When you least expect it, the right one comes your way. Now introduce me."

Before long, Max had the camp stove going, the syrup coming to a boil as the four of them packed fresh snow into the planter and talked about a bunch of stuff. When they all had their taffy balls on Popsicle sticks, Honey ate his almost in one bite before launching into a diatribe about the Steelers' offense.

Alicia kept steering the conversation Jeremy's way, asking him questions about everything from his major to BC sightseeing tips. She tucked her arm through his and asked him to show her where the bathroom was, although clearly it was in the house and it was an excuse to get him alone.

Honey watched them go with a grin. "Maxwell, she has taken to your boy, so you'd better not fuck this up." His grin widened. "You popped that cherry yet?"

"Almost." Max had to grin in return, meeting Honey's fist bump. Excitement skipped through him. He had to get Jeremy alone where they could have real privacy. Not that sneaking around wasn't exciting in its own way. Mmm, the wet breath against his palm when he'd had his hand over Jeremy's mouth…

"I told you so."

"You did." An idea popped into his head with joyful clarity. "You wanna help me set up a date?"

Before long, Max had a bulging backpack of supplies tucked away out of sight and the snowmobile out of the garage.

"Can I drive?" Honey rubbed his hands together gleefully.

"You certainly may not," Valerie said firmly. "Max has taken a snowmobile safety course, and he's the only one allowed to drive."

"Aw, come on, Mrs. N-P!" Honey batted his eyelashes. "Pretty please?"

Valerie gave him a perky smile. "Nope!"

"Dude, trust me." Max laughed. "No way she's backing down."

"No way, no how," Valerie agreed. "Helmets on! Alicia and Jeremy, do you want a turn after Honey? You can use my helmet. It's a bit smaller."

"No, ma'am." Alicia shook her head emphatically. "I'll leave the need for speed to them."

Jeremy looked uncertain, and Max told him, "I can take you out later if you want. It'll be fun." *More fun than you imagine.* Jeremy nodded, and Max tried not to grin too widely, anticipation zipping through him.

"While the boys are out playing, can I buy a bottle of syrup to take home to my mom?" Alicia asked.

Valerie said, "You can't buy one, but you can take whichever bottle you'd like on the house."

"Thank you so much!" Alicia beamed and said to Max, "Your mom is the sweetest."

Max's breath caught, and he was frozen in place. Valerie smiled and thanked Alicia, not seeming fazed at all. "Do you know the differences in flavor from light to dark? You and Jeremy come along with me to the sugar house."

Max watched them go. *My mom.* It wasn't the first time someone had referred to Valerie that way, and it always made Max feel weird and awkward and guilty. Which he knew didn't really make sense. She'd been amazing to him since the day they met, even when he was a sullen little shit. Meg called his father "dad" so easily. What was wrong with Max that he got so stressed about it?

"You good?" Honey asked.

"Uh-huh." He watched them disappear into the sugar house.

"What's up with you? Oh shit, did you get the test results?"

Max refocused on Honey. "No," he lied. Well, he supposed it was true that he *hadn't* gotten the results in that he hadn't seen them yet.

"Okay. Then let's do this." Honey held up his palm.

Max slapped it, shaking off the uncomfortable feelings. He could deal with all of that stuff later. He grabbed the pack from where he'd left it out of the way, and Honey slung it on before they zoomed off along the service road through the acres of maple bush.

They had work to do.

Chapter Thirteen

ARMS SNUG AROUND Max's waist, Jeremy held on, the helmet visor shielding his face from the cold wind as the snowmobile whipped along the narrow road through the forest. He leaned into Max, unable to resist a "Woo!"

Max shook with laughter, slowing for a curve and shouting back, "Told you it would be fun!"

Jeremy had never been on a motorcycle or snowmobile, and without his glasses, which wouldn't quite fit under the helmet, the world was a blur. But he was with Max, so it wasn't scary. Max revved the engine as they hit another straightaway, and Jeremy let out another whoop, adrenaline coursing.

Honey and Alicia had headed back to the city, and Jeremy was excited to have Max to himself for the rest of the afternoon. Valerie had packed them sandwiches and a thermos of hot chocolate, and it felt a lot like a date. Was it a date? He and Max were into each other. But were they officially dating now?

Just enjoy it!

Jeremy tried to quiet his whirling brain as Max slowed and turned off the road, following fresh snowmobile tracks along a trail. A gray blob appeared in the distance, and after a minute, Max parked the snowmobile outside. Jeremy was reluctant to let go of him, but he took off his helmet, his breath pluming in the frosty air. His hair was damp with sweat at the back of his neck. He unzipped his glasses case from his coat pocket and slipped them on.

"Oh!" He peered at the small stone cottage that was now in focus.

Max left his helmet on the snowmobile seat. "This was an original homestead in the pioneer days. We use it sometimes during the season to warm up and have a break."

"Cool. It was built to last."

"Yep. It was mostly log cabins back then, I think, but guess there was a stonemason around."

Smoke curled from the chimney, blending into the gray sky. "Is someone inside?"

"Nope." Max seemed antsy. "Come on."

Curious, Jeremy followed him, kicking his boots against the stone wall. The cabin door creaked, and a wave of warm air fogged Jeremy's glasses. He squinted around the one-room cabin through the misty blur. The cottage's window didn't let in much light, but flames flickered in the big stone fireplace.

Jeremy took off his glasses, unzipping his coat to wipe them on his hoodie impatiently. He put them back on, and his heart skipped. "Oh."

There were fairy lights—looped around a few wooden chairs at a battered old table, others sitting on top. They seemed like the battery-powered LEDs, which made sense since the cabin didn't appear to have electricity. There wasn't much furniture in the small space, the corners empty. But in front of the fireplace, soft-looking burgundy throw blankets had been spread.

It was simple, but Jeremy couldn't think of anything more romantic.

Max shifted from foot to foot. "If I'd had more time, it would be better."

"It's perfect. Thank you." Jeremy went up on tiptoes and kissed Max soundly. "You did all this for me?"

"Honey helped. I know, I know, you should never leave anything burning unattended. But I wanted it to be ready for you."

Jeremy inhaled the sweet, woodsy air deeply. "Am I imagining things, or does the fire smell like maple syrup?"

"It's the candles we sell." Max pointed to a few cans on the table. "You can get them online from a bunch of places too."

"Oh!" Jeremy inspected one. The ridged can was the old-fashioned red and white kind that said it was pure maple syrup with a picture of a snowy, rustic barn on it. "It looks like your farm! I didn't realize these were candles." The wicks were wooden and made a faint crackling sound. He breathed deeply. "It really does smell like maple syrup." He motioned around. "This is all really cozy." *And romantic! And it's for* me!

"I just thought we could hang out. Have some privacy."

"Uh-huh." Jeremy nodded, his excitement taking a decidedly lusty turn. "That would be cool."

"Are you hungry? We could have those sandwiches."

"Right. Sure." He nodded, his throat suddenly dry. "Or we could…"

Max raised an eyebrow, a teasing smile tugging at his lips. "What?"

"We could fuck." He knew he was blushing, but whatever. "Specifically, you could fuck me."

"I could." Max pulled him close, and they kissed deeply. Max nuzzled Jeremy's cheek, his stubble scratching wonderfully. "You ready, Cherry?"

"Cherry is very ready to officially give up his cherry."

They laughed and kissed some more, and when Max rubbed against his swelling cock, Jeremy automatically bit back a moan.

"You get to be as loud as you want out here." Max grinned. "It's just us. No rules."

"Oh my God," Jeremy whispered. "Is this really happening?"

Max bent and swept him into his arms. "It's happening." He grimaced. "But we need to take off our boots and stuff first." He carried Jeremy back to the door, and they quickly stripped off their outerwear and hurried to the blankets to finish getting naked. Max stoked the fire, the flames casting a warm glow over their skin.

Jeremy wasn't sure how long they simply kissed and rubbed their bodies together by the blazing fire. They were hard, and part of Jeremy wanted to rut against Max and come, which he could have done in no time. But he was safe in Max's arms, and he wanted it to last.

He murmured, "I could do this forever."

Max smiled down at him. "We can do whatever you want. No pressure."

"I know." It was still wild to him how unashamed he felt with Max. He was still a little nervous, but he wanted this. Wanted everything. "I'm ready. I really want to lose my virginity. My ass virginity, to get technical."

Max laughed. "I do believe that's the scientific name for it."

"Clearly. I am taking a science major, remember."

"Apologies." Max's shoulders shook, his smile dimpling his cheeks. "You make me laugh. I love that about you."

Love. The word made Jeremy feel like he was flying. No, it hadn't been an actual love declaration, but it made him feel so special. "You too," he managed.

They kissed and kissed and kissed some more, and Max fingered him open with lube until they were both panting, Jeremy's legs spread wide. Max asked, "How do you want to do this?"

"Um, the normal way? However you want."

Max chuckled, a low, breathy sound. "Well, last night you mentioned something about pirates and being *taken.*"

Jeremy shuddered, squeezing his ass around Max's fingers still snug inside him. It wasn't painful anymore but wasn't exactly comfortable either. "Yeah. Like that."

"Once you can take it, I'm gonna bend you over and fuck you so hard you'll barely be able to walk."

"God." Jeremy moaned, bucking his hips and squeezing again. "Yes, please. I can take it."

"I don't want to hurt you." Max ran a fingertip over Jeremy's parted lips. "And today I want to see your face when I'm inside you. I need to make sure you're comfortable. Is that okay?"

Jeremy nodded. Honestly, he would do just about anything Max asked, but his heart soared at Max not wanting to hurt him. Wanting to be face-to-face. He whined as Max withdrew his fingers.

"Don't worry. There's more where that came from." Max grinned and sat back on his heels, stroking his cock. "A lot more." He leered, completely over the top, and they shared another laugh. Jeremy examined his shaft, not sure how it was going to fit.

But he couldn't wait to find out.

Max rolled on a condom and added more lube before he stretched out on his back, urging Jeremy to straddle him. "We'll do it like this for a bit. You can control how much of me you take. Break you in slowly. You can play around, see what feels good."

Max's cock brushed Jeremy's ass, and Jeremy positioned himself. His heart pounded. "Like this?'

"Yep. You're in control for now. Go on." Max grinned, rubbing Jeremy's thighs soothingly. "Use me."

A cock was way bigger than fingers.

Not that this was a surprise, but the reality of the heft of Max's shaft—the weight and power of it, the thickness—filled Jeremy in a way that fingers, either his own or Max's, couldn't compare to. He'd imagined this, fantasized about it, wondered what it would be like.

The reality was so...*much.*

"That's it. Slow and steady." Max ran his hands over Jeremy's chest and caressed his nipples.

Thighs flexing, Jeremy pushed at the head of Max's cock. It stretched his rim, and he breathed deeply through the pain, inhaling the smoky pine scent of the fire with the hint of sweet syrup. He grunted, pushing himself open. On a gasp, he got the head fully inside him and slid down, almost unbearably full but loving it.

"You feel so good, baby." Max stroked Jeremy's spine with his fingers. "Okay?"

"Yeah. It's a lot, but...yeah." He leaned on Max's broad chest. "What do you want me to do?"

"This portion of the program is your show. It's all up to you. We can do anything you want."

Jeremy's breath hitched. "Anything?"

"Of course. Why?" Max's cheeks dimpled. "You got some kinky shit you want to try? Let's hear it." He stroked Jeremy's thighs and hips.

"I... I don't know." He really didn't. Everything was stretch and sensation, and he could barely think while focusing on the fullness in his ass. "I want... I want to make sure you're enjoying it."

"You feel how hard my dick is inside you, right? Trust me. I'm enjoying it." His brows met. "But you don't need to want anything specific. No pressure."

"Right." Jeremy nodded. He was sitting still with Max like iron inside him, neither of them thrusting or pumping or moaning for the moment. They just...were. It suddenly felt more intense than when they were straining for orgasm. It was still. Peaceful.

The intimacy of it was almost too much. They stared at each other in the firelight, the cottage growing darker as the afternoon waned. The delicate fairy lights nearby made it all the more magical, like they were suspended in some fantasy world. Jeremy circled his hips tentatively, and they both groaned.

"That's it," Max said. "Try stuff out. Even if you think it's too dirty. This is a no-judgment zone."

For some reason, that made Jeremy think of their phone sex and Max's tutorial on using the apps. "Okay." He grinned. "You still haven't told me the dirtiest thing you've ever thought of doing with a guy."

Max laughed as he stroked Jeremy's chest and tweaked his nipples, creating sparks. "It's called felching. Have you heard of it?"

Jeremy paused in his slow, experimental circles. "I'm not sure. I don't think so? My parents kept close tabs on the internet."

"It's when you come in a guy's ass and then suck it out and swallow it. I mean, it doesn't have to be with a guy. That's just what I've fantasized about. Cum really gets me off." He quickly added, "If you're not into that, it's okay."

Jeremy rocked on Max's cock slowly and pondered, the stretch and burn lessening. "Have you ever done it?"

"Nah. I've only fucked without condoms with one of my exes, and he wasn't into it. I think most people find it gross." He laughed, but it sounded tense.

"Oh." Jeremy smoothed his hand over Max's chest, rubbing a reassuring circle. "I don't think you should feel bad about it. Sex is pretty gross in general, but somehow amazing too."

"It is, isn't it? Thanks, baby." Max took Jeremy's hand and pressed a kiss to his palm.

"Does it have to be inside? I still want to use condoms, but what if you came on my hole and licked it off?" Jeremy pondered it as he circled his hips in the other direction.

Max thrust upward. Hard. "Jesus, Cherry. You sound so innocent saying something so dirty."

Jeremy blinked, then smiled." You like that idea?"

"You could say that." He gripped Jeremy's hips. "You make me want to lose control."

Yes. "That's what I want." Jeremy wasn't laughing now. "I know it'll hurt, but I want you to be on top. Hold me down and fuck me." His ass felt stretched wide sitting on Max's cock. He was ready. He wanted this. "Then come on my ass."

Fingers pulling Jeremy's hair hard, Max drew him low for a rough kiss before lifting him off his cock, hands firm on Jeremy's hips. His strength was such a turn-on, and Jeremy sighed with pleasure, spreading his legs eagerly as Max covered him with his weight.

Again, the blunt pressure of the head of Max's cock felt big, the stretch burning. But Jeremy tilted his hips, clinging to his shoulders and urging him on. He was panting and sweat slicked his skin where Max's big body met his with a powerful thrust. Jeremy was opened so far, his knees up almost in his armpits now, and the shove of Max's cock into his ass had him trembling and flushed, every nerve ending on alert.

Max looked down at him, one hand caressing Jeremy's face and hair. "Tell me if it's too much."

"Don't stop." His own voice sounded wrecked. It *was* too much, but also not enough. It was *everything.* "I can take it."

And he did.

Max's thrusts were long and powerful, their flesh smacking as he drove home steadily. Jeremy cried out, Max encouraging him to be loud. To be free. He was pinned by Max's muscular body, taking every inch of his cock, his own shaft leaking against his belly.

"You're so tight." Max gasped. "I can't hold out much longer." He worked Jeremy's aching cock as he fucked him powerfully, pinning him down.

Jeremy's orgasm ripped from him, and he shouted as he painted his stomach, shaking under Max's heavy, straining body. The pleasure burned white hot. He shivered with aftershocks when Max eased out slowly and sat back on his heels—then tore off the condom and finished with a few strokes.

Holding himself open with trembling hands, Jeremy watched Max come on his ass, feeling the wet smacks of jizz before Max dove down and licked with hot gasps, his tongue almost frantic as he cleaned around Jeremy's tender hole.

Jeremy whimpered, the friction a bit too much, and Max slowed, moving up his body and easing his legs down, licking Jeremy's load from his stomach, then holding him close and kissing his throat.

"I'm really not a virgin anymore." Jeremy had the crazy thought that he might look different and laughed out loud. "That always felt like the final frontier or something."

Max chuckled with a gust of warm breath. "I get it. Cherry no more." He reached down and grazed Jeremy's tender hole with his fingertips. "Final frontier, huh? To boldly go where no man has gone before?"

Jeremy shivered at the delicate, delicious touch. "Does that make you Captain Kirk?"

"Excuse you—I'm clearly Picard."

"Sorry, I wasn't thinking. You fucked my brains out."

Max laughed, nuzzling Jeremy's cheek, his fingers just lightly pressing now against Jeremy's hole. "I'll forgive you," Max murmured against his skin. "You're amazing."

"Am I?" Although Jeremy's eyes were heavy, his mind snapped into gear. Max had certainly seemed to get off, but surely he'd been with guys with more experience. Jeremy probably could have done things better. Like when he'd—

"Baby."

He opened his eyes to find Max above him, propped on one arm. "You're amazing," he repeated. "That was incredible. Stop second-guessing. I can hear you worrying."

Jeremy had to laugh. "Guilty as charged. And that really was amazing." He blinked drowsily. "Best pirate sex I could ask for."

Chuckling, Max kissed his forehead with a simple press of lips. "Arrgh, matey. Glad I could shiver your timbers."

"You definitely won't have to walk the plank." Jeremy was drifting off now.

Max yawned. "I feel like there's a booty joke here somewhere." He tugged one of the blankets over them, and Jeremy snuggled against him, smiling against Max's sweaty chest.

"WHAT'S WRONG?" JEREMY paused in rolling the throw blankets.

Dressed again, Max stood by the table in the fairy lights' soft glow. He stared at his phone, the screen going dark. He didn't answer.

"Max?" Jeremy abandoned the blankets on the hearth, pushing to his feet and rubbing his hands on his jeans nervously. "You look like you saw a ghost."

"It's nothing." Max jammed his phone in his pocket and smiled, but it wasn't a real smile. Jeremy definitely knew him well enough now to spot that.

"Doesn't seem like nothing." He tried for a smile himself. "I'm surprised there's even service out here."

"Didn't used to be." Max hooked a thumb over his shoulder. "It's dark. We should get back or they'll worry."

"Okay. Are you sure—"

"It's fine!" Max snapped. He inhaled sharply. "I'm sorry. I don't want to talk about it. It's nothing for you to worry about."

"Oh." Jeremy nodded and went back to rolling the blankets. He kept his head down, telling himself not to get upset. Not to feel ridiculously *hurt*.

Tense silence stretched out as they packed up. Jeremy had felt incredible—waking from a doze warm and snug in Max's arms. After they had full-on sex. He'd *had sex*. His ass was sore in the best way, and Max had been so considerate, and everything had been perfect.

Max said with forced cheer, "Ready to head back?"

This was the part where Jeremy was supposed to go along with it and act like nothing was wrong. Max had apologized. Jeremy should just leave it alone. They were still getting to know each other. It wasn't his place to pry. But pretending was what he'd been doing with his parents.

He didn't want to be *civil* with Max.

He took a deep breath. "Maybe it's none of my business, but I wish you'd tell me what's wrong. I want to help."

Max sighed. "Baby, you have enough to worry about."

Jeremy motioned to the hearth. "I thought we had a connection. Not just sex. The things we did together—it was special to me. You brought me home with you for Christmas. I know we just met, but…" He ordered himself to stop talking. He was going to ruin everything.

He'd never been more vulnerable with another person. Not his parents or Sean, or any friends. He'd opened up to Max completely. Body and soul. Maybe he wasn't being fair, but Max's silence felt like a slap in the face. Like rejection.

Max was shaking his head with a pinched expression. Jeremy barreled on. "I know you have this whole fairy godfather thing. And I love how protective and sweet you are. But I don't want it to be one-sided. I've told you so many things. Big things. After what we just did, it hurts that you're not telling me what's upsetting you. I trust you. Don't you trust me?"

He ran out of steam, sucking in a breath in the silence and staring at the blanket gripped in his hands. Maybe he was being ridiculous. Max didn't owe him anything. When he'd invited Jeremy for the holidays, he'd explicitly said it was only as friends. Even if Jeremy had felt closer to him than anyone else in the world, he was probably being an over-emotional loser. So many people had sex like it was nothing. Even if it felt like everything to him.

Kneeling on the hearth, Max took hold of Jeremy's shoulders. "You're right. I'm sorry."

"No, I'm being dramatic. My mom says I overreact."

Max huffed. "That's rich coming from her." He lifted Jeremy's chin with one finger, his brown eyes sincere. "Honestly? I haven't talked to anyone about this. I'm afraid you'll think I'm a selfish asshole. Because I feel like one. And I don't want you to think that. I want you to like me."

"I do. I like you more than anyone."

Max smiled, puffing out a breath. "I like you too. So, so much."

"Are you seeing someone else or something?" Jeremy wasn't sure he wanted to know, but he had to ask.

"What? No, nothing like that." Max peered at him seriously. "Honestly. What's wrong isn't about you and me." He pulled out his phone. "I got another email notification. LSAT people reminding me to look at my results."

"Oh! They came in?" Jeremy blinked. "But you don't want to look."

In the dying embers of the fire, Max's face was half in shadow. "Correct." He tapped his phone, the screen lighting up. "Before, I just wanted the results already. Now I'm afraid to look at them."

"Even if you didn't do as well as you'd like, you can take them again, can't you?"

Max stared at the home screen. "I can. The problem is, I'm not sure what I'm really afraid of at this point. Part of me hopes I bombed and the choice is out of my hands. I mean, yeah, I can take them again and the schools I've applied to won't have made a decision yet. But it feels like, if I did badly, that's a sign or something."

Jeremy pondered it. It seemed clear to him now that he thought back that Max's instant tension when the topic of law school came up wasn't nerves about the test. "Doesn't that wish...kind of tell you?" He held up his hands. "But I don't know. Don't listen to me." He cringed at his reflex to add that.

A smile tugged on Max's lips. "I thought you wanted me to listen to you. And I do. Please. Tell me what you really think."

Again, he took time to consider. "If you look at the results right now and you failed, will you be relieved? Don't think about it—yes or no."

Max opened and closed his mouth. "Yes." He nodded with certainty. "I'd be glad."

"I think that means you don't really want to go to law school. Why does that scare you so much?" He reached for Max's free hand, squeezing his fingers. "You can tell me anything."

Adam's apple bobbing, Max whispered, "I'm afraid I'll disappoint everyone. It's been my plan since I was a kid. I've told everyone I know at some point or another."

"Plans change. When I was fifteen, I was sure I was going to be a doctor. But I realized I'd rather be in a lab. You don't think less of me, do you?"

"Of course not. But this is different." He gripped Jeremy's hand, his gaze on the smoldering fire, his phone dark again. "When my mom died, I promised I'd be a lawyer like her."

It all fell into place, and Jeremy ached for him. He inched closer, their knees pressing as he caressed Max's hair. "Changing your mind doesn't mean you didn't love her. It doesn't diminish anything."

Max stared at him hopefully. "You really think it's okay?"

Jeremy nodded. His mind whirled, searching for the right words. "I know following in her footsteps is a kind of tribute to her, but you can still admire her and remember her without being a lawyer. You can still honor her memory. You already do. She would understand."

"Yeah?" Max's voice trembled.

"Absolutely. Whatever you do, she would be so proud. You're amazing."

Max's eyes glistened as he met Jeremy's gaze. "Even if I don't follow through on my promise?"

"*Yes.*"

"When she died, I made all sorts of vows to her and God. I don't even know if I believe in God anymore. I'm definitely not a good Catholic."

"Is anyone?"

He laughed softly. "Probably not so much. My mom seemed perfect to me, but I know she wasn't. But law school was the plan for almost as long as I can remember. Shifting gears is scary. I like plans."

"You can make a new one. Have you thought about what else you might do?"

"I think I want to be a teacher."

"Oh, you'd be great at that. That feels so right for you."

"Yeah?" Max's shoulders relaxed, his face animated. "I can see myself in a classroom. When I think about courtrooms… It feels like an obligation. It doesn't excite me. But I don't know. I don't want to make the wrong choice."

"You'd probably have to wait a year to apply for teachers college, right? If you get into law school, you could defer. Apply to be a teacher and give yourself the time to really think about it."

Max half laughed. "I guess if you want to be logical and reasonable about it instead of wound up and stressed."

"It's just an idea." Jeremy grinned as Max pulled him into a hug.

"Thank you. Guess we both needed to get out of our own way." He leaned back. "I should look at the email, shouldn't I?"

"You look at the email, and I'll tell my parents that we're more than friends."

He hadn't planned on saying it—hadn't even thought about telling his parents after his mother's outburst. But now that the words were out, he knew this was what he needed to do. This wasn't a phase. He wasn't going to hide, and if that meant his family cut him off, so be it.

Max nodded. "Deal. Here goes nothing." He tapped his phone, his face lit by the harsh light. He mumbled, "Click here. Then there. Loading…" His spine zipped up straight. "Whoa. Aced it."

"Congrats?"

"Yeah. You know what? That feels good. I worked hard for that." He looked at Jeremy. "And I don't think I want to go to law school."

"That's okay."

"It is, isn't it?"

They held each other on the hearth in silence, simply breathing together. Jeremy imagined he could feel Max's stress melting away and acceptance taking its place.

There was a faint buzz, and Max looked down at his phone again. "Shit, a text from my dad. We'd better get back for dinner." He tapped a reply, and they hurriedly finished packing and gearing up.

With his glasses off and helmet on, the world was a blur of snow and shadows. He held onto Max as they drove back along the winding road, Max going slowly in the dark, a light snow falling. Jeremy's butt was tender, and he reveled in it.

The house and barn glowed with colored Christmas lights, the starbursts of red, green, blue, yellow, and pink beautiful. While Max put away the snowmobile in the garage, Jeremy put his glasses back on, the lights no less beautiful for being in focus. He inhaled deeply.

"This feels like peace on Earth."

"And good will to men?"

"I think there's something about bells?"

"We can ask Valerie. She's a walking encyclopedia of Christmas carols."

Their boots crunched in the snow as they strolled toward the house. The porch was awash in color from the outdoor bulbs and the golden-lit tree in the front window. Jeremy took out his phone and held it up. "Think a selfie will come out?"

Slinging his arm about Jeremy, Max took the phone and positioned them, turning this way and that until he was satisfied. "Smile." He lowered the phone. "Yeah. That's a great one. Can you send it to me?"

Jeremy stared at the pic. He and Max had their heads together, the pom-poms on their toques meeting. Their smiles were bright in the glow of the flattering Christmas lights. Before he could talk himself out of it, he tapped out a text to his parents and attached the pic.

Hope you guys had a great day in Honolulu. This is Max. Mom, you were right—we're more than friends. This isn't a phase I'm going through. I'm gay. I hope you can accept that. Please tell Sean I miss him. I miss you all. I love you.

He tilted the phone at Max. "Does this sound okay?" His mouth was suddenly dry.

Max nodded. "That sounds perfect. Are you sure you're ready? There's no pressure. If you want to think about it more, take your time."

He'd spent so long thinking and thinking and thinking. His finger hovered over the screen.

The front door opened and Meg stuck out her head. "There you are! Get in here, you goobers. Dinner's ready."

Jeremy looked at the message one more time, then hit *send*.

Chapter Fourteen

M AX SWORE UNDER his breath as the tape on his thumb caught another piece and got twisted as he tried to keep the wrapping paper straight. He was going to make a joke about how he was all thumbs, but when he looked over at Jeremy on the love seat across the coffee table, he bit his tongue.

It had been two days since Jeremy had sent the pic of them together to his parents. Nothing in reply. Now it was Christmas Eve, and Jeremy had been understandably subdued through dinner, only picking at his tourtière. He'd offered to help Max wrap presents, but he sat with a box of fancy mints half-wrapped on his lap, staring into the fire.

The Christmas music station was on the TV, the mournful "In the Bleak Midwinter" seeming appropriate. Max wanted to tell Jeremy for the hundredth time that it would be okay, no matter what. He wanted to *fix* this. He wanted to call the cruise ship, have the Rourkes paged, and rip them a new one.

"You don't have to stay up to help," Max said quietly. "It's my fault I always leave it to the last minute."

Jeremy snapped to attention, blinking at the mints like he was surprised to find them in his lap. "No, I don't mind." He folded the snowman paper over the box.

Max still had Jeremy's present to wrap, but he could quickly put it in a gift bag if all else failed. While Jeremy had been meeting Levi, Max had picked him up a new case for his glasses. Which was probably stupid, since the glasses had come with a case. But this one was smooth leather and marked with his initials. A kiosk in the mall had offered all sorts of personalized leather goods, and this had felt perfect. He hoped it was.

"This one's for Meg?" Jeremy asked.

"Yep. It's an old joke about how her breath stinks. It really doesn't, but one time she ate so much garlic she was sweating it out. Her breath was a deadly weapon."

Smiling absently, Jeremy wrote the tag and got up to tuck the box onto one of the tree's thick boughs. The golden lights on the tree reflected off his glasses. He wandered to the fire, adding another log, then peered at the photos that covered the wall.

Noticing Max watching, he asked, "Is this your mom?"

"Yeah." His throat was suddenly tight, but Max forced an even tone as he joined Jeremy and pointed to the four pictures in the big frame. "Her and my dad's wedding. She always wanted a Princess Diana dress with poufy sleeves, even though it was out of style by then. Her law school graduation. With me as a hairy baby. The three of us on vacation in Goa at the beach. I have a vague memory of her in that red bathing suit helping me build a sandcastle."

"She was beautiful."

"Thanks." His laugh was strained. "I don't know why I said that. Not like I had anything to do with it."

Jeremy smiled and gazed at the other framed photos of the family—Valerie, Dad, Meg, Mamy and Papy, Max, and various aunts and uncles and cousins. Grinning, Jeremy pointed to the grade nine uniformed school photo of Max with zits and his hair slicked down with half a bottle of gel.

"I never imagined you having an awkward phase."

"Glad to hear it, but clearly inaccurate, as you can see."

Jeremy laughed, and Max would happily bust out his embarrassing yearbooks if it would cheer up Jeremy, who slowly walked the wall, eyes roving over the photos. Max found himself stuck at the pics of his mom, the ache familiar. Dependable. Her smile had been a little crooked, and she squinted into the sun in the beach photo.

"I know all these pics so well. Like, if I close my eyes, I can see the images of her in my mind as if I'm looking right at them. But I don't remember the real her. Not really."

Jeremy took Max's hand. "You were young, right?"

"Yeah." He cleared his throat as he stared at the beach photo. "I've lived more of my life without her. Thirteen years."

"It doesn't seem fair."

"Nope." He squeezed Jeremy's hand. "But life isn't always fair. Especially when it comes to family."

"True. But I shouldn't complain. Compared to what you went through—"

"No comparing. You get to be upset. Okay?"

Jeremy nodded. His gaze wandered the wall. "Is that your mom at court?"

"Yeah, her first case at the Superior Court of Justice wearing the robes." Max gazed at the photo: Mom with her wavy hair pulled back into a bun, the traditional black waistcoat and long black robe a bit too big for her, the white collar and tabs around her neck. She should have looked utterly serious, but in the picture, she had her hands on her hips and a grin lighting up her face. "Her friend took it in the bathroom before she went into the courtroom."

"How do you feel looking at it now knowing that might never be you?"

Max stared at his mom's cocky grin. "Pretty good, actually. I think she'd tell me to get over myself already." He laughed, and it really did feel good. But when he looked back to Jeremy beside him, his smile vanished.

Rigid, Jeremy stared at his phone. "My dad texted," he croaked. Hands trembling, he unlocked the phone and read the message.

Please be decent humans, Max begged the Rourkes in his head. *Please see how incredible your son is. Please don't have waited until Christmas Eve to crush him even more.*

Jeremy cleared his throat and read aloud, "Hello, son. Honolulu was too crowded for our tastes. We have really enjoyed Maui. Sean sends his love. We all do. Max looks like a nice young man. We look forward to meeting him some time. Merry Christmas."

Exhaling the breath he'd been holding, Max asked, "How do you feel?"

Jeremy blinked back tears. "Good, I think? Better, at least."

"C'mere." Max hugged him tightly, and Jeremy pressed his face into Max's chest, his sob muffled.

The stairs creaked, and Valerie called, "Are you two still up? Santa will—" Wearing matching pajamas decorated with reindeer, she skidded to a halt in the living room, her slippers making a *whooshing* sound. Her ponytail swayed. "My goodness. Is everything all right?"

Jeremy swiped at his face and nodded, slipping out of Max's arms. "Uh-huh! It is. Sorry."

Valerie gave him a kind smile. "Don't be, hon."

"I'm just going to—" Jeremy motioned to the stairs. "I'll be back."

"Take your time," Max said, giving him smile.

Valerie watched him go, then whispered, "I hope his parents are still being '*civil*.' Oh, I'd really like a word with them sometime."

"Get in line. But I think they're coming around. I hope so."

"Glad to hear it. Now, I'm not staying up all night, so you'll just have to pretend you don't see me putting the presents from Santa under the tree." She ducked into the dining room and took a half-filled black garbage bag from the bottom of a rustic sideboard.

Max clutched his chest. "Childhood. Illusions. Shattered."

"Yes, I'm afraid to tell you that your father and I are Santa Claus." She clucked her tongue. "We've tried to shield you from life's harsh realities as best we could."

Laughing, Max joined her by the tree. As a teenager, he'd rolled his eyes at Valerie's insistence at still putting presents from Santa under the tree on Christmas Eve, but now he liked the tradition. He grabbed presents from the bag, reattaching a bow to one of them. He checked the tag.

"Wait, this says 'Jeremy.'"

Valerie glanced over from where she was squeezing presents into his dad's stocking. "I got him some stocking stuffers, nice thick socks, a turtleneck, and some of those great hand-warmers from Canadian Tire. He won't be used to real winter if he grew up in Victoria. Oh, and I hope you kids are still using Spotify. The little box for him is a year's subscription."

Max stared at her as she hummed along to "Up on the Rooftop" playing on the TV and filled the stockings—including the non-personalized guest stocking, which was clearly for Jeremy. When she turned back to the garbage bag, she jolted.

"Max? What is it?"

"Does it bug you that I don't call you 'mom'?" Oh God. He'd finally asked it out loud.

Valerie blinked, her eyebrows shooting up. "What? No, sweetheart."

He fidgeted, trying to say it the right way now that he'd brought it up after so long. "It's just, sometimes I feel like I should. But it doesn't feel right because she was my mom and that's what I called her."

"Of course." Valerie was using her best soothing voice, and it helped Max breathe.

"But Meg calls Dad that." Max grimaced. "You know what I mean."

"Yes. And that's her choice." She smiled wryly. "As you know, her birth father didn't hang around long enough for her to call him anything, so it's easier for Meg. But you can call me whatever you want."

In unison, they said, "As long as you don't call me late for dinner."

It felt damn good to laugh. Valerie smiled fondly. "You used to roll your eyes whenever my mamy said that, but you always secretly loved her corny sayings."

"I did," Max admitted. He smiled tremulously, on the edge of crying and he wasn't even sure why.

"Max, your mom was a wonderful woman. I wish I could have

known her, which probably sounds a little funny since I'm married to your dad. I could never take her place. But we can love people in different ways. There's a whole world of love to give."

Throat tight, he nodded, tears burning his eyes. "You've been—" He motioned to the stockings and the presents under the tree. "You've always been an amazing mother to me. And thank you for thinking about Jeremy."

She smiled, blinking away her own tears. "You've been the most wonderful son I could ask for. And we can't have poor Jeremy sitting there watching us all open presents. That's just being a good host."

"It's more than that. Thank you."

She swatted the air. "Oh, don't be silly." She sniffed and put on a bright smile. "Here's Jeremy. How are you doing, hon?"

Jeremy entered the living room hesitantly. "I'm okay. Are...you guys okay?"

"Yep!" Valerie answered. "How about a midnight snack? It's Christmas, after all. Jeremy, there's a jug of Papy's cider in the bottom of the fridge. Can you get it heating on the stove? Do you know how to work a gas range?"

Jeremy nodded eagerly and hurried out. Valerie said, "Let's finish this up quick smart." She took Max's chin and kissed his cheek with a loud smack the way she used to when he was still a kid.

Soon, all the presents were in place, the cider was steaming, and the leftover *pets-de-soeur* from a batch Papy had made that morning were warming. The door to his room opened with a creak, his shuffling steps nearing the kitchen.

"Dad, you're supposed to be fast asleep!" Valerie chided.

"I had to piss, and I smelled what you're up to out here."

"We all smelled it!" Max's father said as he entered the kitchen. "Is this for Santa?"

Meg followed him. "I was watching YouTube, but I'm not missing out."

Valerie huffed in exasperation. "It's after midnight!"

"And since we skipped out on mass this year, we can worship at the altar of Papy's treats." Meg grinned and crossed herself. "Amen." She gave Jeremy a wink and led him out of the kitchen.

Max stayed to help Valerie and Dad ladle out the cider into mugs while the others relaxed in the living room, their off-key singing of "Jingle Bells" ringing out.

It had nagged at him that Jeremy had told his parents they were dating, and since it was apparently the night for confessions, he blurted, "Jeremy and I... Well, I think we really like each other."

After a beat of silence, Valerie and Dad shared a look. "You don't say!" Valerie struggled to keep a straight face.

Max had to laugh. "Okay, you figured it out. Or Meg blabbed."

"Your sister did not blab," Dad said. "No need. No need whatsoever."

Valerie grinned. "Jeremy looks at you like you hung the moon, the stars, and Pluto to boot. And you beam it right back to him."

"Poor Pluto." Dad shook his head solemnly. "I still say it got a raw deal."

"Yes, yes, justice for Pluto. But back to me and Jeremy." Max suddenly had no idea what to say next. "Um..."

Valerie squeezed his arm. "He's a lovely young man. Why on Earth would you think we'd have an issue with him?"

"I didn't. But it's still new, and I guess I got freaked out. I really like him. But you guys have the rule about separate rooms if we bring someone home. So I figured it was a good excuse to slow down. Just be friends for a couple of weeks and figure out some stuff."

Dad's brow furrowed. "We have a rule?"

Valerie seemed just as puzzled. "Sweetheart, you're an adult. Of course we always appreciate discretion, but it's not as if we think you and Meg are going to be chaste until marriage."

"Wait, what?" He sputtered. "*What*? No way. You made a big deal about it! Remember? When Meg was a frosh and she was dating that guy Craig? She brought him home for Thanksgiving, and you two were super weird about it."

"Oh!" Valerie burst out laughing. "We couldn't stand that Craig! Thank goodness Meg regained her senses soon enough. But in the meantime, that greasy, obsequious little man wasn't sleeping with our daughter under our roof."

Dad screwed up his face. "What did she ever see in him?"

Max gaped. "Yeah, he was the worst. But you're telling me you don't actually have some weird Puritanical rule about us not sharing a room with our SO unless we're married?"

They laughed a little too hard. "It's not the seventies, Max." Valerie wheezed, her pale face flushing red. "Oh my goodness. I can't believe you thought that was a real rule. Just imagine if this had gone on for years!"

"Wait until we tell Meg." Dad's shoulders shook. "Wait, wait. Maybe we should hold off until she has another boyfriend, then add *more* arcane rules."

Max shook his head. "You guys are such dorks. I love you."

They drew him into a group hug. "We love you too," Valerie murmured, and they broke apart, laughing, as the living room contingent— particularly Papy—loudly shouted for refreshments.

It was very late when they finally trooped up to bed. Dad and Valerie had confessed to Meg that the no-sex rule had been specific to her bad choice in boyfriends, and after Meg's outrage, they'd all laughed and laughed. Max nodded to his room in the hallway, snagging Jeremy's hand.

"You're allowed now. If you want."

Jeremy smiled, glancing down the empty hall. "Is it okay if I still stay in the guest room? I feel weird otherwise." He ducked his head, clearly embarrassed, and Max could understand it.

"Of course." Max said, leaning in to whisper in his ear. "Besides, it's fun sneaking across the hall."

He kissed Jeremy softly. Slowly. Cider and buttery pastry lingered on their tongues, and it really did taste like Christmas.

Epilogue

One year later

J EREMY PULLED OFF his helmet, breathing the crisp air deeply. He reached into his pocket for the smooth leather case, his fingers skimming over his initials before he removed his glasses and pushed them up his nose.

Valerie called, "Trail's all set?"

Max gave her a thumbs-up before pushing the snowmobile into the garage. Jeremy hadn't really needed to go along for the ride, but it was the first chance he'd had since early March. He'd missed zooming along, holding onto Max, his heart thumping.

The morning had been a whirlwind of activity as they prepared for the final open house before Christmas. Jeremy helped Max set up the taffy station as the first vehicles arrived. They had a steady line of customers, and Jeremy was so busy handing out Popsicle sticks he didn't realize Levi was there until he was handing sticks to him and his nieces.

"Hey!" Jeremy leaned over the snow-packed planter and gave Levi a hug. "I didn't know you were coming."

"They wouldn't miss it for the world." He motioned to the girls, who were eagerly spinning hot syrup onto their sticks. "Hey, Max!" He held out his hand.

Max shook it with a genuine smile, the pom-pom on his old U of T toque swaying. "Great to see you, man. Sorry I couldn't make the show. Had to cover for the other bartender at the last minute."

"No worries. If you can come next time, the band got another gig in TO thanks to playing our set at the rainbow pub night on campus. Thanks again for suggesting us to the committee, Jer."

Jeremy flushed with pleasure. "That's awesome! We'll be there. I'm sure Honey and Alicia and the guys will come too. I'm actually helping organize a Valentine's Day event for the queer club too. Not sure yet if we'll have bands, but if we do, I'll get you in. They asked me to take over as treasurer, and I have some say on activities."

Max grinned. "He'll be president next year. Mark my words."

Jeremy shrugged but couldn't hide his smile. And why should he? He'd worked really hard after joining the club. "We'll see. Marjorie might go for prez, and I don't want to run against a good friend."

"Hey, if we come down for another gig, is it cool if we crash in your dorm again? Your roomie won't mind?"

"It's totally cool. I'll sleep at Max's, and Doug's never there on weekends." Now that he actually had a life, Jeremy appreciated that Doug was often absent.

"By the way, we just came from the Christmas tree farm." Levi whistled softly. "*Damn*, that is one fine lumberjack. His twinky partner's hot too."

Max laughed as he stirred the bubbling syrup on the camp stove. "Oh yeah. Always enjoy the eye candy at the Spini farm." He winked at Jeremy. "Nadeau farm's not bad for it either."

Blushing, Jeremy rolled his eyes, definitely unable to stop his grin this time.

The day flew by, hundreds of visitors passing through. Jeremy's phone buzzed as he mounted the porch with Max, the sun setting behind snowy treetops. "My parents," he said. Breathing deeply, Jeremy answered the video call. "How's Jamaica?"

His mother's face filled the screen. "Hello, Jeremy. We're having a lovely time." She moved the phone, and Sean's pimply face appeared.

"Hey, bro! How's it hangin'?" Sean asked, clearly delighting in their mom's grimace of distaste.

"I'm good. Lots of snow on the farm. Say hi to Max."

Max slipped his arm over Jeremy's shoulders and greeted them. Jeremy's dad appeared too, and they talked about the resort, detailing the food options while Jeremy and Max nodded and smiled.

"We wish you were here," Jeremy's mother said after a few minutes. "Talk to you soon."

Jeremy ended the call, leaning against Max's shoulder. "Well, that went okay."

"It's been steadily more than civil," Max agreed. He pressed a kiss to Jeremy's temple beneath the brim of his hat. "Maybe next Christmas we should brave Victoria, unless they're off on some other vacation."

"Hmm. Maybe." Jeremy had gone home alone for a few weeks before starting summer school, and it had been mostly awkward with his parents. But they were trying, and they hadn't cut him off financially. He'd told Sean he was gay, and Sean had rolled his eyes and said, *"Duh. Who cares?"*

"Christmas here is pretty perfect," Max mused. "Peak winter wonderland."

"Victoria cannot compete in so many, many ways."

"If I'm in teachers college, probably can't afford to go away anyway. We'll see."

"You'll get in."

Max groaned. "I dunno. Maybe."

"Definitely." Jeremy truly had no doubts. Max's application was stellar. He'd get in. Jeremy had bought him a glass-blown apple for when he did but didn't want to jinx it by giving it to him until it was official. He hoped Max liked the gift of a deluxe mixology kit that Jeremy had put under the tree, along with presents for the rest of the family. Bartending was temporary, but Max had really gotten into making cocktails.

Late that night when everyone else was in bed, Jeremy helped Max wrap presents since Max was determined not to wait until the very last minute this year. The fire blazed and carols played on the TV. Jeremy noticed something by the mantel he somehow hadn't spotted earlier. He stepped closer, running his finger over the glittery cursive letters on red felt. "There's a stocking for me."

Max was concentrating on taping the wrapping paper shut on one end of the box. "Yeah, of course. You had one last year too. Everyone who's here for Christmas gets a stocking."

"But my name's on this one." He tentatively scratched at one of the letters. "Like, permanently."

Max came over, peering at it with a smile. He squeezed Jeremy's shoulders. "Looks good to me. Like it belongs there."

Jeremy's throat was too thick, his eyes burning. "I love you."

"I love you too, baby."

They shared a kiss by the crackling fire, "Silent Night" filling the warm silence.

Upstairs, Jeremy shut the door to Max's room behind him. It still felt strangely momentous even though they'd shared the bed at Max's apartment plenty of times, and sometimes the narrow twin bed in his dorm. Scared, lonely Jeremy of a year ago seemed a lifetime away.

Max stripped off his sweater by the double bed. Old football trophies gleamed on the bookcase in the low light. Their gazes met, and heat rushed through Jeremy at the hunger in Max's eyes.

"Think we can be quiet enough?" Max whispered.

Jeremy grinned, then lifted his finger to his lips. "Shh."

THE END

Thank you so much for reading *Merry Cherry Christmas*! I hope it brings you warm and fuzzy holiday feels. I'd be grateful if you could take a few minutes to leave a review on Amazon, Goodreads, BookBub, social media, or wherever you like. Just a couple of sentences can really help other readers discover the book. ☺

Wishing you and yours a happy and safe holiday season—and many happily ever afters!

Keira
<3

P.S. Keep reading for a peek at how Hunter and Nick from the Christmas tree farm met!

SITTING ON THE too-hard bench, Nick watched as Hunter reached to straighten his elf hat. His green jacket rode up, giving Nick an excellent view of his perky, rather spectacular ass. He was quite pretty, what with his golden hair wisping over his forehead, a round face and pink lips, freckles on his nose, and deep blue eyes. Too bad he was apparently one of those spoiled millennials who showed up late and only cared about money.

Hunter looked to be in his twenties and probably still lived at home. By his mid-twenties, Nick had been working full time for years and owned a truck and a house. It hadn't been easy, and he'd worked his way up, learning about forestry and eventually tree farming. He hadn't expected anything on a silver platter. People of all ages these days seemed more entitled than ever, and Nick had no patience for any of it.

Well, Hunter wasn't Nick's business, or his problem. He was playing Santa for two days, and two days only. When the usual Santa had fallen that morning, John had called in a panic, and considering John and

Desmond were Nick's only friends, he'd given in. So this weekend he'd have to deal with people whether he liked it or not.

He thought of John's instructions: What would Eric have said and done?

As Nick watched Hunter lead a little redheaded girl along the path toward him, he had to smile to himself, hearing Eric's voice—low, with a mischievous hint to his Scottish brogue.

I'd say you're being a miserable grouch and that you need to remove the stick from your ass, stat. That's my professional medical opinion.

Of course Eric was gone, so what did he know? But no, he was right, and Nick made an effort to smile genuinely at the girl, who clung to Hunter's hand. Maybe Nick's smiling skills were rusty, since Hunter said to her, "It's okay, Jessica. Santa's really friendly, I promise." He shot Nick a pointed look, eyebrows raised as if daring Nick to prove him wrong. Okay, perhaps there was a bit of sass there, not just eye-rolling millennial petulance.

Nick cleared his throat, pitching his voice a little higher and softer than usual, mimicking the way Eric had spoken to young children. "Hi there, Jessica. It's wonderful to meet you. Do you want to sit down and tell me what you'd like for Christmas?"

As Jessica hesitantly told him about wanting a sled and some kind of doll that was probably the latest fad, Nick nodded and smiled and pretended he knew exactly what she was talking about. From the corner of his eye, he was aware of Hunter watching, and when Nick glanced at him while he and Jessica shifted for their picture, Hunter's cheeks went red, and he hurried back down the candy path.

The picture was taken as Hunter brought up the next kid, and Nick smiled and nodded to the steady stream of children coming to sit with him. He also tried to ignore Eric in his head.

Admit it—the kids are adorable. You don't hate this. Especially with the sexy elf eye candy.

Eric had always called him on his shit, and eight years after his death, his voice in Nick's head was a familiar comfort. It wasn't *real*, of course, and it wasn't always there. But Eric would show up once in a while, usually when Nick needed a swift kick in the ass.

Yes, sometimes Daddy needs the spanking.

He snorted out loud, and Hunter, who had brought up another girl, glared and hissed, "What are you laughing at?" His fair cheeks flushed red, and when he had the girl seated, he tugged at the hem of his green jacket. Clearly, he was uncomfortable in the too-small costume, but he also seemed anxious and jittery in his own skin. Any traces of sass vanished, replaced by a flash of raw vulnerability.

Nick instinctively wanted to reassure him, but before he could, the little girl was providing detailed evidence of her being very, *very* good and deserving of soccer cleats and a princess dress with puffy sleeves she really, *really* wanted so, *so* much.

The stream of kids seemed unending, and Nick's ass was numb and his entire body uncomfortably damp with sweat by the time John closed off the line and put up a sign saying they'd be back in half an hour. Nick's cheeks actually hurt from all the smiling, and he couldn't wait to take off the beard and hat.

While John grabbed them lunch, Nick and Hunter retreated to the storeroom. As soon as they were inside, Hunter rounded on him and snapped, "Seriously, could you stop laughing at me? I feel ridiculous enough already in this costume."

Nick blinked in surprise. "I wasn't." He dropped his gaze over Hunter's body. Yes, the costume was comical, but those lean legs were enticing in the tights, and the way the green jacket just skimmed the bulge of Hunter's package... "There's nothing wrong with the way you look." He'd meant it to be reassuring, but it had come out decidedly flirty.

But Hunter rolled his eyes, his arms crossed tightly. "Yeah, right. Now you're just messing with me."

He bit back a surge of irritation. This was exactly why Nick spent most of his time with his trees and his dog. People were so much damn work. He clamped down on his urge to soothe. "If you say so."

"I just..." Hunter clenched his jaw. "Forget it." He swiped off his hat with attached ears, running a hand through his damp hair, sweat glistening on his forehead. "Jesus, it's hot out there."

"That we can agree on." Nick tried to unfasten the long beard, which fit with a string around his head that hooked together at the side, but the hook seemed to be caught in his hat by his ear. He tugged, but it was no use. "Can you give me a hand?"

After a beat of silence, Hunter pointed to himself and asked, "Me?"

"I don't see any other elves here." He motioned to his ear. "The hook's caught."

"Oh. Right. Um…" Hunter neared as if he was afraid Nick would bite.

And goddamn if that didn't rattle the cage of Nick's inner dom.

Tentatively, Hunter tugged on the snag, his knuckles brushing the corner of Nick's jaw. Nick watched from the corner of his eye as Hunter frowned and said, "It's really tangled somehow." He leaned closer, going up on his tip-toes, the bells on his shoes dinging softly. He wavered, and Nick took hold of Hunter's waist with one hand to steady him.

Hunter sucked in a breath, a tremor rippling through the firm muscles under Nick's palm. "These shoes are too tight," he mumbled. "Hard to get my balance."

"Take your time." Nick spread his fingers, wondering what Hunter's body would feel like naked.

Hunter stuck out the pink tip of his tongue as he concentrated on the hook. "There." He lifted off the hat, and the beard mercifully came free as he stepped back and Nick let go of him.

The fake beard made his real hair itchy, and Nick rubbed at his face. "Thanks." He unbuckled the thick black belt and dropped it to the concrete floor with a thud before stripping off his coat and padding. His white tank top stuck to his skin, and goosebumps spread over him in the chill of the room compared to the heat out in the mall. He tugged at the scooped neck of the cotton, tempted to peel it off, but he'd only have to put it back on damp.

When he looked up, a new shiver ran through him—one that had nothing to do with the temperature. Hunter was staring at Nick's chest, his full lips parted, a shine glistening as if he'd just licked them. He jerked his gaze up to Nick's, his Adam's apple bobbing. "Oh, um... You're welcome." He spun away with a decidedly guilty expression on his pretty face to go along with the lust.

Despite himself, Nick's balls tingled, and as John opened the door, Nick found himself flushing as well even though nothing had happened. Hunter stared at his feet, and silence stretched out. Holding a bulging paper bag and cardboard cup holder, John looked between them with arched eyebrows.

"How are my Santa and elf holding up?"

Read the rest of Hunter and Nick's sexy age-gap romance in *Santa Daddy*!

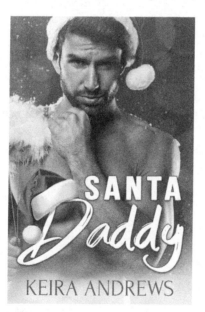

Mall Santas aren't supposed to be hot!

Hunter is hopelessly adrift after college. He's still romantically inexperienced, can't find a real job, and has no clue what to do with his life. Desperate, he returns to his humiliating old gig as an elf at the Santa's

Village in his hometown's dying mall.

Enter the sexiest Santa ever.

Twice Hunter's size and age, lumberjack Nick makes Hunter tingle. Too bad he's super grumpy and intimidating. Years after the tragic death of his partner, Nick has his beagle and long, hard days on his Christmas tree farm. That's plenty. But he can't refuse a loyal friend's plea for help and finds himself filling in as Santa. Despite Nick's attempt to stay aloof, the beautiful, anxious young man playing elf brings out his long-dormant daddy instincts.

Then a surprise blizzard traps them alone in Nick's isolated forest home. Will they surrender to the sizzling spark between them and find the release and comfort they crave?

Santa Daddy is a sweet and spicy holiday gay romance from Keira Andrews featuring an age gap, m/m first times, role playing, Christmas romance feels, and of course a happy ending.

Read more steamy and sweet holiday romance from Keira Andrews!

Will fake boyfriends become the real deal this holiday?

It's the most wonderful time of the year—except ex-Marine Logan is jobless and getting evicted. Worse, he's a new single dad with a stepson who hates him. A kid needs stability—not to mention presents under the tree—and Logan's desperate.

Then he meets lonely Seth and makes a deal.

Can Logan temporarily pretend to be live-in boyfriends to increase Seth's chances at a promotion? If it provides a roof over their heads for the holidays, hell yeah. Logan considers himself straight—he doesn't count occasional hookups with guys—but he can fake it. Besides, with his shy little smile, Seth is surprisingly sexy.

Make that *damn* sexy.

Shocked that Seth has only been with one man, Logan can't resist sweetening their deal to teach him the joys of casual sex. No strings attached. No feelings. No kissing. No commitment.

No falling for each other.

Easy, right?

The Christmas Deal is a steamy holiday gay romance from Keira Andrews featuring fake boyfriends, bisexual awakening, a clueless single dad with an angry preteen, and of course a happy ending.

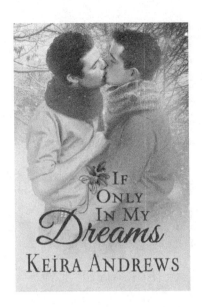

To be home for Christmas, they must bridge the distance between them.

Charlie Yates is desperate. It's almost Christmas and his flight home from college has been delayed. For days. Charlie promised his little sister Ava he'd be home for her first holiday season since going into remission from leukemia. Now he's stuck on the opposite coast and someone else grabbed the last rental car. Someone he hasn't even spoken to in four years. Someone who broke his heart.

Gavin Bloomberg's childhood friendship with Charlie ended overnight after a day of stolen kisses. With years of resentment between them, they don't want to be in the same room together, let alone a car. But for Ava's sake, Gavin agrees to share the rental and drive across the country together.

As they face unexpected bumps along the road, can Charlie and Gavin pave the way to a future together?

This gay holiday romance from Keira Andrews features new adult angst, enemies to lovers, steamy first times, and of course a happy ending.

Join the free gay romance newsletter!

My (mostly) monthly newsletter will keep you up to date on my latest releases and news from the world of LGBTQ romance. You'll also get access to exclusive giveaways, free reads, and much more. Join the mailing list today and you're automatically entered into my monthly giveaway. Go here to sign up: subscribepage.com/KAnewsletter

Here's where you can find me online:
Website
www.keiraandrews.com
Facebook
facebook.com/keira.andrews.author
Facebook Reader Group
bit.ly/2gpTQpc
Instagram
instagram.com/keiraandrewsauthor
Goodreads
bit.ly/2k7kMj0
Amazon Author Page
amzn.to/2jWUfCL
Twitter
twitter.com/keiraandrews
BookBub
bookbub.com/authors/keira-andrews

About the Author

Keira aims for the perfect mix of character, plot, and heat in her M/M romances. She writes everything from swashbuckling pirates to heart-warming holiday escapism. Her fave tropes are enemies to lovers, age gaps, forced proximity, and passionate virgins. Although she loves delicious angst along the way, Keira guarantees happy endings!

Discover more at:
keiraandrews.com

Made in the USA
Coppell, TX
06 December 2023

25447038R00132